SUPERMAN ISN'T JEWISH

(BUT I AM...KINDA)

JIMMY BEMON & EMILIE BOUDET

SUPERMAN ISN'T JEWISH

(BUT I AM...KINDA)

Life Drawn

JIMMY BEMON
Story

ÉMILIE BOUDET
Art

✻

NANETTE McGUINNESS
Translation

✻

**FABRICE SAPOLSKY
& ALEX DONOGHUE**
US Edition Editors

AMANDA LUCIDO
Assistant Editor

**VINCENT HENRY
& FRANCIS ADAM**
Original Edition Editors

JERRY FRISSEN
Senior Art Director

FABRICE GIGER
Publisher

Rights & Licensing - licensing@humanoids.com
Press and Social Media - pr@humanoids.com

SUPERMAN ISN'T JEWISH (BUT I AM...KINDA)
This title is a publication of Humanoids, Inc. 8033 Sunset Blvd. #628, Los Angeles, CA 90046.
Copyright © 2018 Humanoids, Inc., Los Angeles (USA). All rights reserved.
Humanoids and its logos are ® and © 2018 Humanoids, Inc.
Library of Congress Control Number: 2018946023

Life Drawn is an imprint of Humanoids, Inc.

First published in France under the title *"Superman n'est pas Juif (...et moi un peu)"*
Copyright © 2014 La Boîte à Bulles, Jimmy Bemon & Émilie Boudet. All rights reserved. All characters, the distinctive
likenesses thereof and all related indicia are trademarks of La Boîte à Bulles Sarl and / or of Jimmy Bemon & Émilie Boudet.

I always thought I had super powers. Something that others didn't have and that made me better, stronger, smarter...

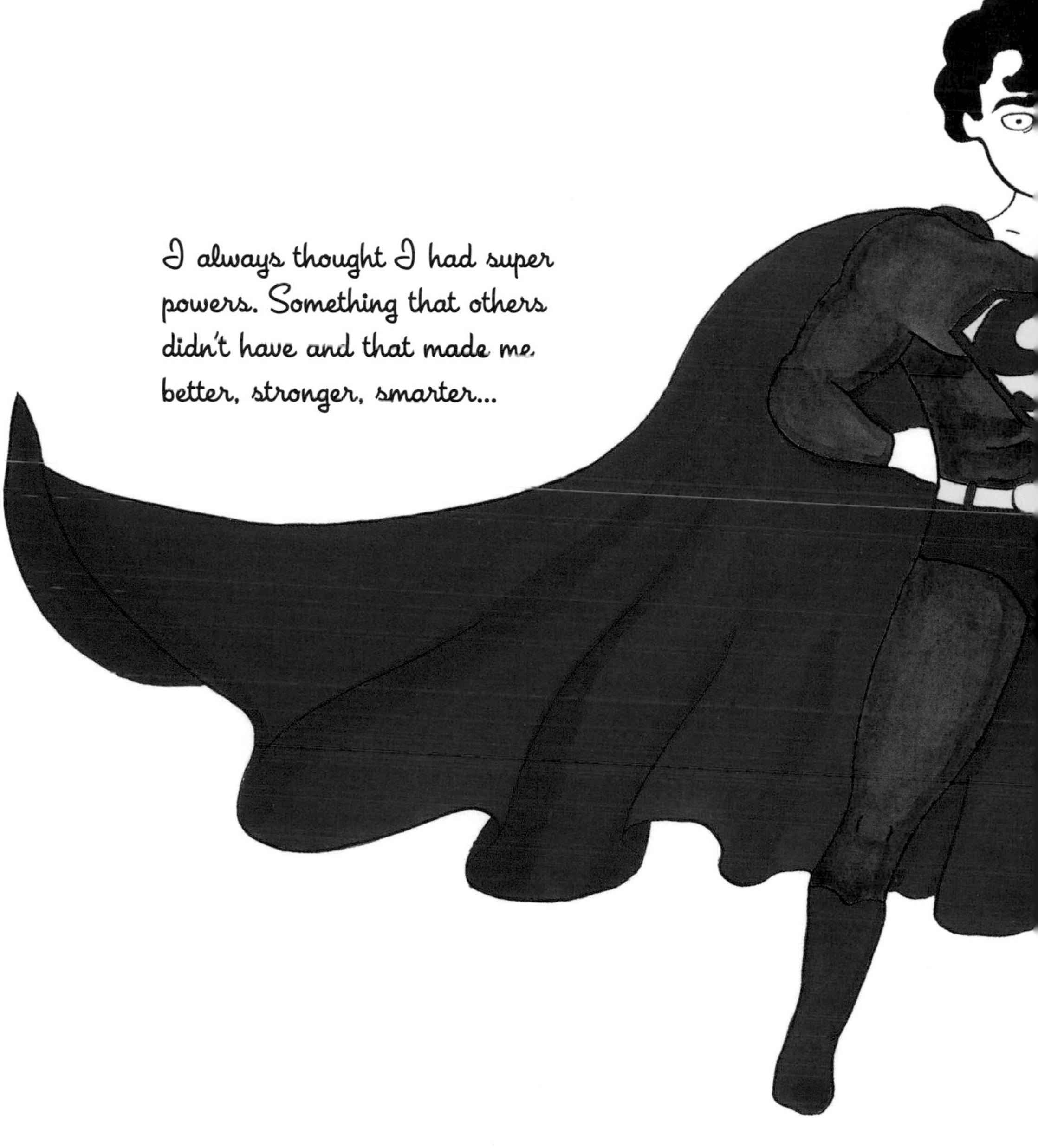

When I really think about it, it all traces
back to the day my parents separated...

Nice, January 1984

...when my father took me aside and told me:

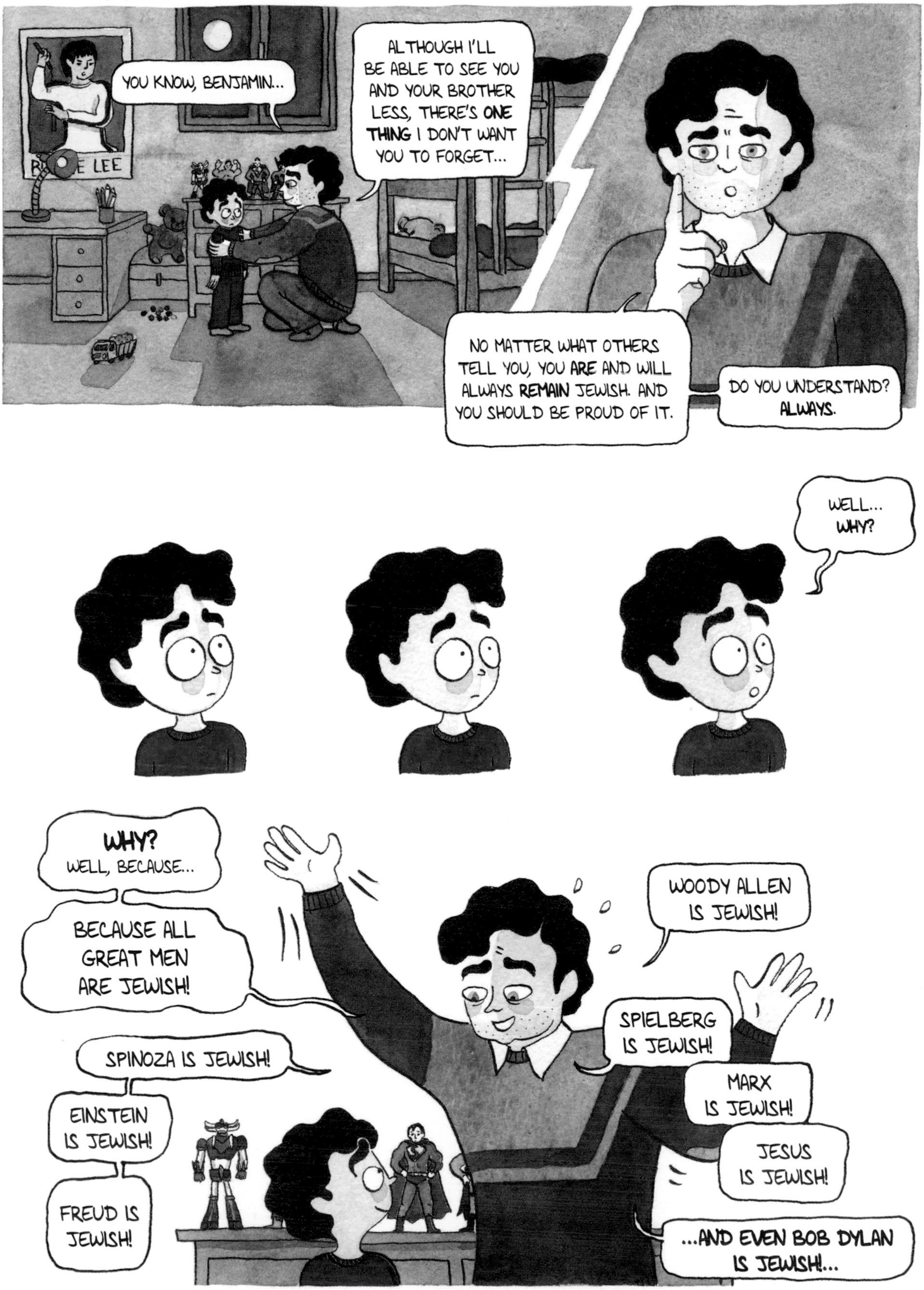
YOU KNOW, BENJAMIN...
ALTHOUGH I'LL BE ABLE TO SEE YOU AND YOUR BROTHER LESS, THERE'S **ONE THING** I DON'T WANT YOU TO FORGET...
NO MATTER WHAT OTHERS TELL YOU, YOU **ARE** AND WILL ALWAYS **REMAIN** JEWISH. AND YOU SHOULD BE PROUD OF IT.
DO YOU UNDERSTAND? **ALWAYS.**
WELL... **WHY?**
WHY? WELL, BECAUSE...
BECAUSE ALL GREAT MEN ARE JEWISH!
WOODY ALLEN IS JEWISH!
SPIELBERG IS JEWISH!
SPINOZA IS JEWISH!
MARX IS JEWISH!
EINSTEIN IS JEWISH!
JESUS IS JEWISH!
FREUD IS JEWISH!
...AND EVEN BOB DYLAN IS JEWISH!...

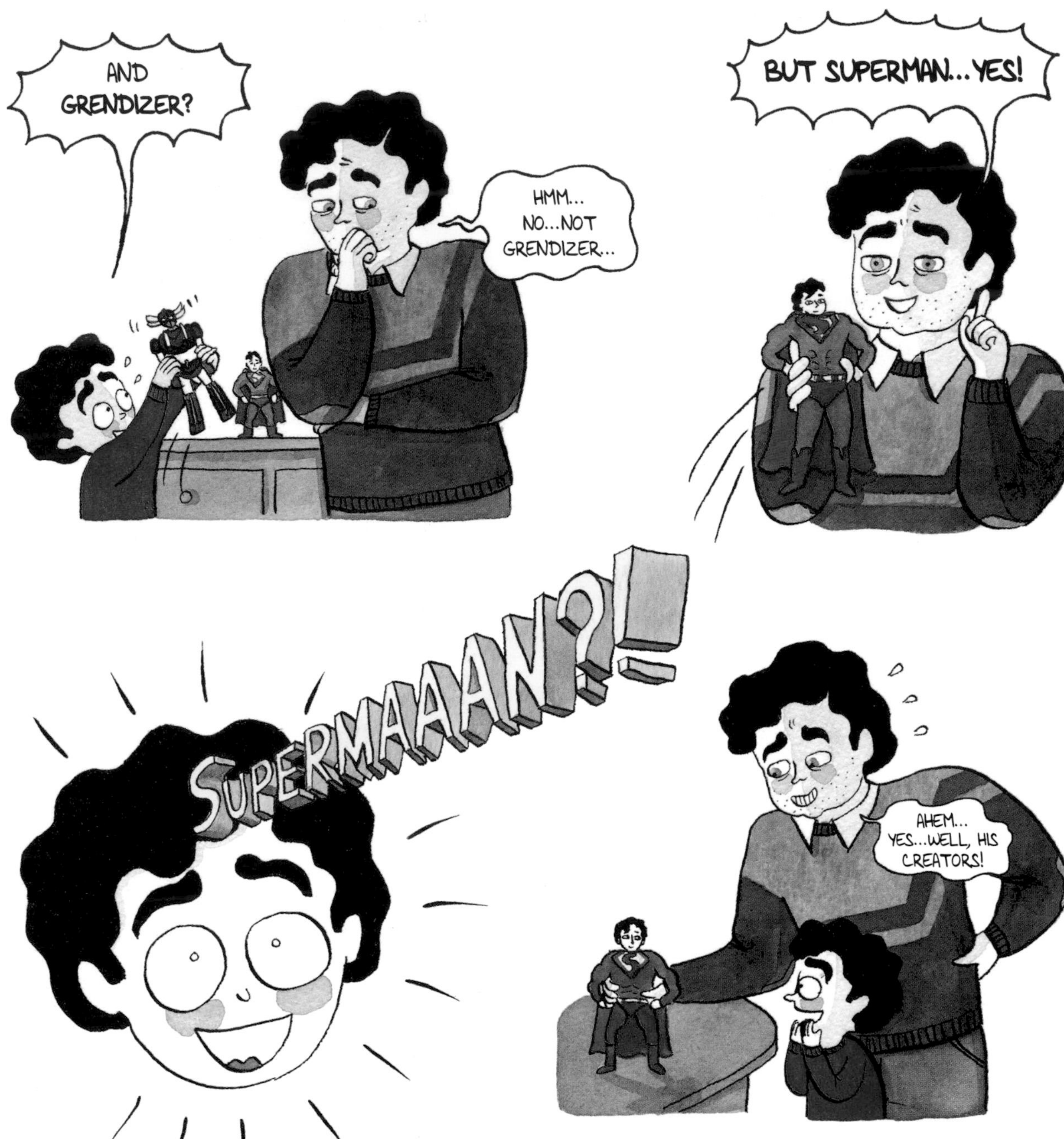
AND GRENDIZER?
HMM... NO...NOT GRENDIZER...
BUT SUPERMAN...YES!
SUPERMAAAN?!
AHEM... YES...WELL, HIS CREATORS!

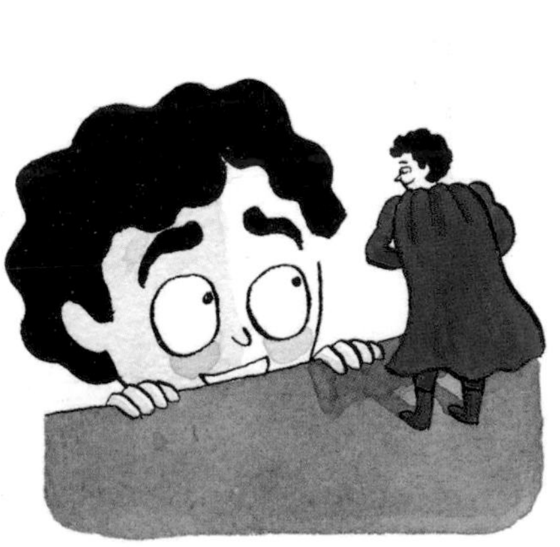

To be honest, I didn't really know what "being Jewish" meant... But that day, if there was one thing I really understood...

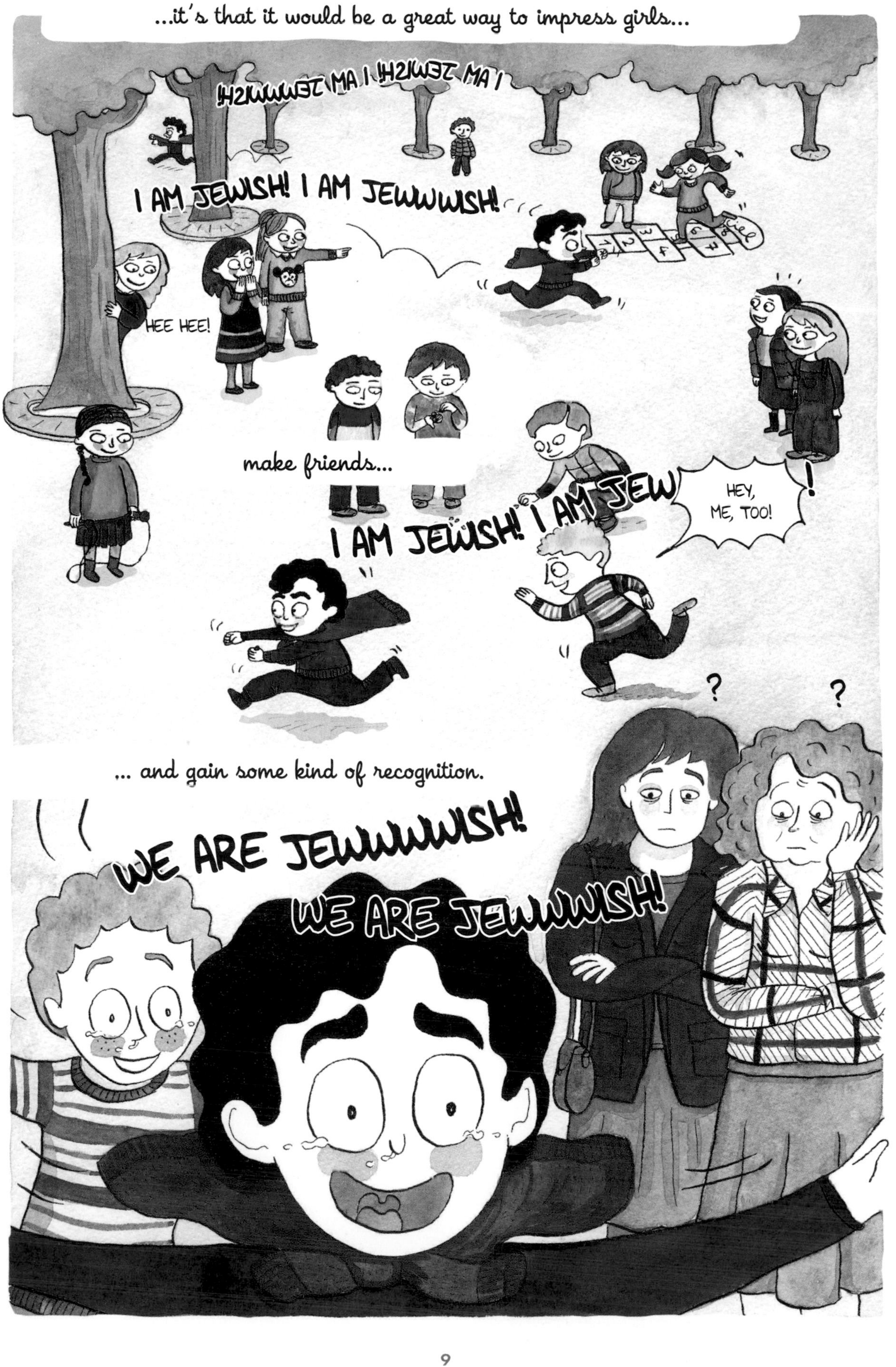
...it's that it would be a great way to impress girls...
I AM JEWISH! I AM JEWWWISH!
HEE HEE!
make friends...
I AM JEWISH! I AM JEW
HEY, ME, TOO!
... and gain some kind of recognition.
WE ARE JEWWWWISH!
WE ARE JEWWWISH!

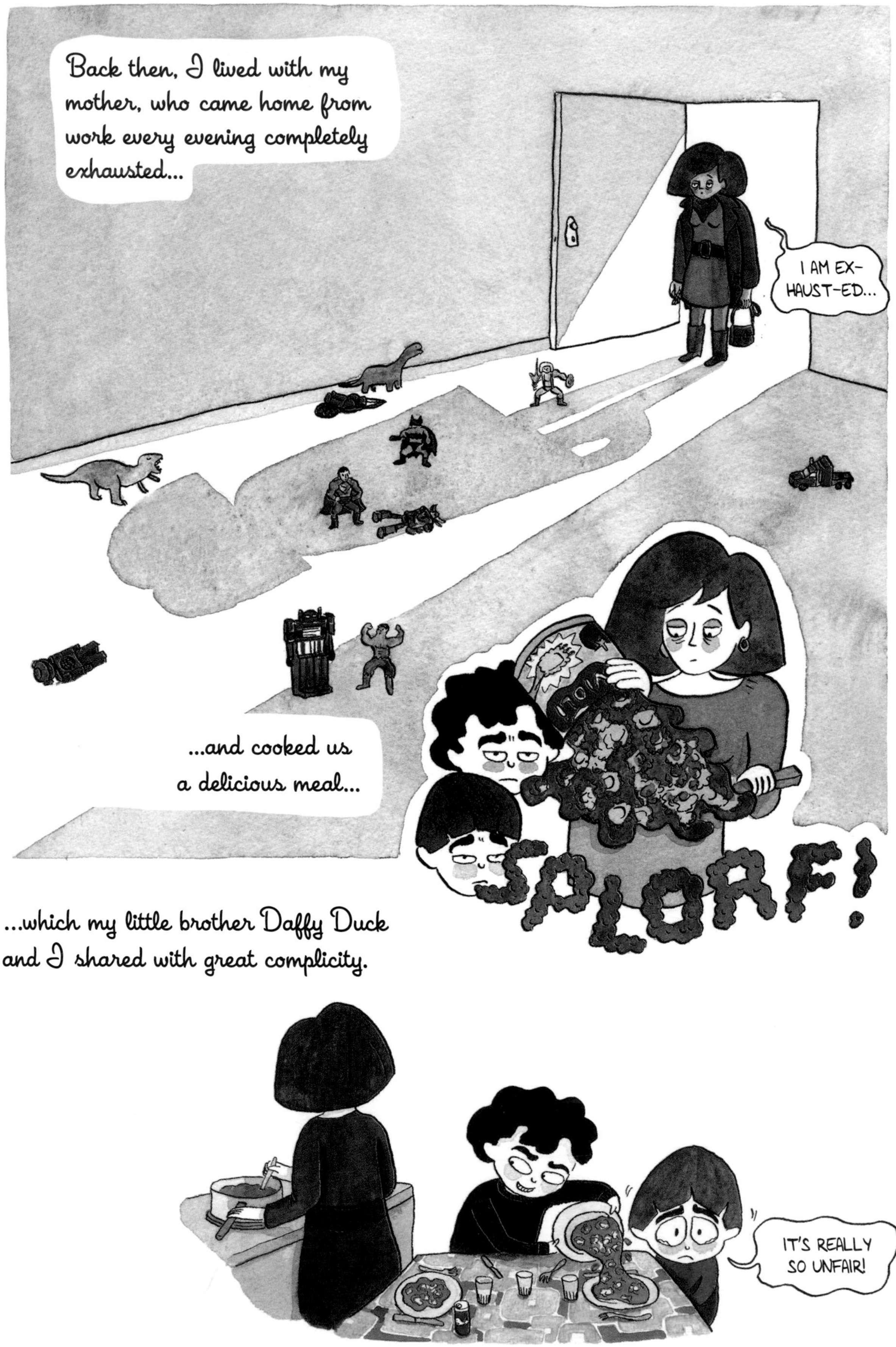
Back then, I lived with my mother, who came home from work every evening completely exhausted...
I AM EX-HAUST-ED...
...and cooked us a delicious meal...
SPLORF!
...which my little brother Daffy Duck and I shared with great complicity.
IT'S REALLY SO UNFAIR!

Every other weekend, my mother took us to visit my father, who took us to my grandparents', where we ate...

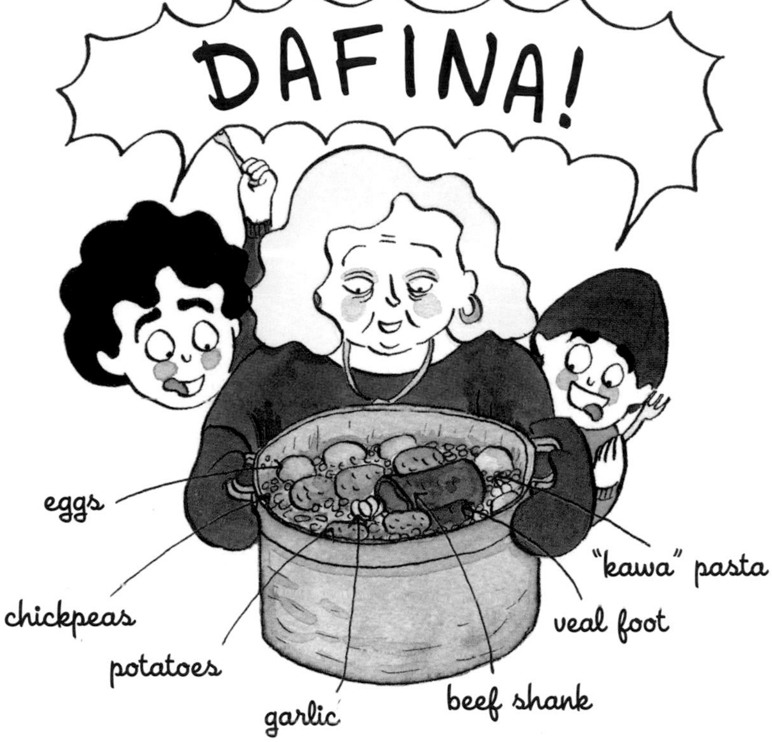
DAFINA!
eggs
chickpeas
potatoes
garlic
beef shank
veal foot
"kawa" pasta

There we sang some prayers that sounded like a mixture of French, Arabic, and Kryptonese–the language of Superman!

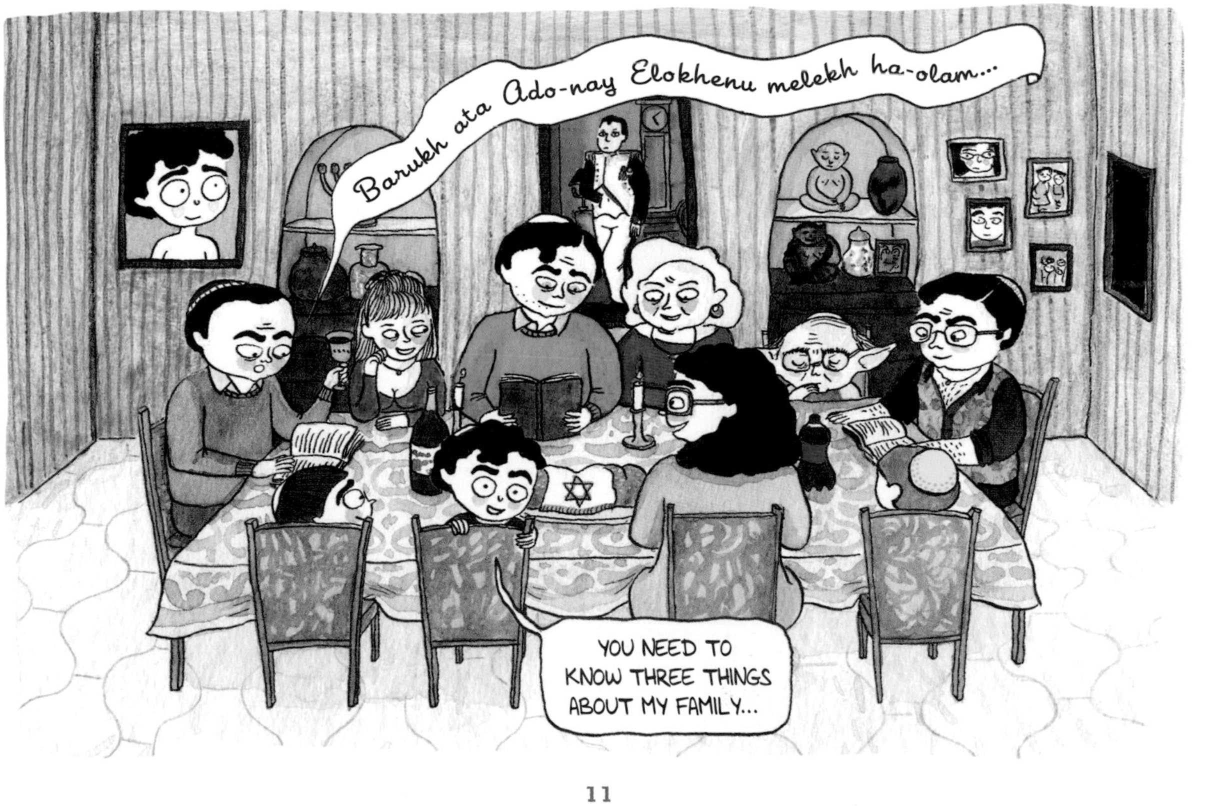
Barukh ata Ado-nay Elokhenu melekh ha-olam...
YOU NEED TO KNOW THREE THINGS ABOUT MY FAMILY...

The more they love each other, the louder they get...

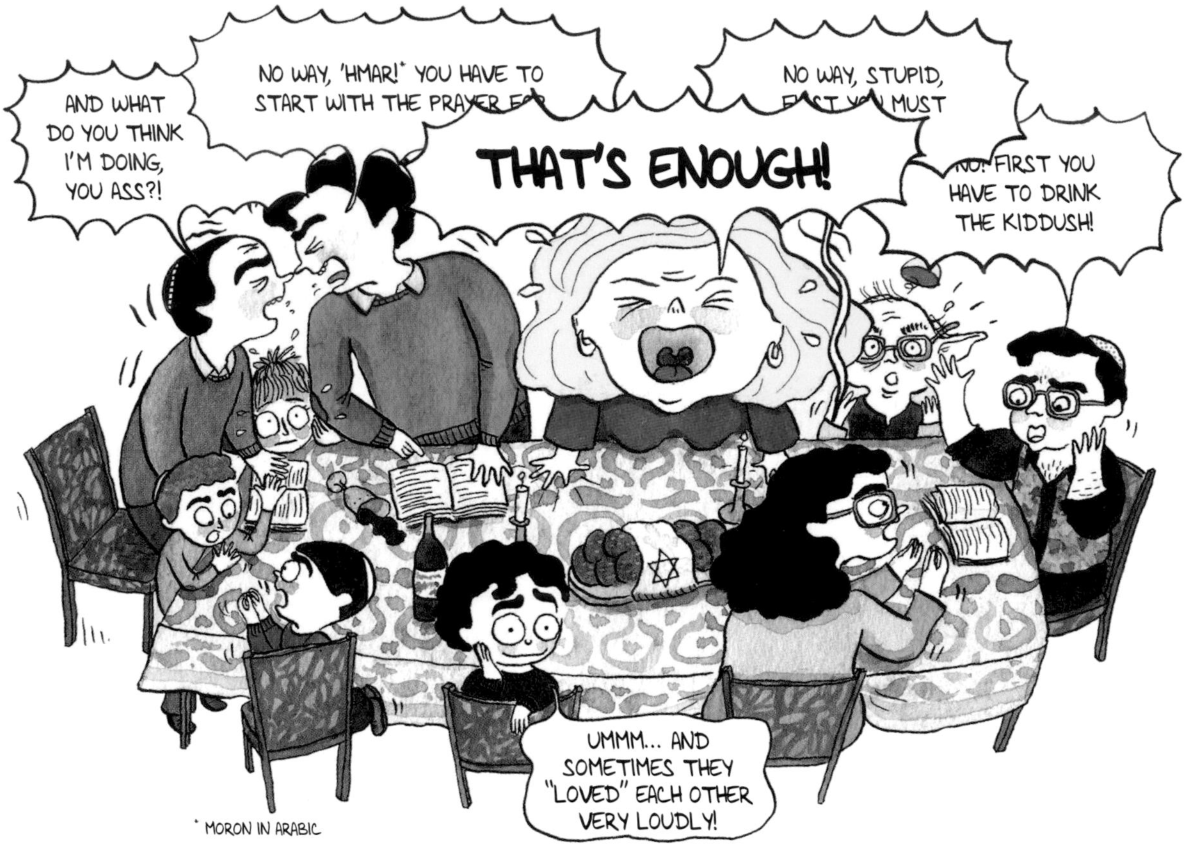
AND WHAT DO YOU THINK I'M DOING, YOU ASS?!
NO WAY, 'HMAR!* YOU HAVE TO START WITH THE PRAYER
NO WAY, STUPID,
THAT'S ENOUGH!
FIRST YOU HAVE TO DRINK THE KIDDUSH!
UMMM... AND SOMETIMES THEY "LOVED" EACH OTHER VERY LOUDLY!
* MORON IN ARABIC

Being a success is veeery important for them...

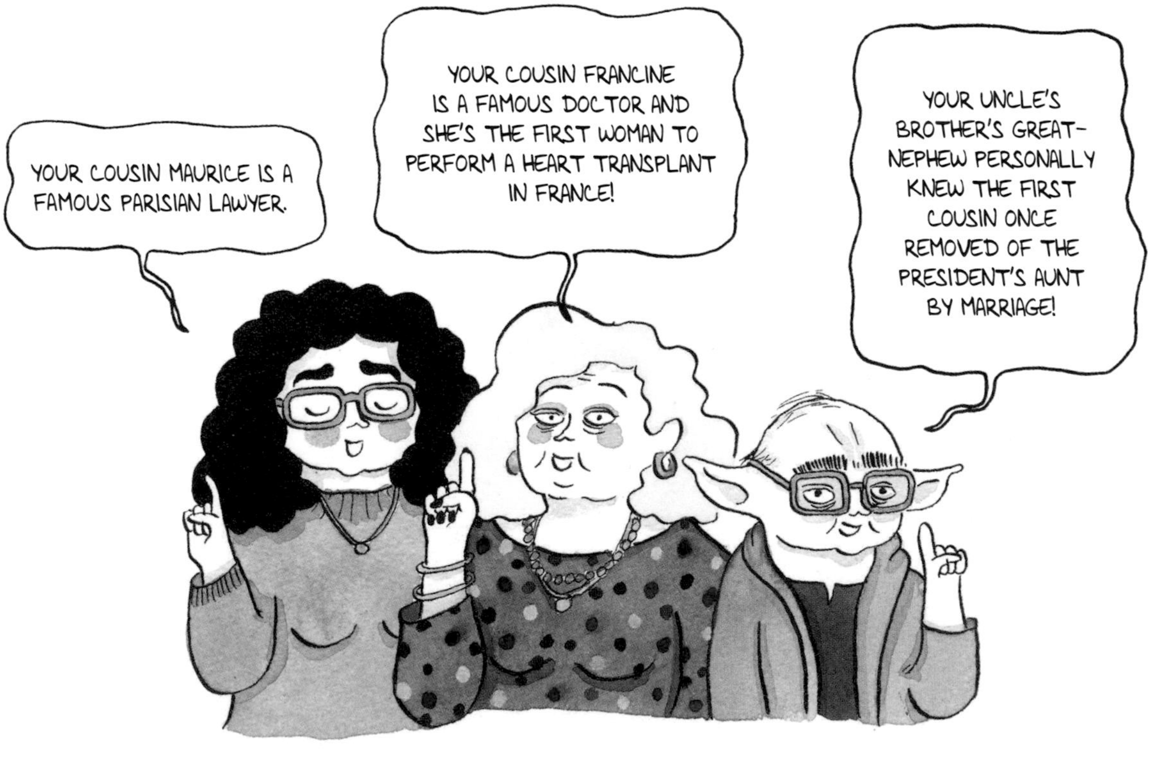
YOUR COUSIN MAURICE IS A FAMOUS PARISIAN LAWYER.
YOUR COUSIN FRANCINE IS A FAMOUS DOCTOR AND SHE'S THE FIRST WOMAN TO PERFORM A HEART TRANSPLANT IN FRANCE!
YOUR UNCLE'S BROTHER'S GREAT-NEPHEW PERSONALLY KNEW THE FIRST COUSIN ONCE REMOVED OF THE PRESIDENT'S AUNT BY MARRIAGE!

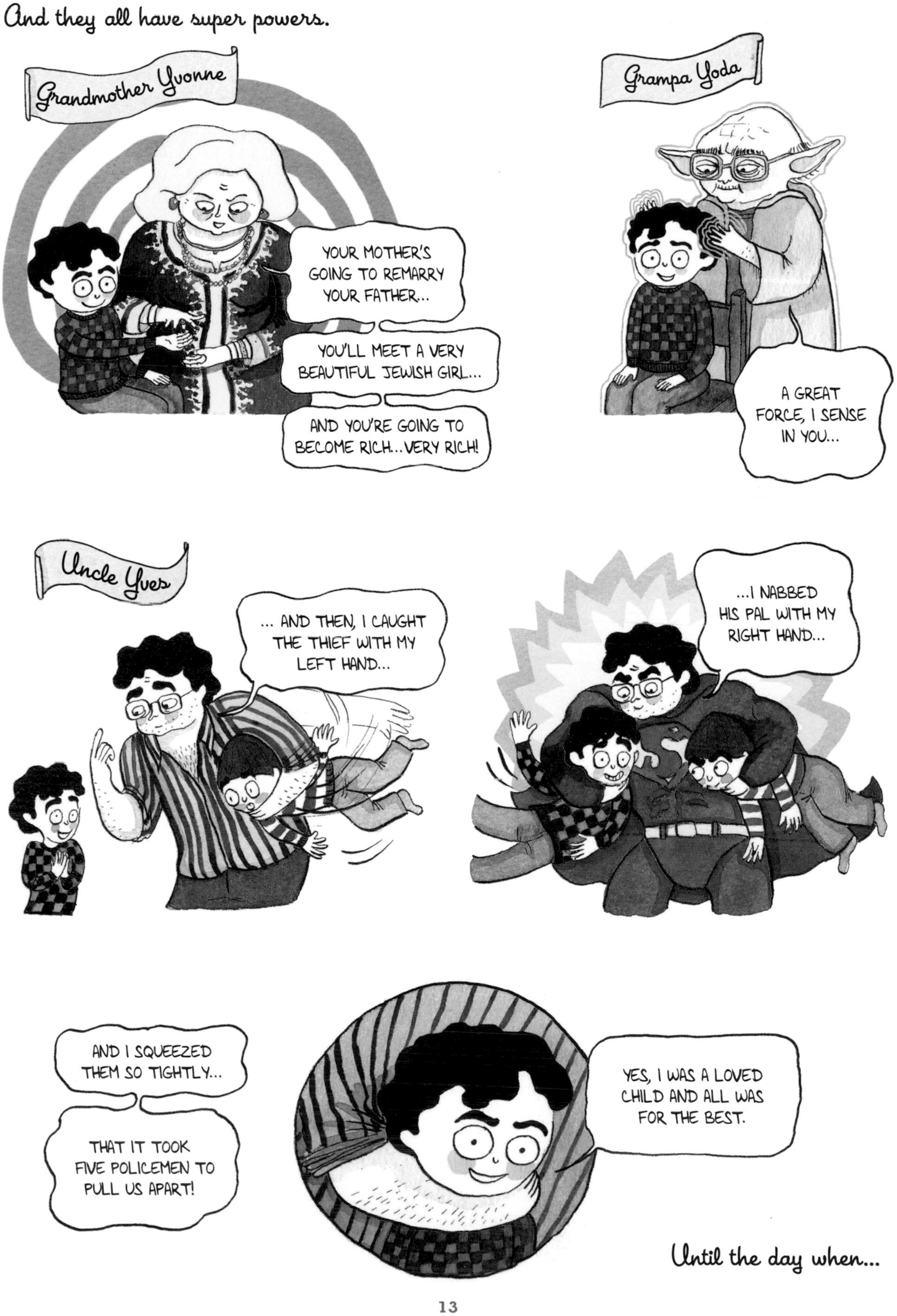
And they all have super powers.
Grandmother Yvonne
YOUR MOTHER'S GOING TO REMARRY YOUR FATHER...
YOU'LL MEET A VERY BEAUTIFUL JEWISH GIRL...
AND YOU'RE GOING TO BECOME RICH... VERY RICH!
Grampa Yoda
A GREAT FORCE, I SENSE IN YOU...
Uncle Yves
... AND THEN, I CAUGHT THE THIEF WITH MY LEFT HAND...
...I NABBED HIS PAL WITH MY RIGHT HAND...
AND I SQUEEZED THEM SO TIGHTLY...
THAT IT TOOK FIVE POLICEMEN TO PULL US APART!
YES, I WAS A LOVED CHILD AND ALL WAS FOR THE BEST.
Until the day when...

I needed to understand...

So that evening...

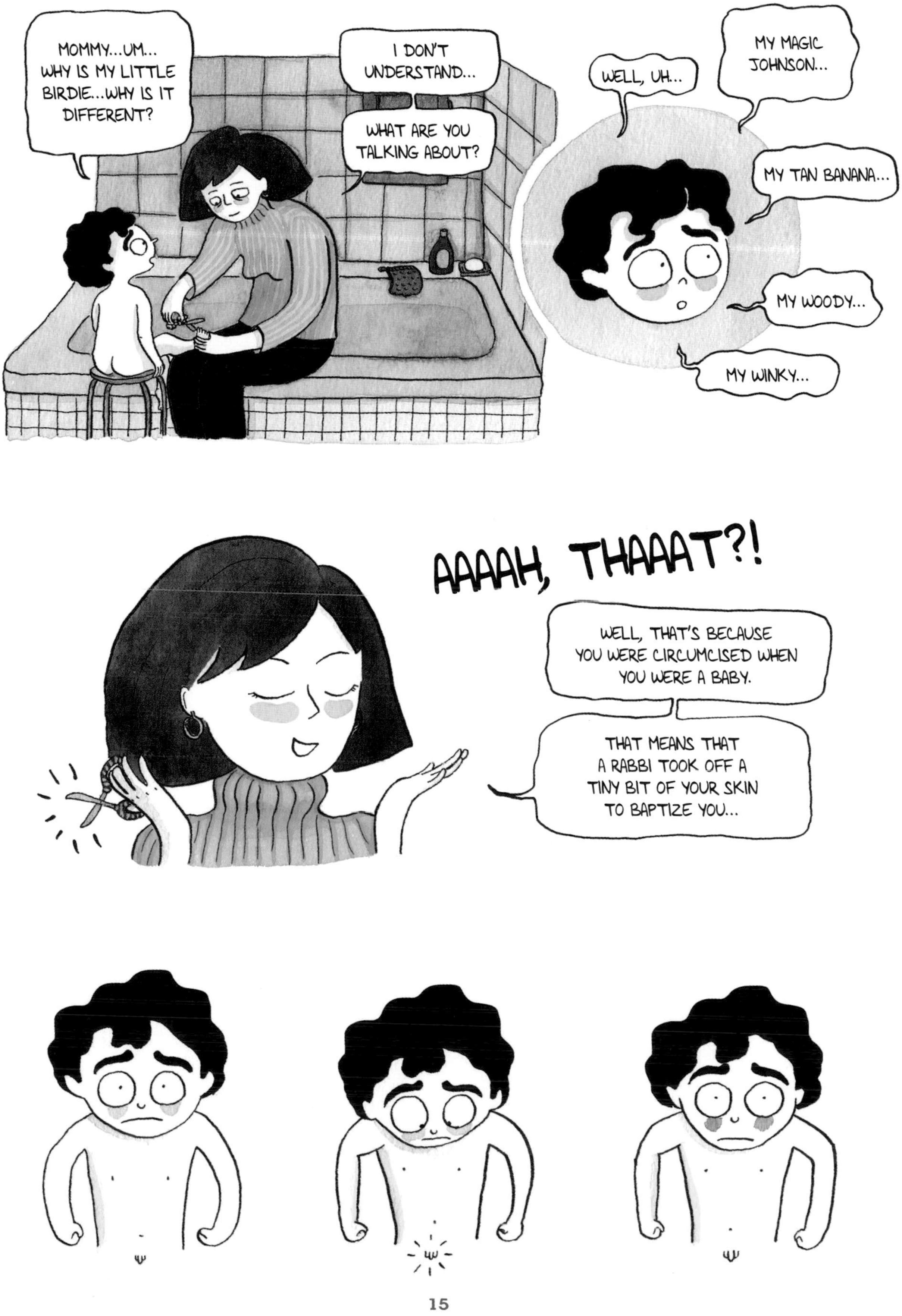

MOMMY...UM... WHY IS MY LITTLE BIRDIE...WHY IS IT DIFFERENT?
I DON'T UNDERSTAND...
WHAT ARE YOU TALKING ABOUT?
WELL, UH...
MY MAGIC JOHNSON...
MY TAN BANANA...
MY WOODY...
MY WINKY...
AAAAH, THAAAT?!
WELL, THAT'S BECAUSE YOU WERE CIRCUMCISED WHEN YOU WERE A BABY.
THAT MEANS THAT A RABBI TOOK OFF A TINY BIT OF YOUR SKIN TO BAPTIZE YOU...

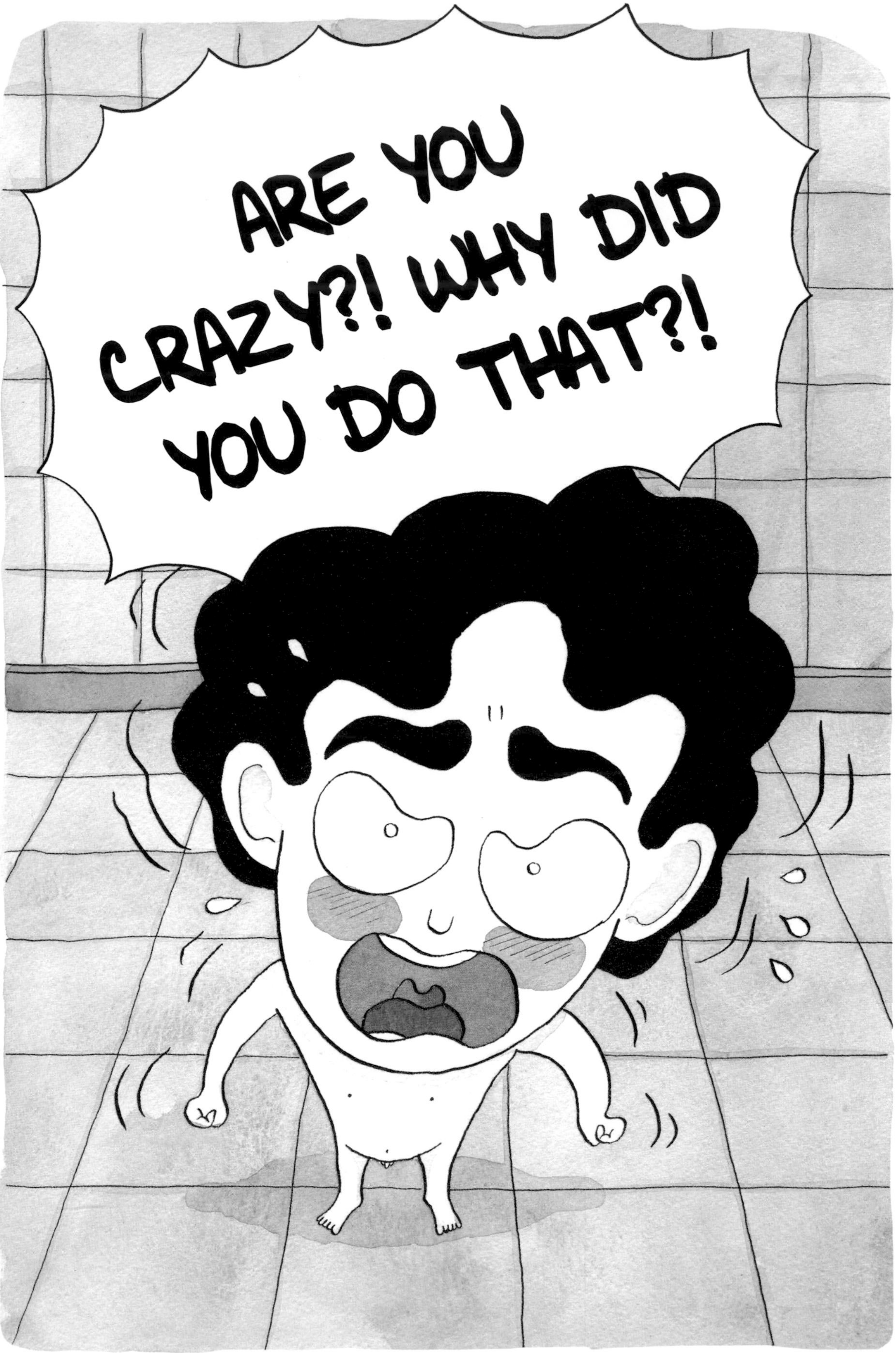
ARE YOU CRAZY?! WHY DID YOU DO THAT?!

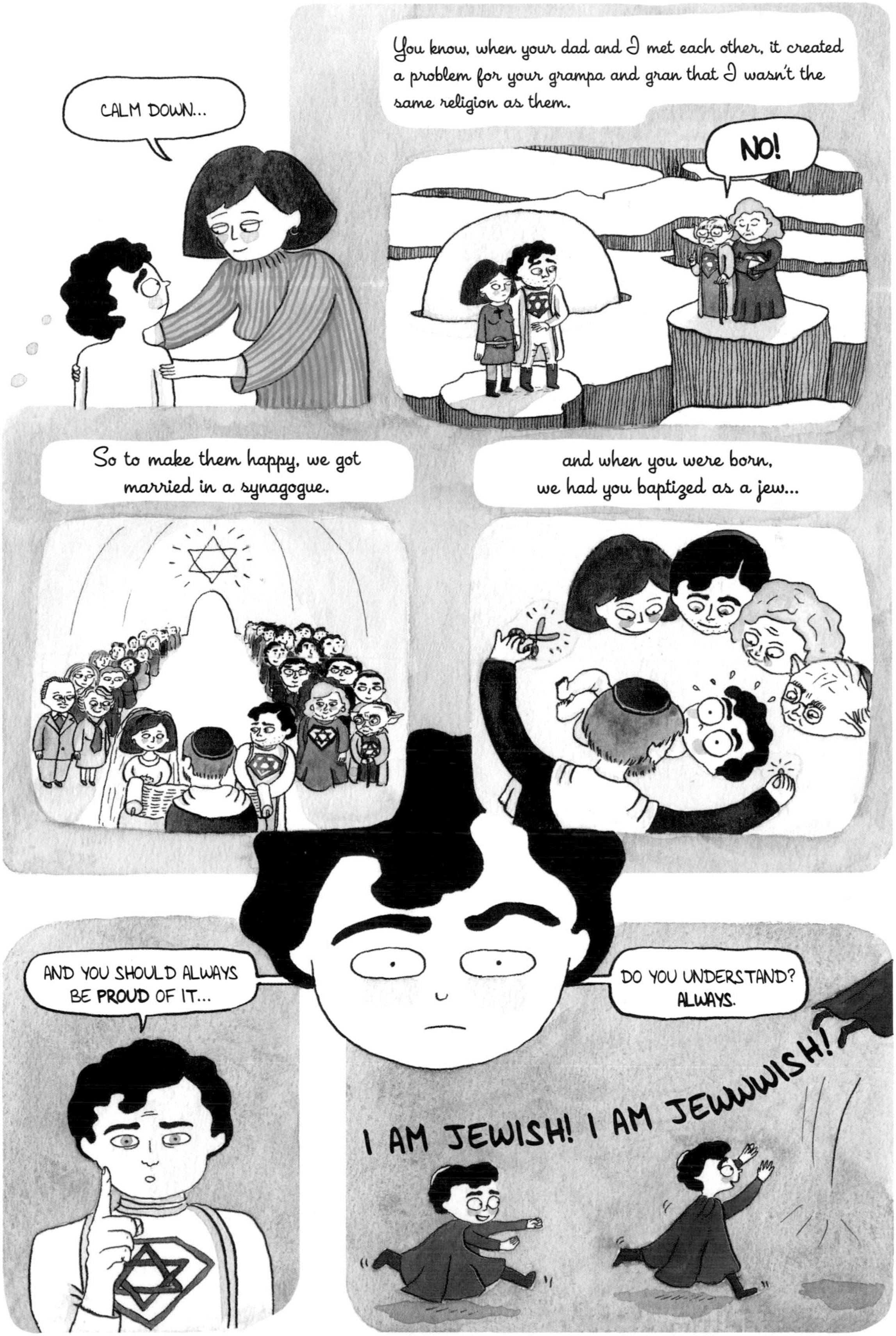

CALM DOWN...
You know, when your dad and I met each other, it created a problem for your grampa and gran that I wasn't the same religion as them.
NO!
So to make them happy, we got married in a synagogue.
and when you were born, we had you baptized as a jew...
AND YOU SHOULD ALWAYS BE PROUD OF IT...
DO YOU UNDERSTAND? ALWAYS.
I AM JEWISH! I AM JEWWWISH!

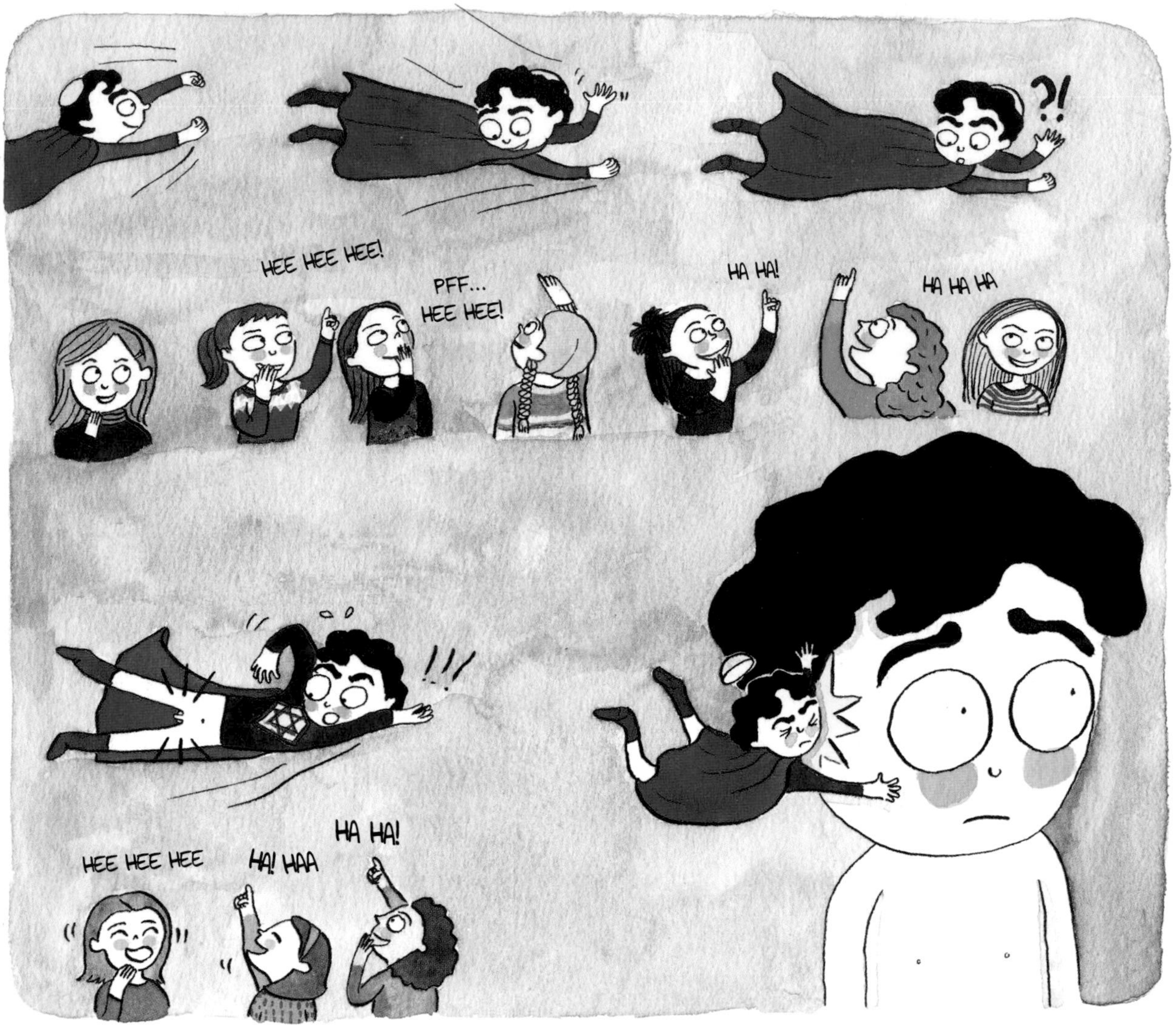
HEE HEE HEE!
PFF... HEE HEE!
HA HA!
HA HA HA
HEE HEE HEE
HA! HAA
HA HA!

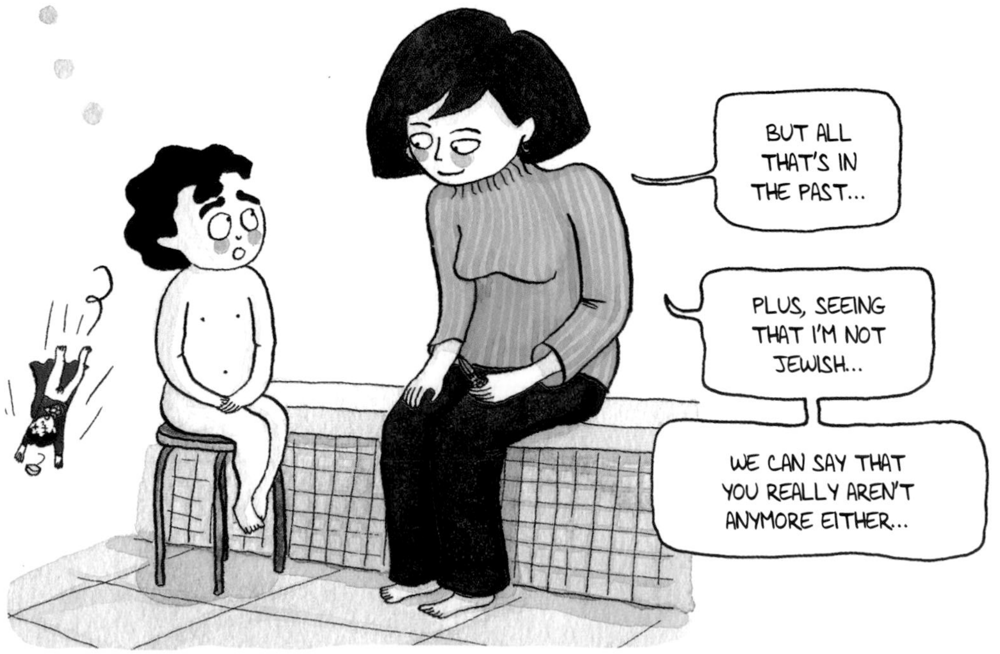
BUT ALL THAT'S IN THE PAST...
PLUS, SEEING THAT I'M NOT JEWISH...
WE CAN SAY THAT YOU REALLY AREN'T ANYMORE EITHER...

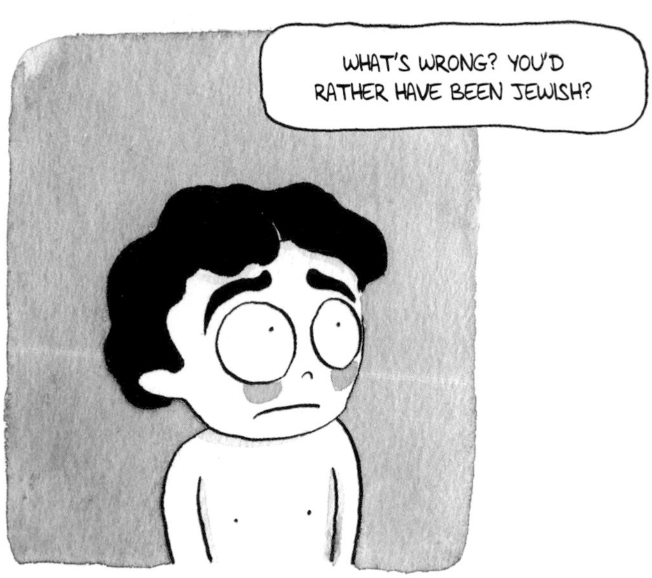
WHAT'S WRONG? YOU'D RATHER HAVE BEEN JEWISH?

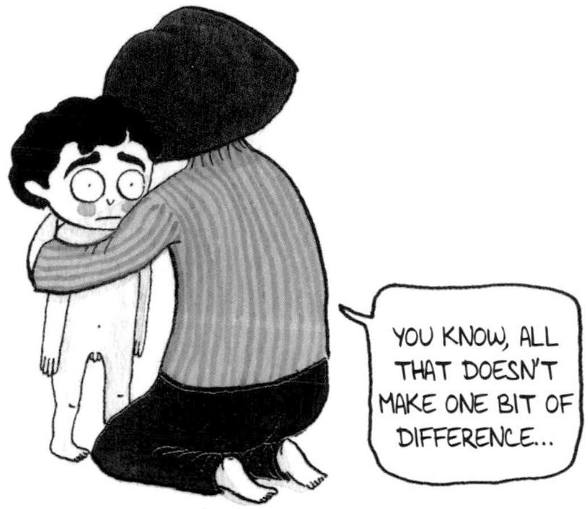
YOU KNOW, ALL THAT DOESN'T MAKE ONE BIT OF DIFFERENCE...

Actually, for me, it wasn't important whether I was Jewish or not...
I still didn't even know what that meant!

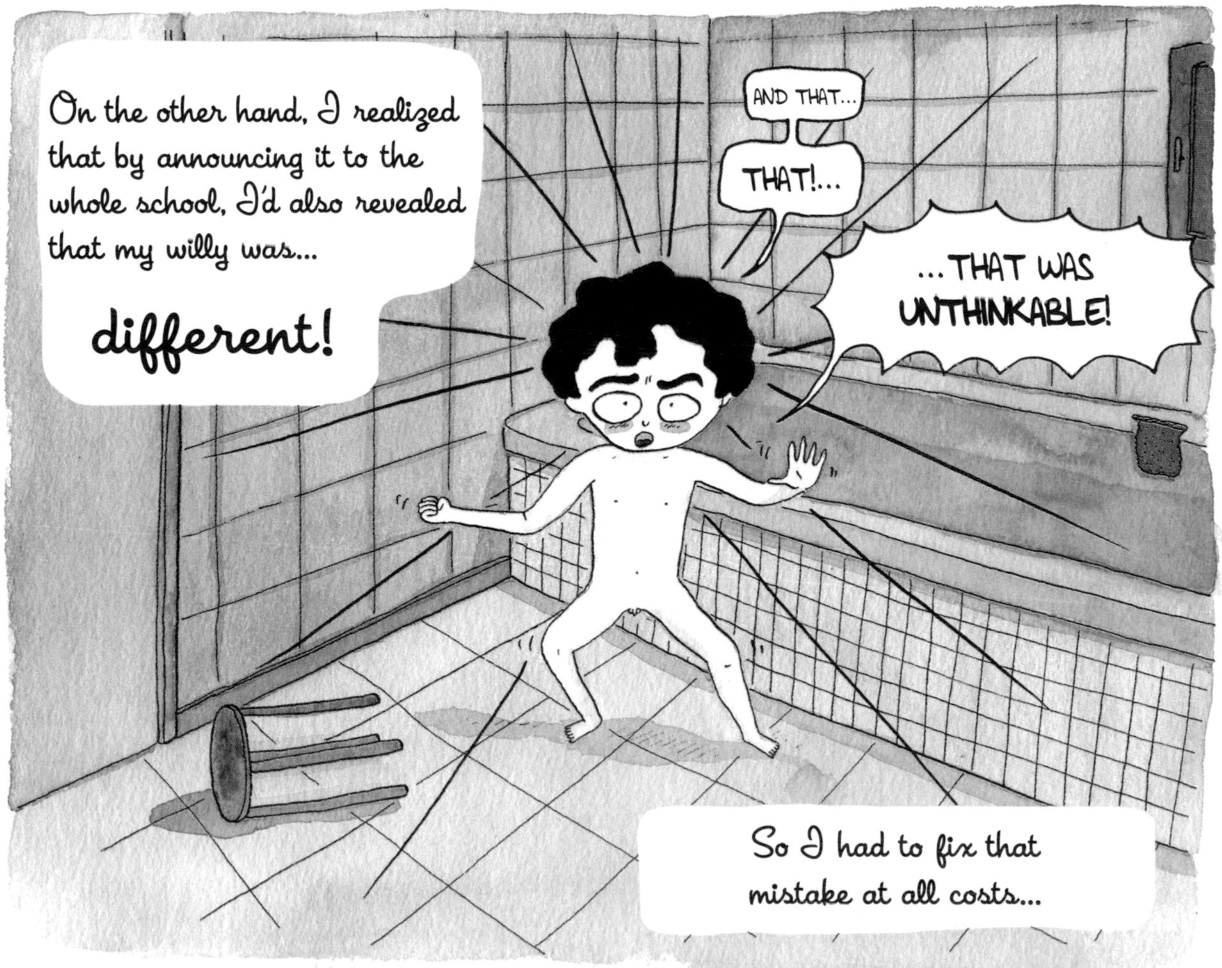
On the other hand, I realized that by announcing it to the whole school, I'd also revealed that my willy was...
different!
AND THAT...
THAT!...
...THAT WAS UNTHINKABLE!
So I had to fix that mistake at all costs...

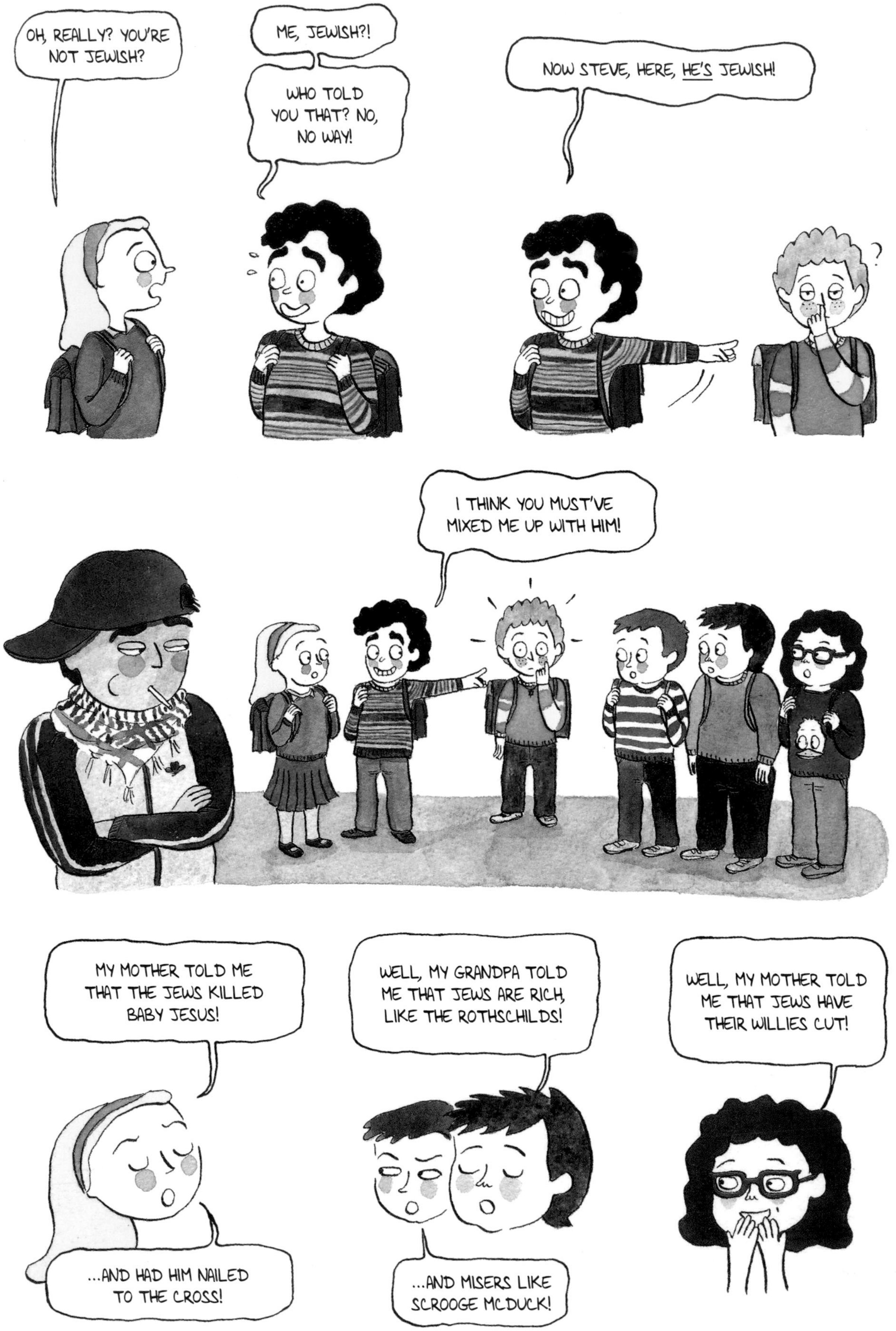
OH, REALLY? YOU'RE NOT JEWISH?
ME, JEWISH?!
WHO TOLD YOU THAT? NO, NO WAY!
NOW STEVE, HERE, HE'S JEWISH!
?
I THINK YOU MUST'VE MIXED ME UP WITH HIM!
MY MOTHER TOLD ME THAT THE JEWS KILLED BABY JESUS!
...AND HAD HIM NAILED TO THE CROSS!
WELL, MY GRANDPA TOLD ME THAT JEWS ARE RICH, LIKE THE ROTHSCHILDS!
...AND MISERS LIKE SCROOGE MCDUCK!
WELL, MY MOTHER TOLD ME THAT JEWS HAVE THEIR WILLIES CUT!

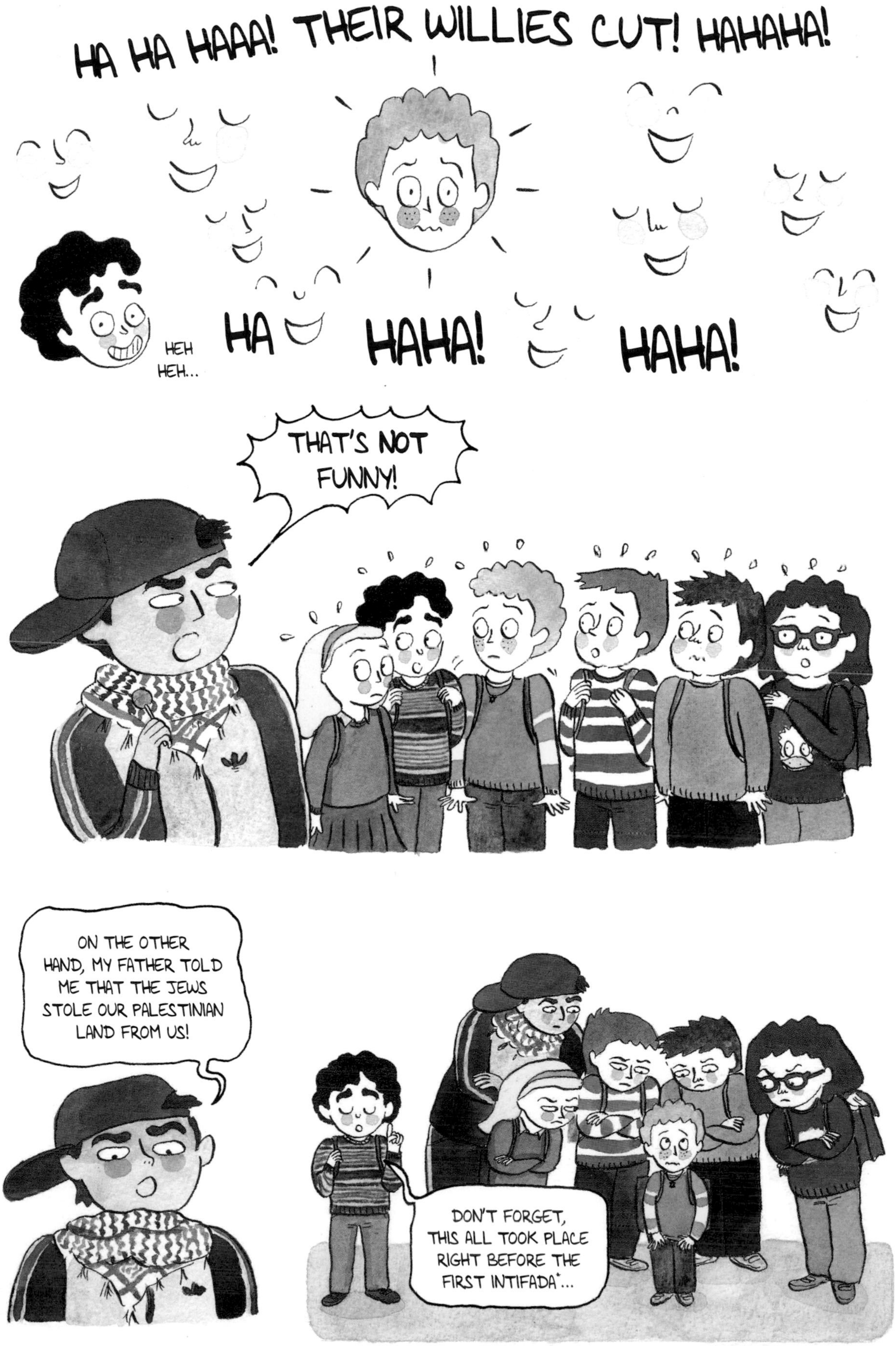
HA HA HAAA! THEIR WILLIES CUT! HAHAHA!
HEH HEH...
HA
HAHA!
HAHA!
THAT'S NOT FUNNY!
ON THE OTHER HAND, MY FATHER TOLD ME THAT THE JEWS STOLE OUR PALESTINIAN LAND FROM US!
DON'T FORGET, THIS ALL TOOK PLACE RIGHT BEFORE THE FIRST INTIFADA*...

*PALESTINIAN REVOLT THAT FIRST OCCURRED IN 1987

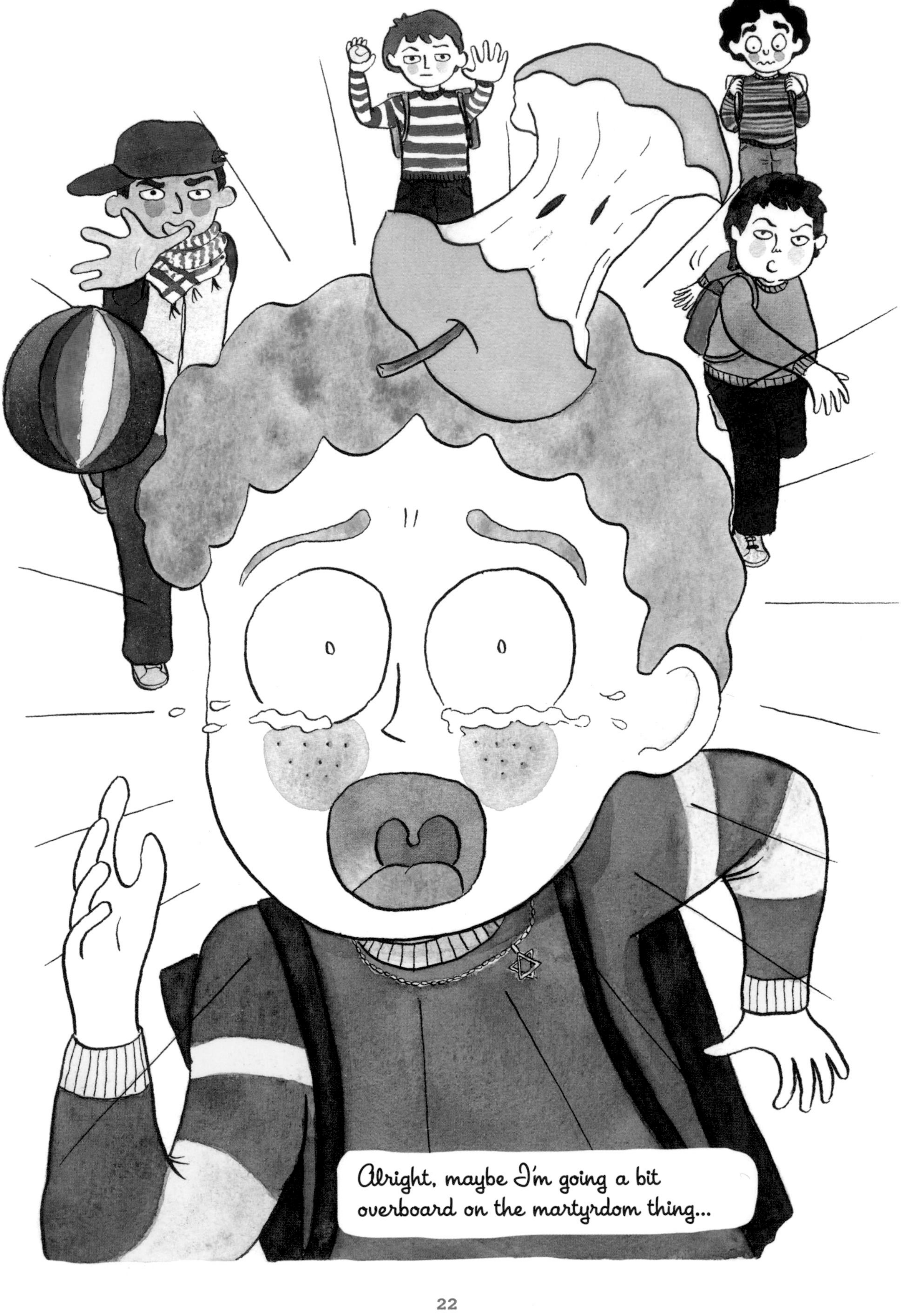
Alright, maybe I'm going a bit
overboard on the martyrdom thing...

...but at my school, whether you were big, little, red-headed, nearsighted, or effeminate...

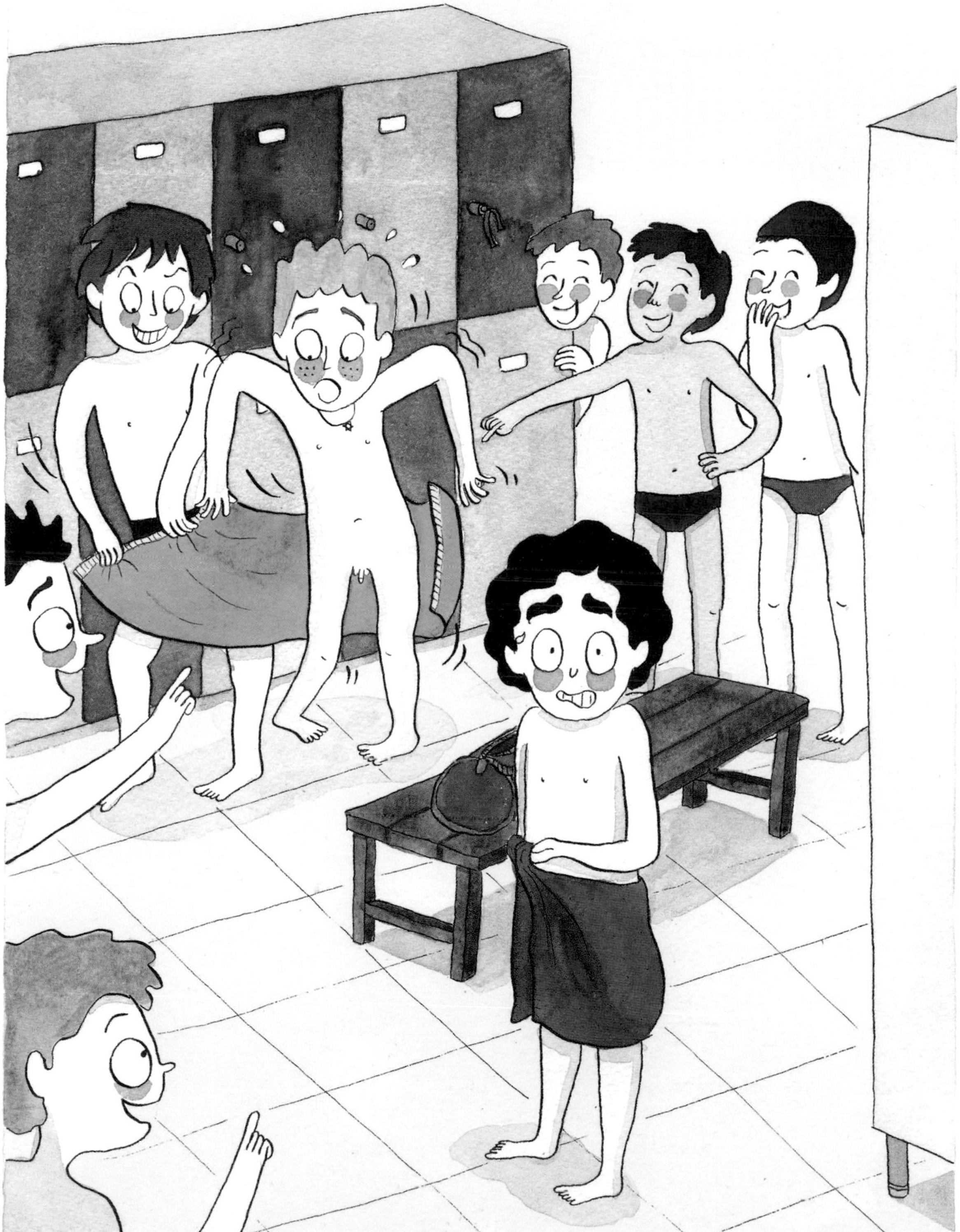

...it didn't feel too good to be different.

And so, when they asked me:

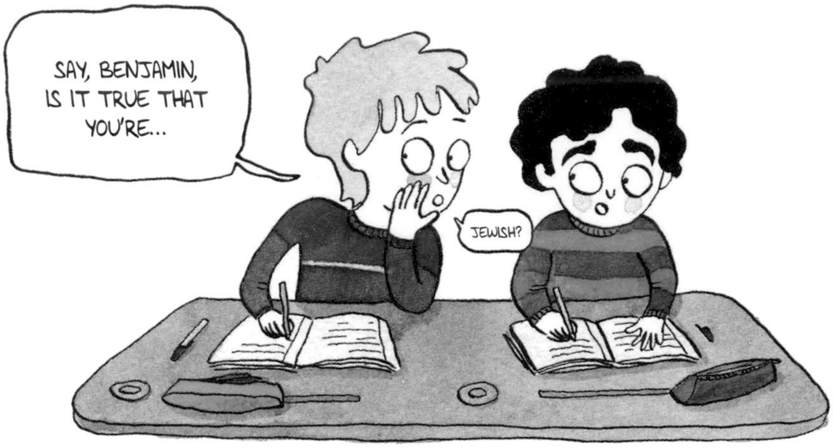
SAY, BENJAMIN, IS IT TRUE THAT YOU'RE...
JEWISH?

I went for the educational approach, explaining that...

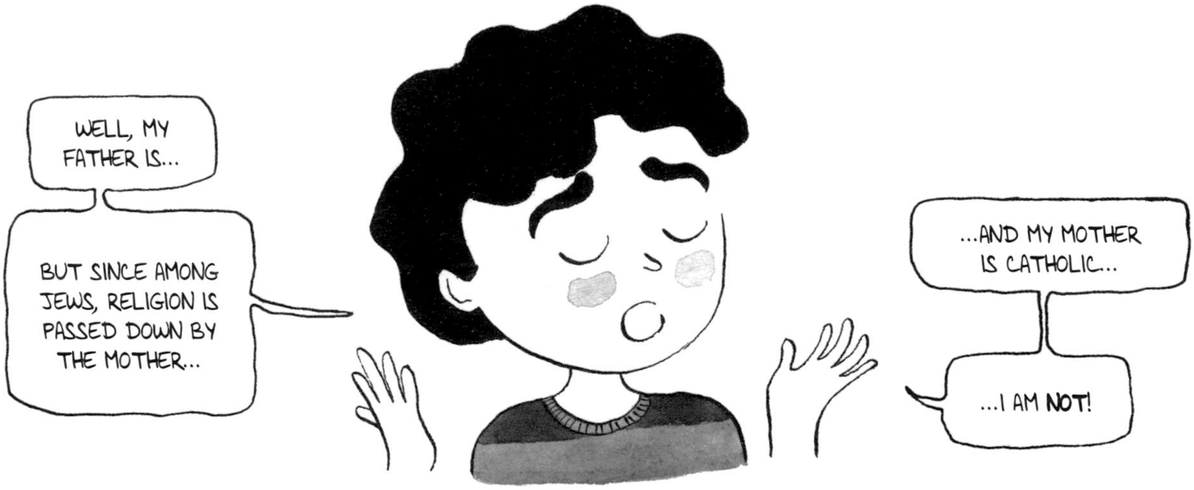
WELL, MY FATHER IS...
BUT SINCE AMONG JEWS, RELIGION IS PASSED DOWN BY THE MOTHER...
...AND MY MOTHER IS CATHOLIC...
...I AM NOT!

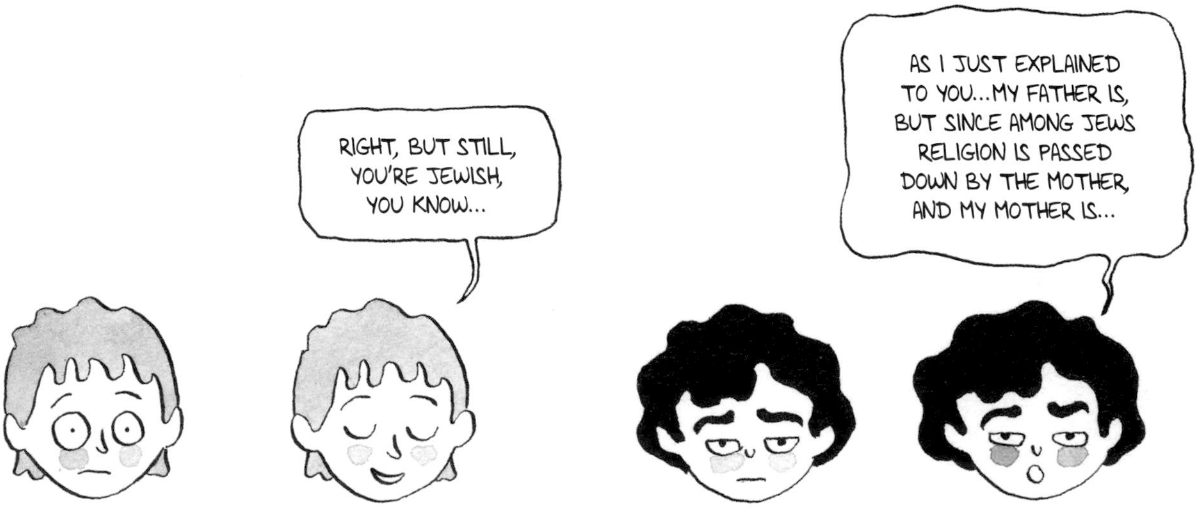
RIGHT, BUT STILL, YOU'RE JEWISH, YOU KNOW...
AS I JUST EXPLAINED TO YOU...MY FATHER IS, BUT SINCE AMONG JEWS RELIGION IS PASSED DOWN BY THE MOTHER, AND MY MOTHER IS...

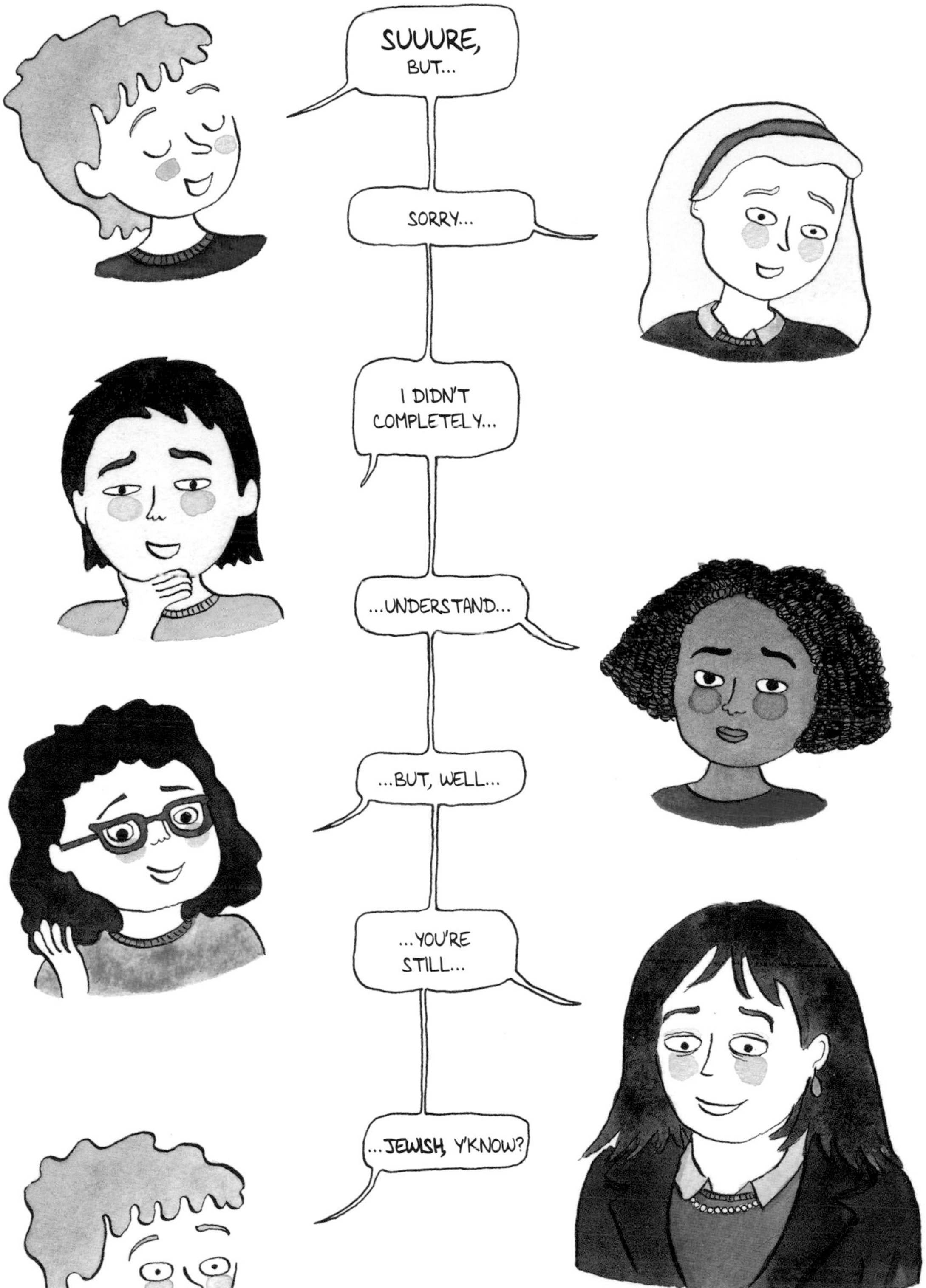
SUUURE, BUT...
SORRY...
I DIDN'T COMPLETELY...
...UNDERSTAND...
...BUT, WELL...
...YOU'RE STILL...
...JEWISH, Y'KNOW?

Then one day...

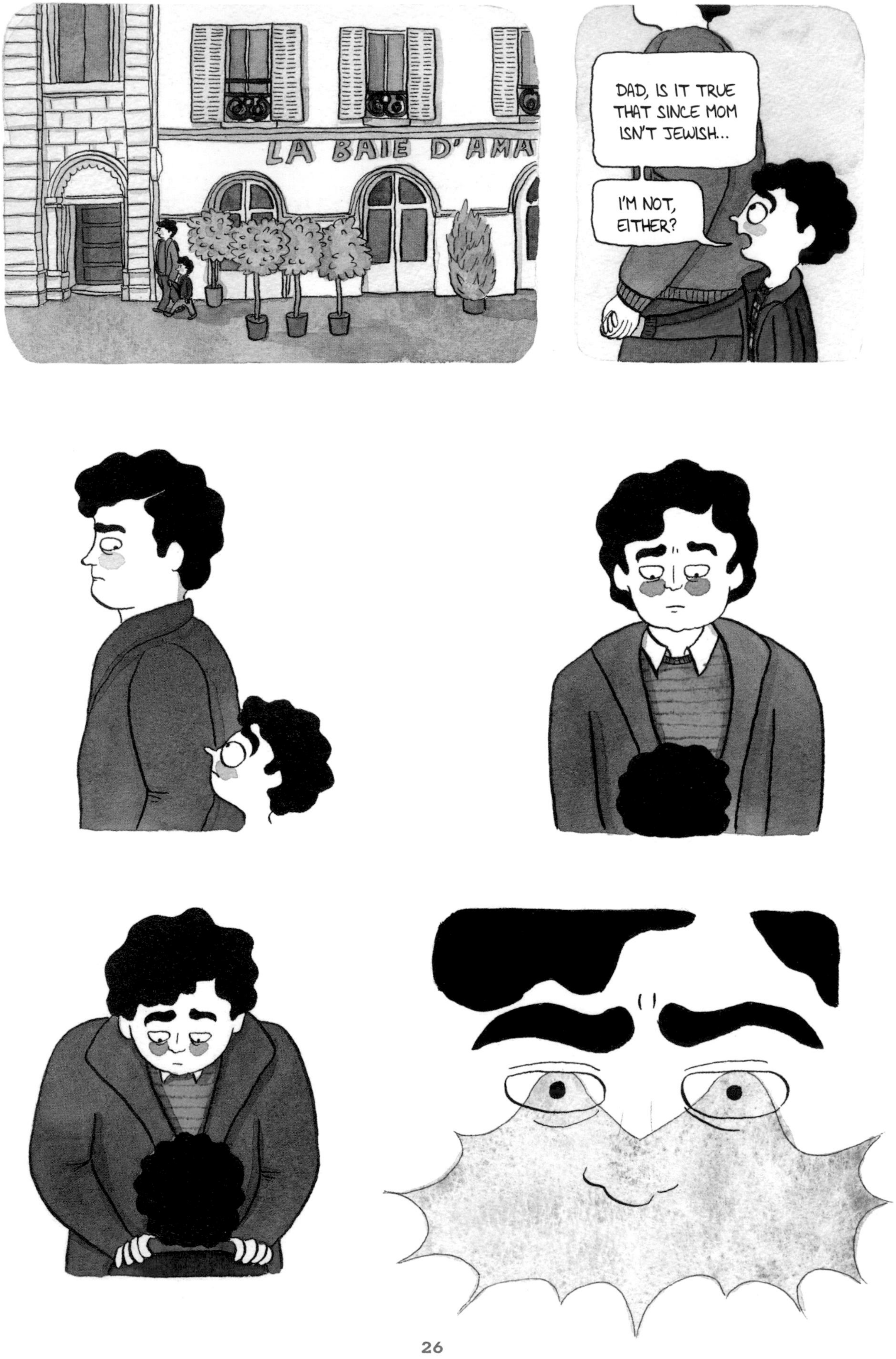
LA BAIE D'AMA
DAD, IS IT TRUE THAT SINCE MOM ISN'T JEWISH...
I'M NOT, EITHER?

WHAT'S ALL THIS ABOUT?

Ah, yes. I didn't tell you: even though my father had been eating in secret since the Big Pardon, religion was still very important to him.

WHO TOLD YOU THAT?!

IT WASN'T ME... IT WAS MOM!

YOUR MOM'S TALKING TOTAL NONSENSE!

BESIDES, IF THAT WERE THE CASE, HOW WOULD WE HAVE BEEN MARRIED IN A SYNAGOGUE?

HUH?! HOW?

You need to know that there were three competing theories in my family...

According to my mother...

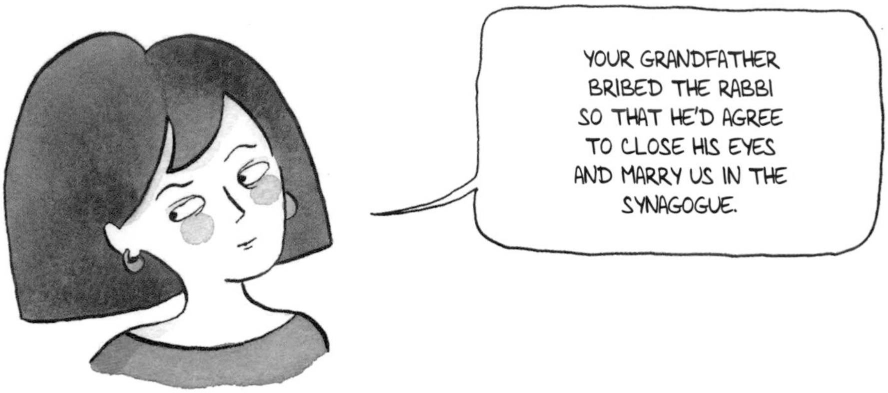
YOUR GRANDFATHER BRIBED THE RABBI SO THAT HE'D AGREE TO CLOSE HIS EYES AND MARRY US IN THE SYNAGOGUE.

According to my father...

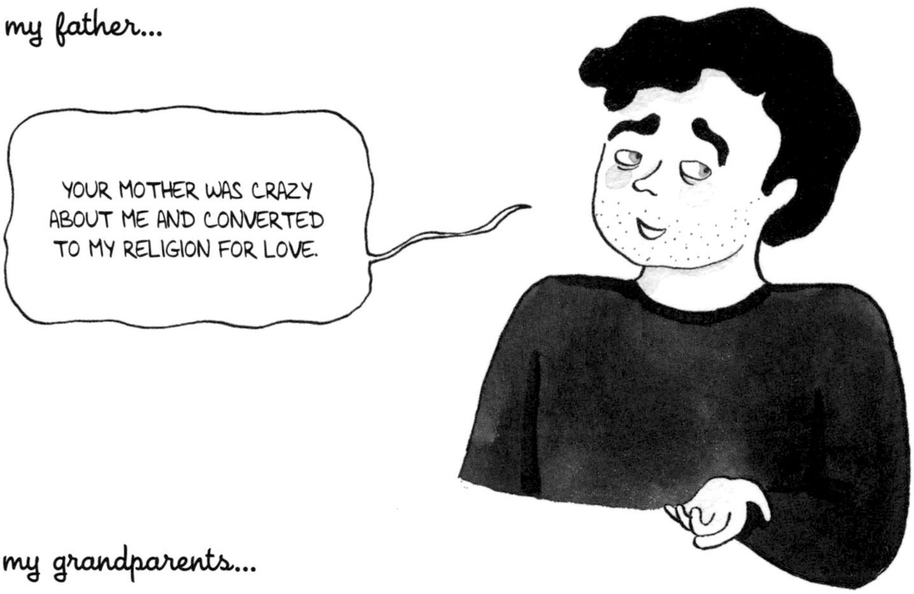
YOUR MOTHER WAS CRAZY ABOUT ME AND CONVERTED TO MY RELIGION FOR LOVE.

According to my grandparents...

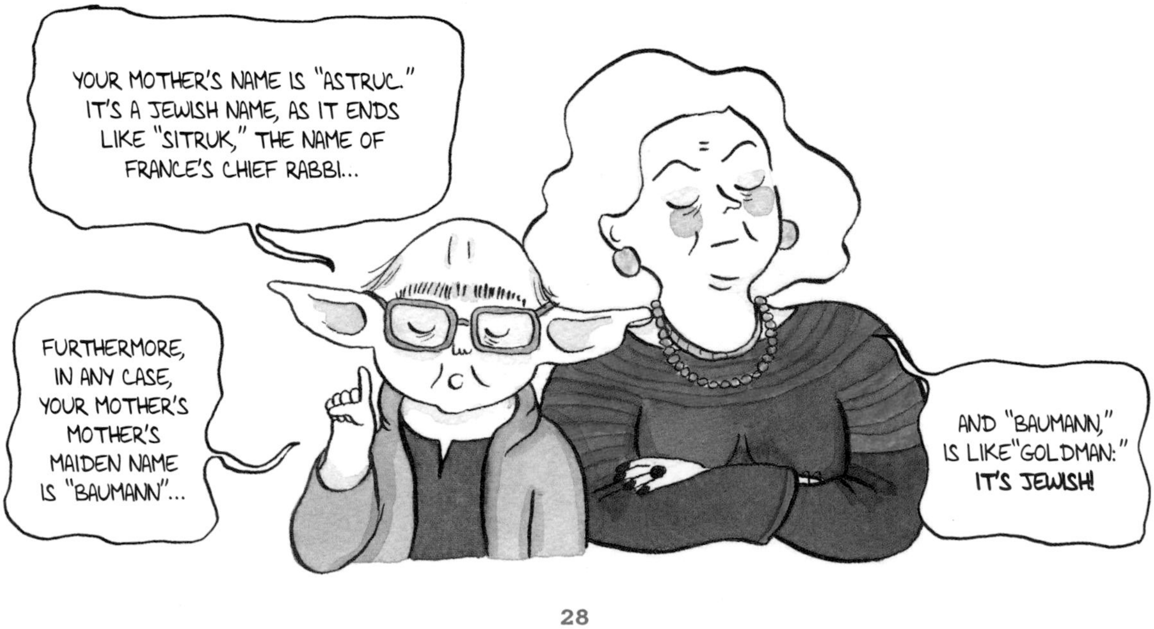
YOUR MOTHER'S NAME IS "ASTRUC." IT'S A JEWISH NAME, AS IT ENDS LIKE "SITRUK," THE NAME OF FRANCE'S CHIEF RABBI...
FURTHERMORE, IN ANY CASE, YOUR MOTHER'S MOTHER'S MAIDEN NAME IS "BAUMANN"...
AND "BAUMANN," IS LIKE "GOLDMAN:" **IT'S JEWISH!**

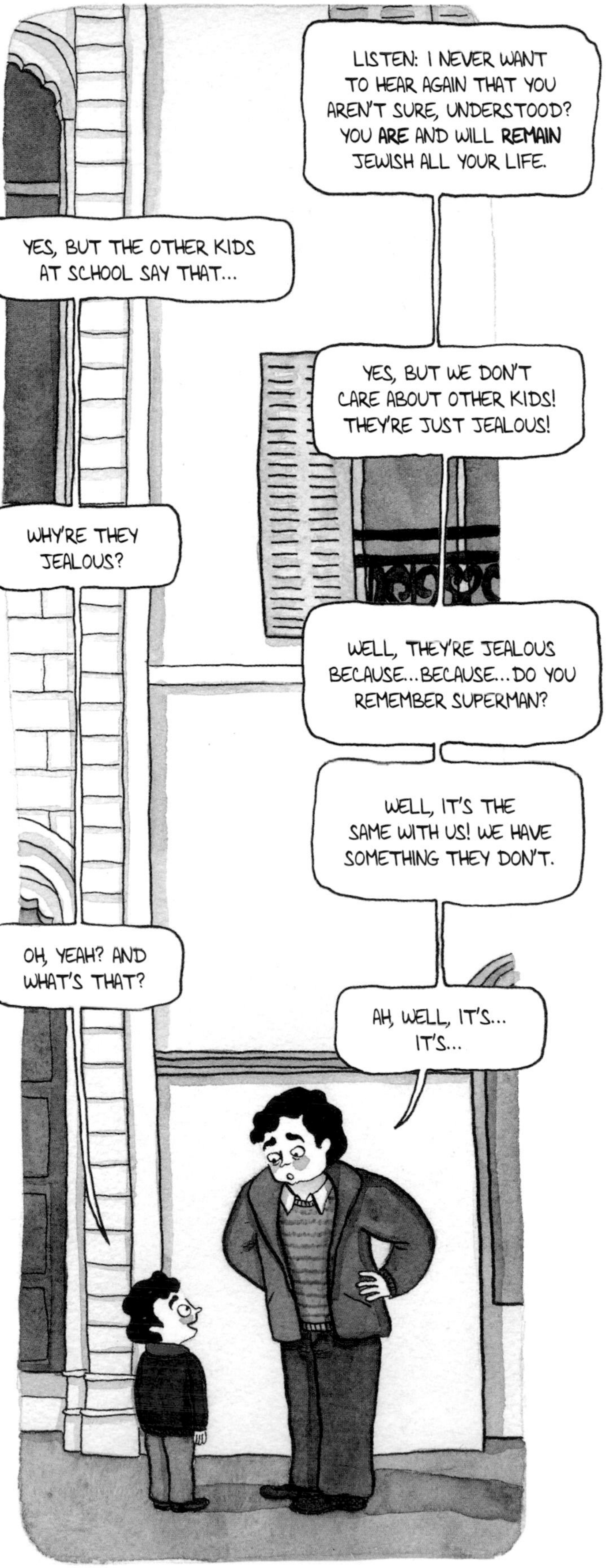
LISTEN: I NEVER WANT TO HEAR AGAIN THAT YOU AREN'T SURE, UNDERSTOOD? YOU **ARE** AND WILL **REMAIN** JEWISH ALL YOUR LIFE.
YES, BUT THE OTHER KIDS AT SCHOOL SAY THAT...
YES, BUT WE DON'T CARE ABOUT OTHER KIDS! THEY'RE JUST JEALOUS!
WHY'RE THEY JEALOUS?
WELL, THEY'RE JEALOUS BECAUSE...BECAUSE...DO YOU REMEMBER SUPERMAN?
WELL, IT'S THE SAME WITH US! WE HAVE SOMETHING THEY DON'T.
OH, YEAH? AND WHAT'S THAT?
AH, WELL, IT'S... IT'S...

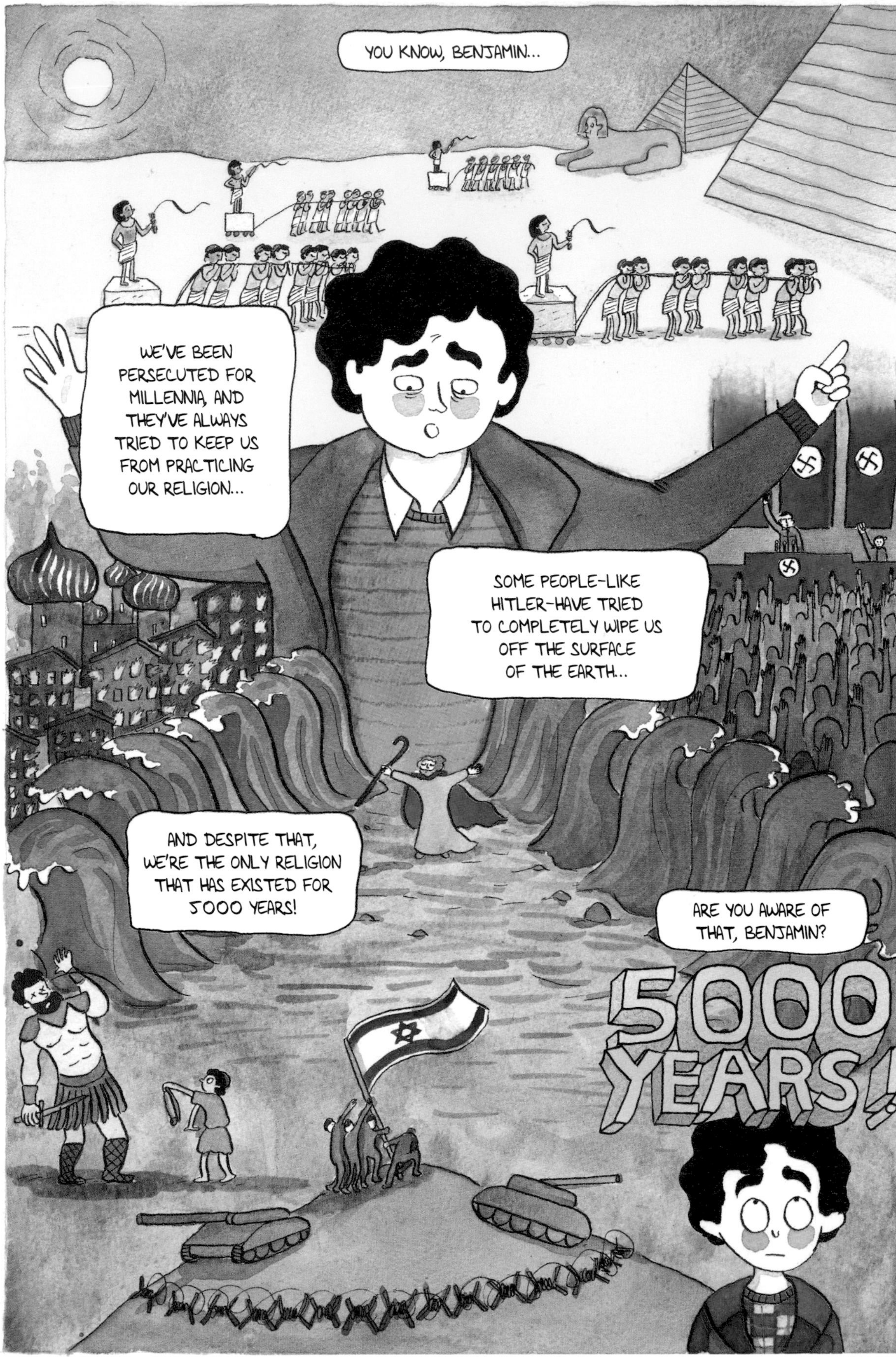
YOU KNOW, BENJAMIN...
WE'VE BEEN PERSECUTED FOR MILLENNIA, AND THEY'VE ALWAYS TRIED TO KEEP US FROM PRACTICING OUR RELIGION...
SOME PEOPLE–LIKE HITLER–HAVE TRIED TO COMPLETELY WIPE US OFF THE SURFACE OF THE EARTH...
AND DESPITE THAT, WE'RE THE ONLY RELIGION THAT HAS EXISTED FOR 5000 YEARS!
ARE YOU AWARE OF THAT, BENJAMIN?
5000 YEARS!

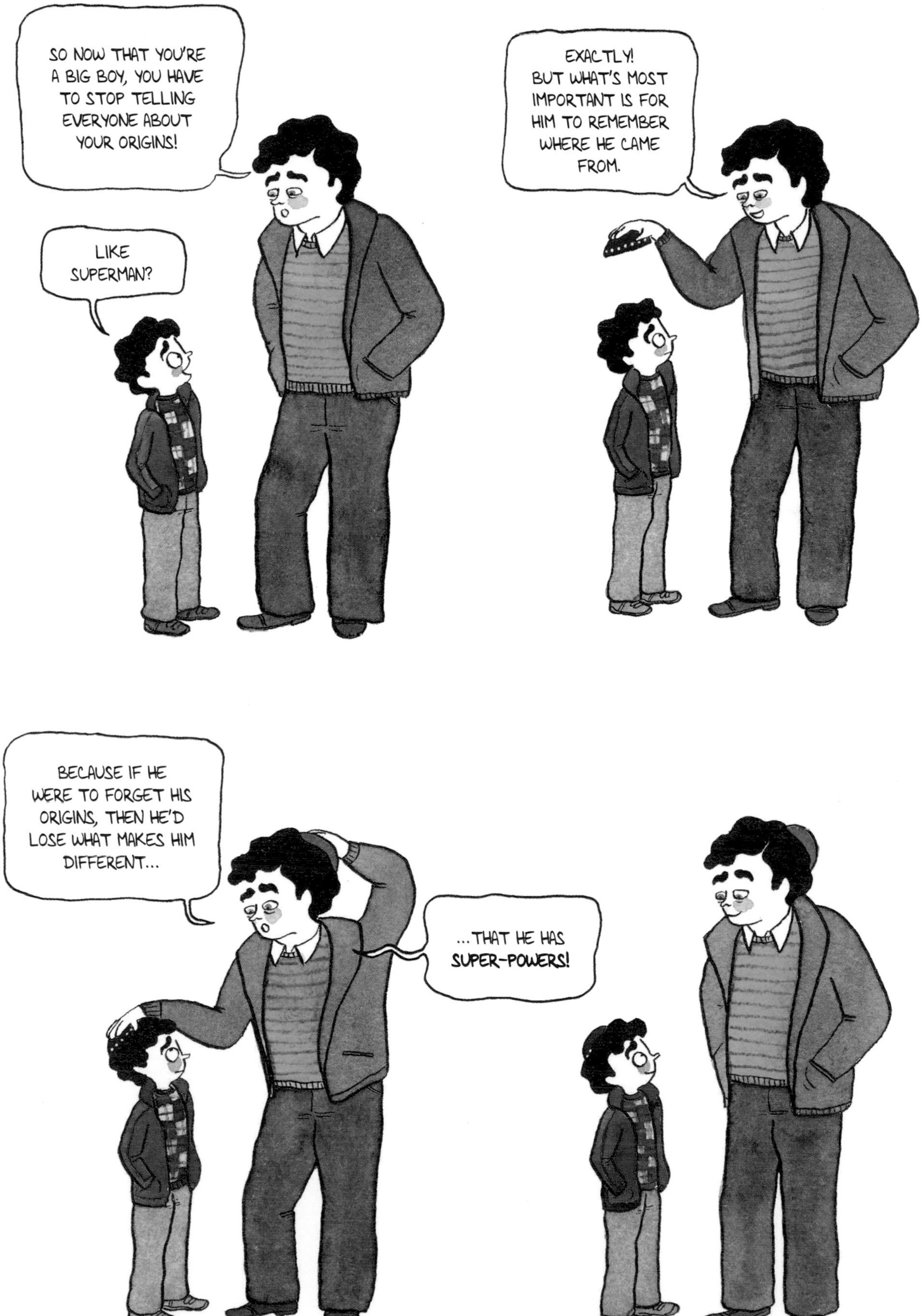
SO NOW THAT YOU'RE A BIG BOY, YOU HAVE TO STOP TELLING EVERYONE ABOUT YOUR ORIGINS!
LIKE SUPERMAN?
EXACTLY! BUT WHAT'S MOST IMPORTANT IS FOR HIM TO REMEMBER WHERE HE CAME FROM.
BECAUSE IF HE WERE TO FORGET HIS ORIGINS, THEN HE'D LOSE WHAT MAKES HIM DIFFERENT...
...THAT HE HAS SUPER-POWERS!

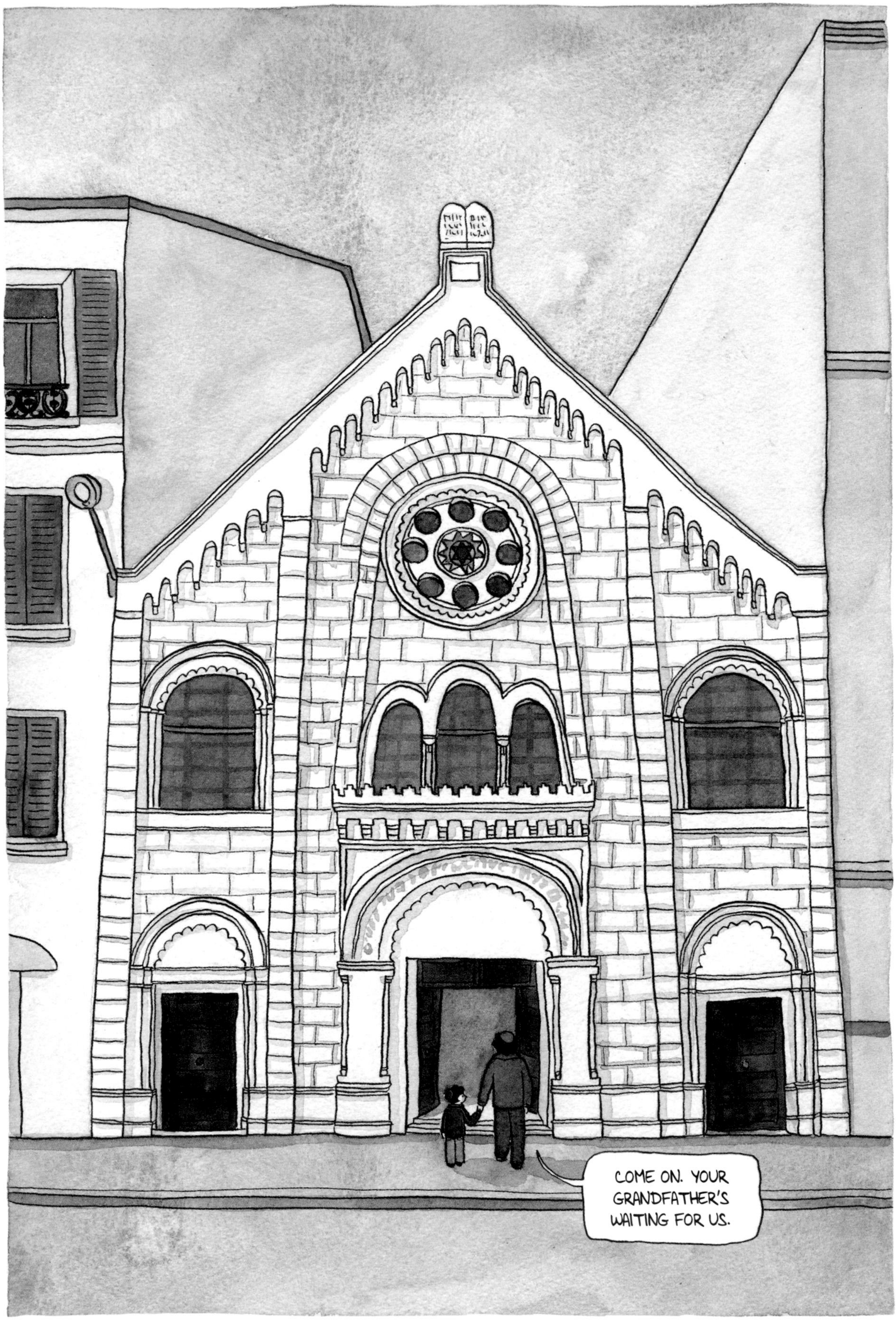
COME ON. YOUR GRANDFATHER'S WAITING FOR US.

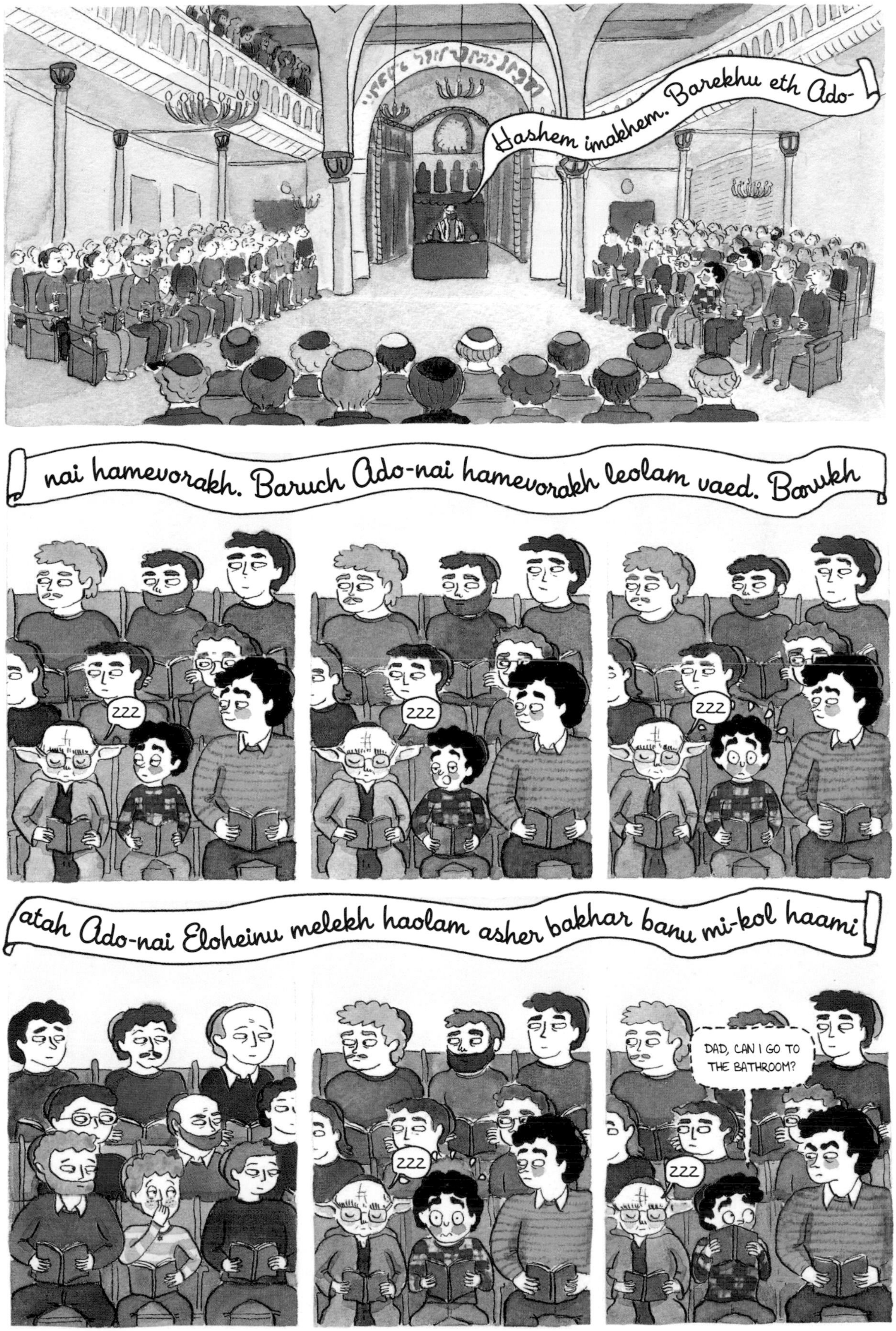
Hashem imakhem. Barekhu eth Ado-
nai hamevorakh. Baruch Ado-nai hamevorakh leolam vaed. Barukh
ZZZ
ZZZ
ZZZ
atah Ado-nai Eloheinu melekh haolam asher bakhar banu mi-kol haami
ZZZ
ZZZ
DAD, CAN I GO TO THE BATHROOM?

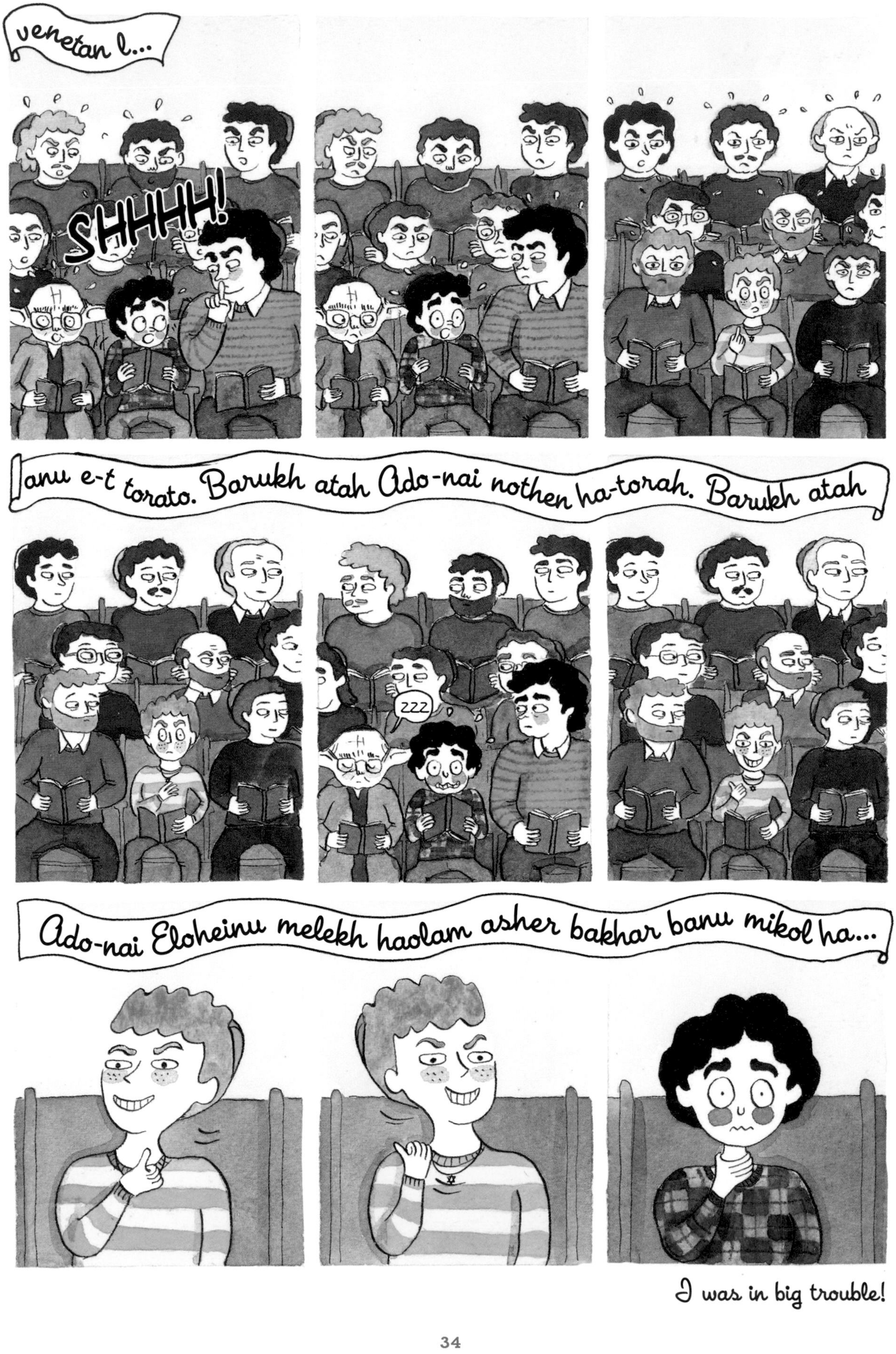
venetan l...
SHHHH!
anu e-t torato. Barukh atah Ado-nai nothen ha-torah. Barukh atah
zzz
Ado-nai Eloheinu melekh haolam asher bakhar banu mikol ha...
I was in big trouble!

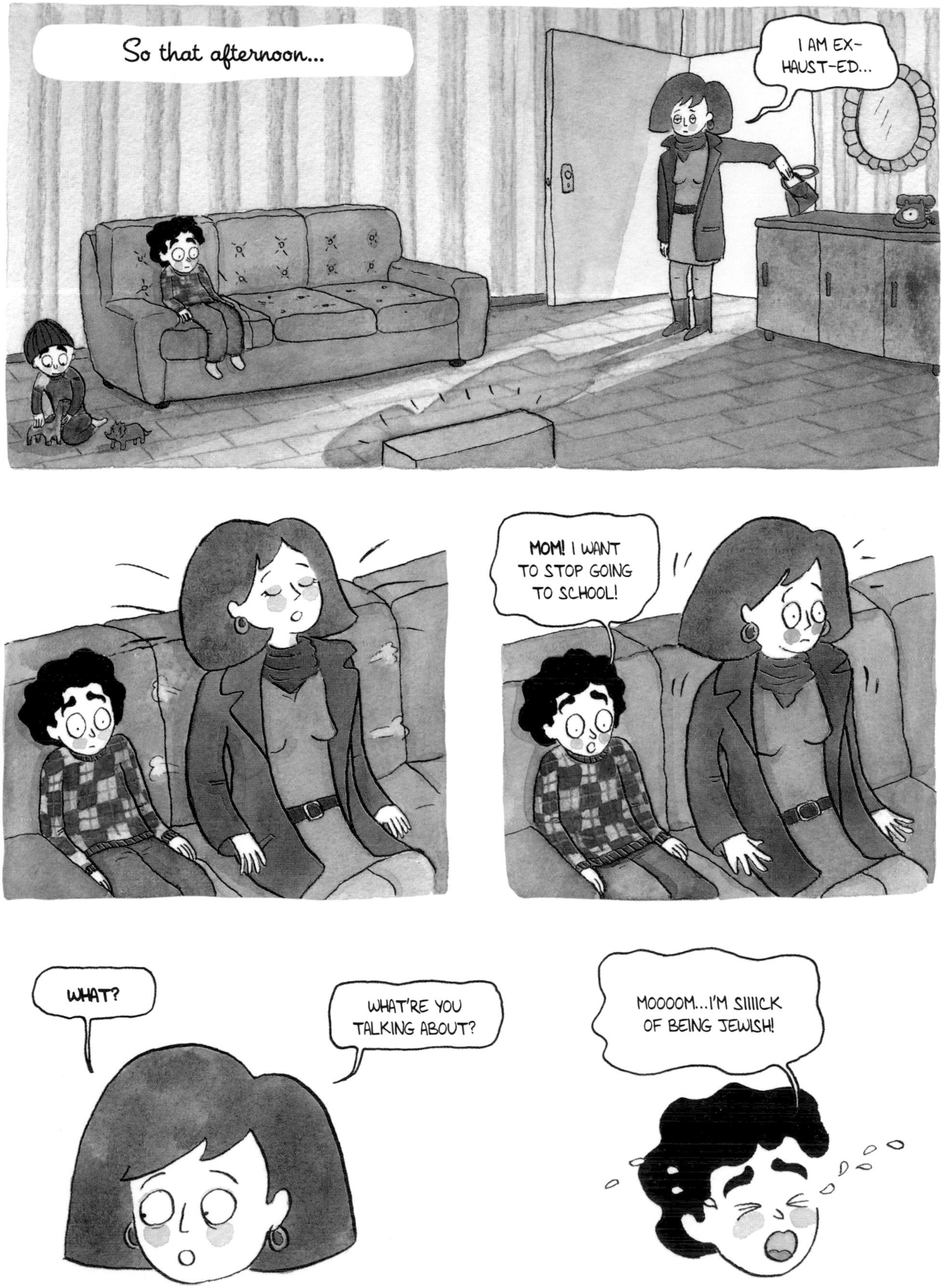
So that afternoon...
I AM EX-HAUST-ED...
MOM! I WANT TO STOP GOING TO SCHOOL!
WHAT?
WHAT'RE YOU TALKING ABOUT?
MOOOOM...I'M SIIIICK OF BEING JEWISH!

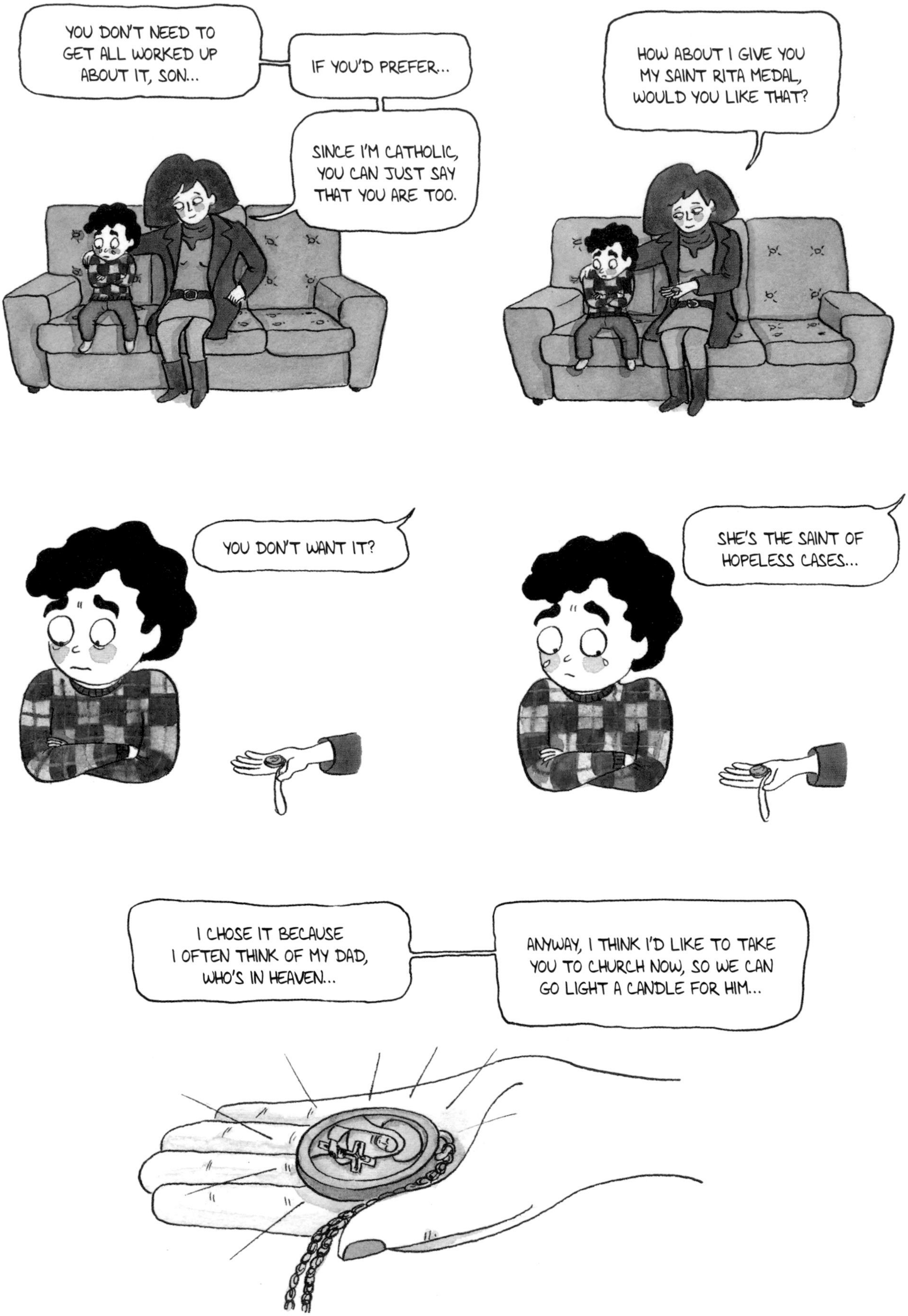
YOU DON'T NEED TO GET ALL WORKED UP ABOUT IT, SON...
IF YOU'D PREFER...
SINCE I'M CATHOLIC, YOU CAN JUST SAY THAT YOU ARE TOO.
HOW ABOUT I GIVE YOU MY SAINT RITA MEDAL, WOULD YOU LIKE THAT?
YOU DON'T WANT IT?
SHE'S THE SAINT OF HOPELESS CASES...
I CHOSE IT BECAUSE I OFTEN THINK OF MY DAD, WHO'S IN HEAVEN...
ANYWAY, I THINK I'D LIKE TO TAKE YOU TO CHURCH NOW, SO WE CAN GO LIGHT A CANDLE FOR HIM...

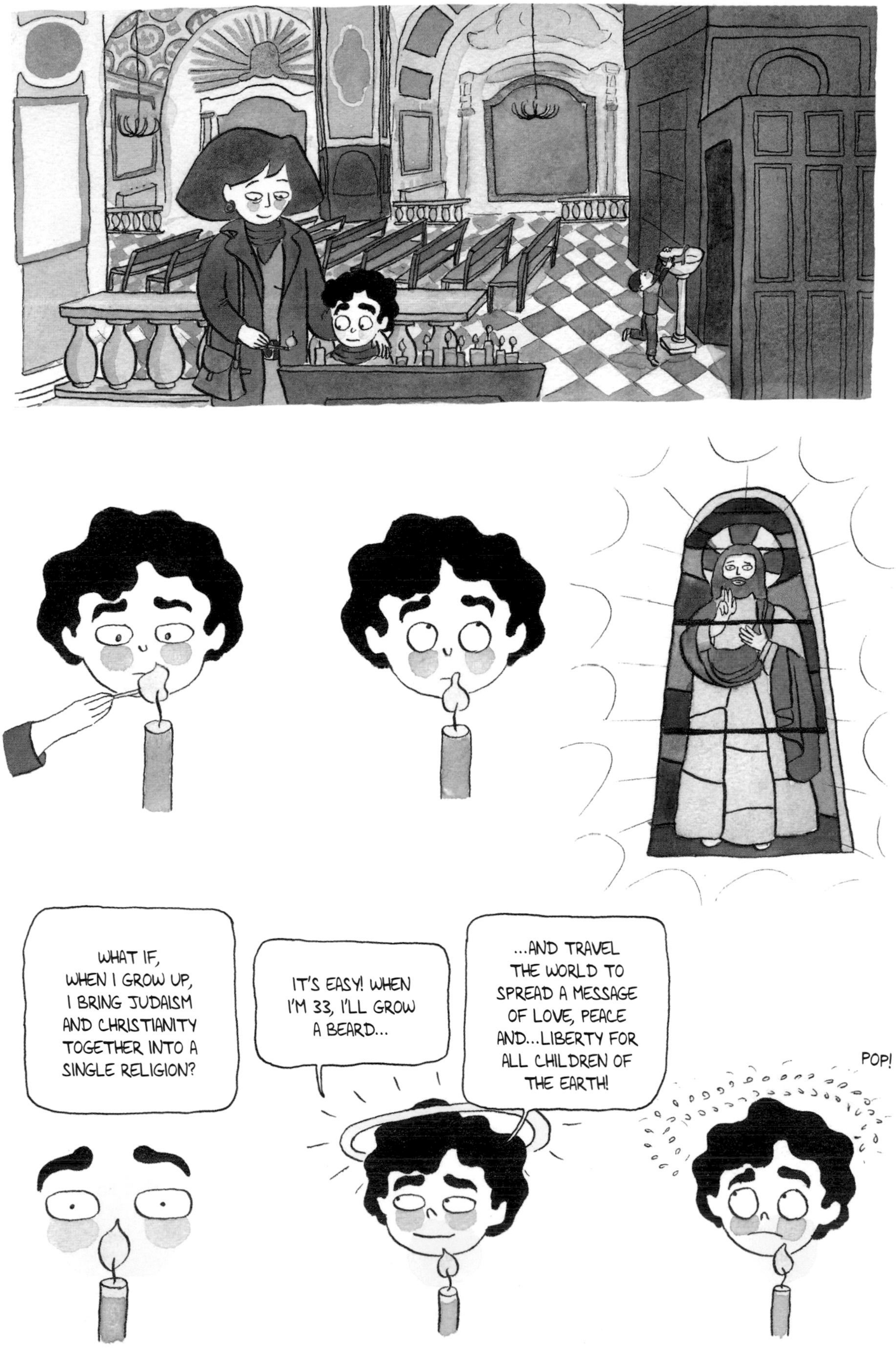
WHAT IF, WHEN I GROW UP, I BRING JUDAISM AND CHRISTIANITY TOGETHER INTO A SINGLE RELIGION?
IT'S EASY! WHEN I'M 33, I'LL GROW A BEARD...
...AND TRAVEL THE WORLD TO SPREAD A MESSAGE OF LOVE, PEACE AND...LIBERTY FOR ALL CHILDREN OF THE EARTH!
POP!

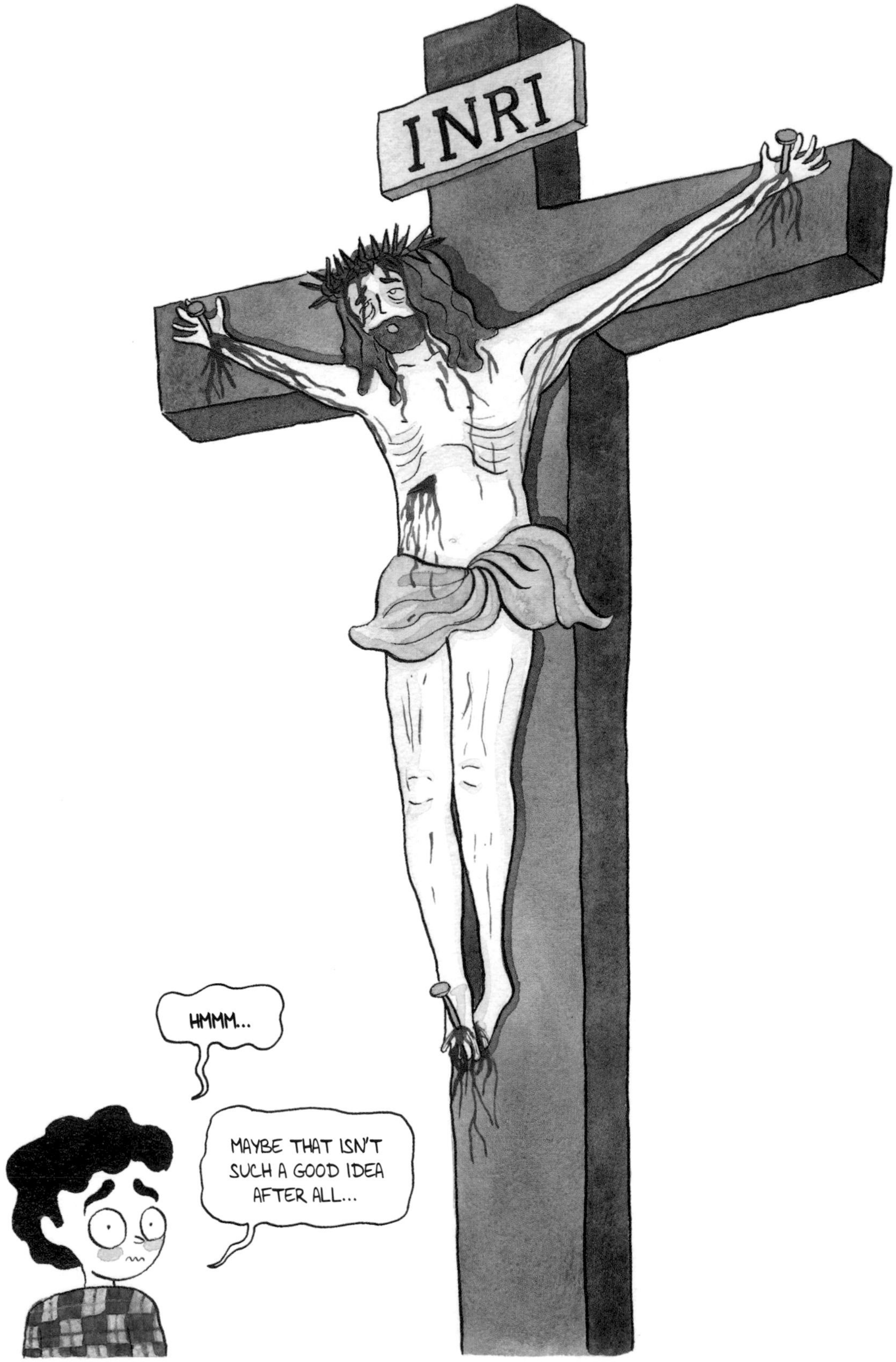
INRI
HMMM...
MAYBE THAT ISN'T SUCH A GOOD IDEA AFTER ALL...

So the next day...

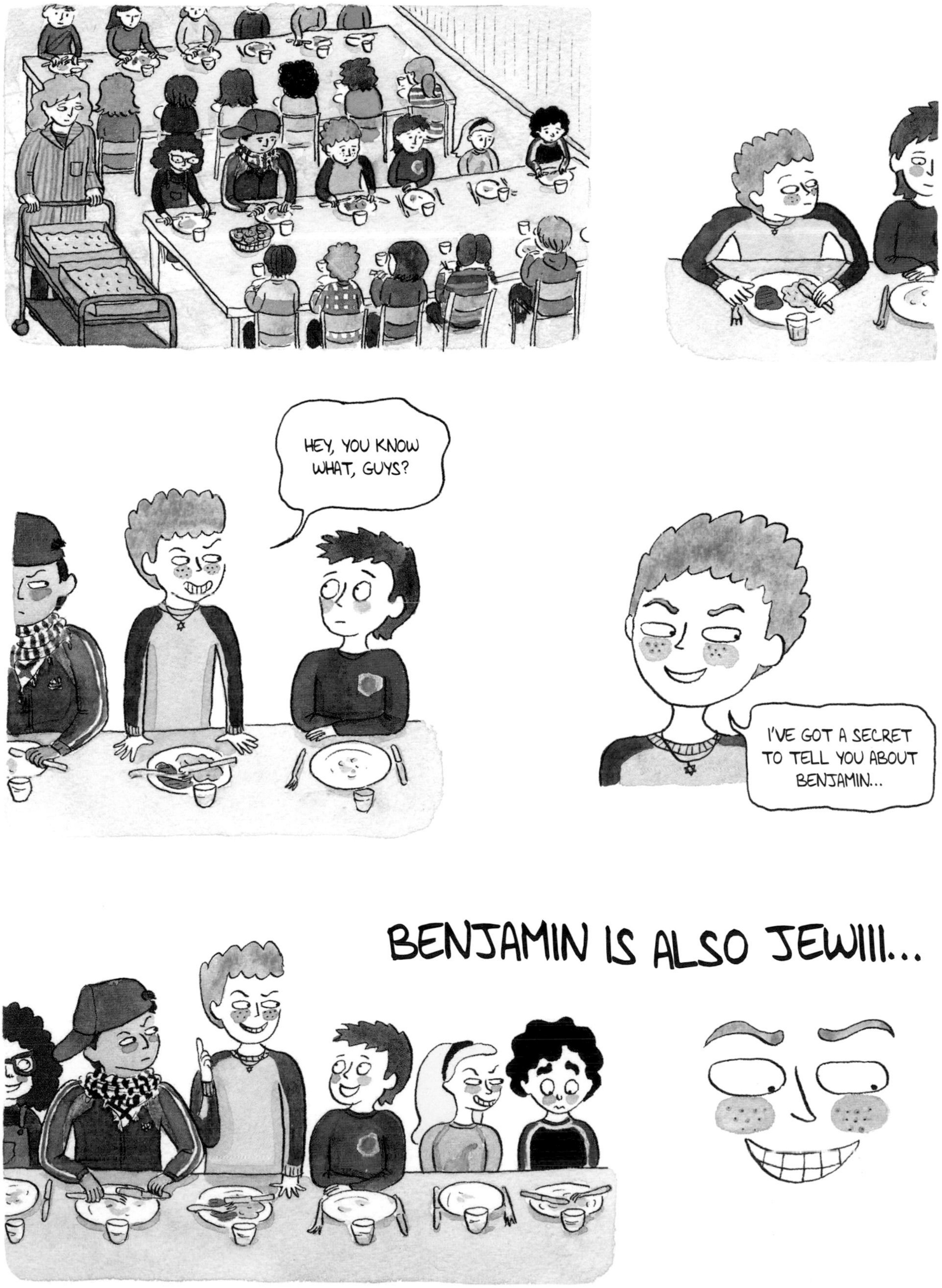
HEY, YOU KNOW WHAT, GUYS?
I'VE GOT A SECRET TO TELL YOU ABOUT BENJAMIN...
BENJAMIN IS ALSO JEWIII...

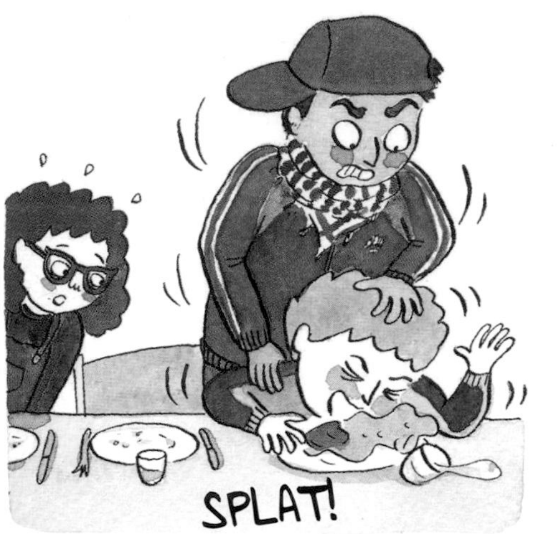
SPLAT!

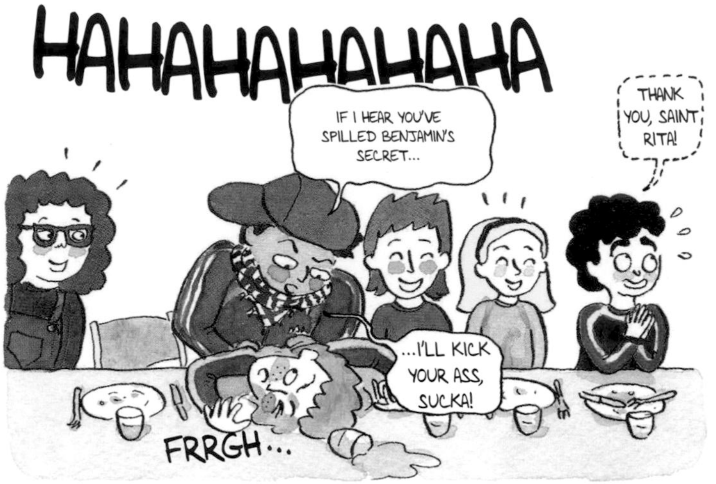
HAHAHAHAHAHA
IF I HEAR YOU'VE SPILLED BENJAMIN'S SECRET...
...I'LL KICK YOUR ASS, SUCKA!
THANK YOU, SAINT RITA!
FRRGH...

Mohammed saved my life...but why'd he do it?

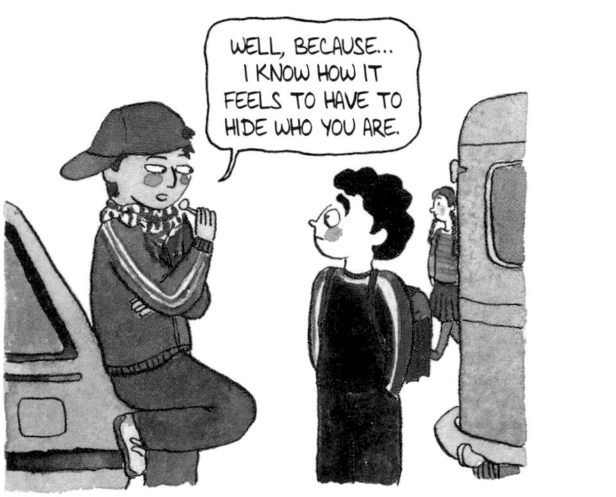
WELL, BECAUSE... I KNOW HOW IT FEELS TO HAVE TO HIDE WHO YOU ARE.

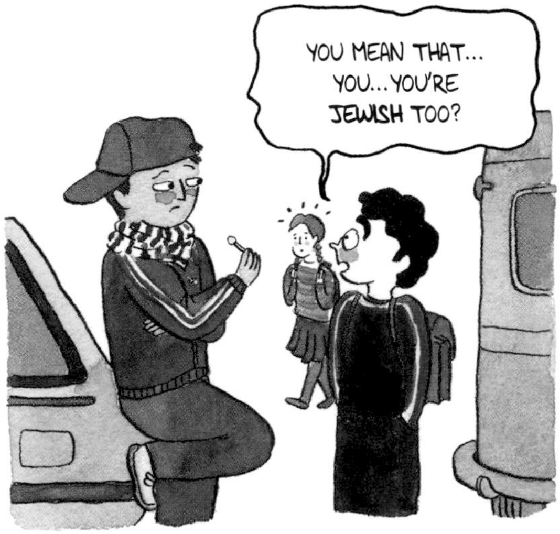
YOU MEAN THAT... YOU...YOU'RE **JEWISH** TOO?

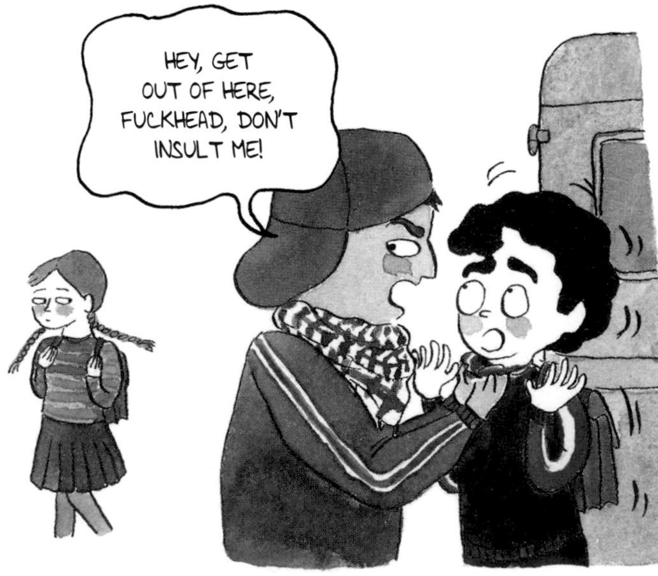
HEY, GET OUT OF HERE, FUCKHEAD, DON'T INSULT ME!

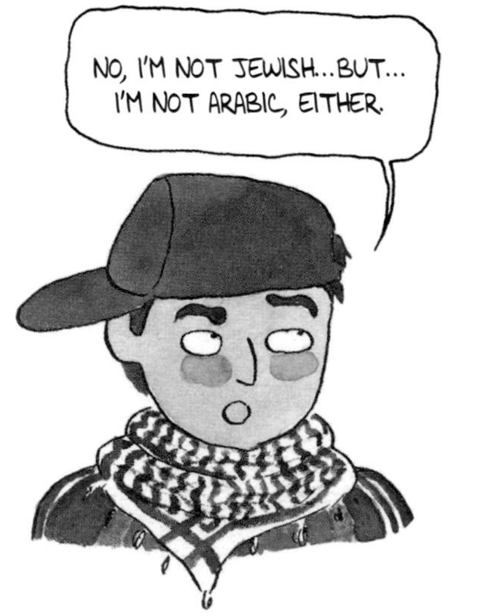
NO, I'M NOT JEWISH...BUT... I'M NOT ARABIC, EITHER.

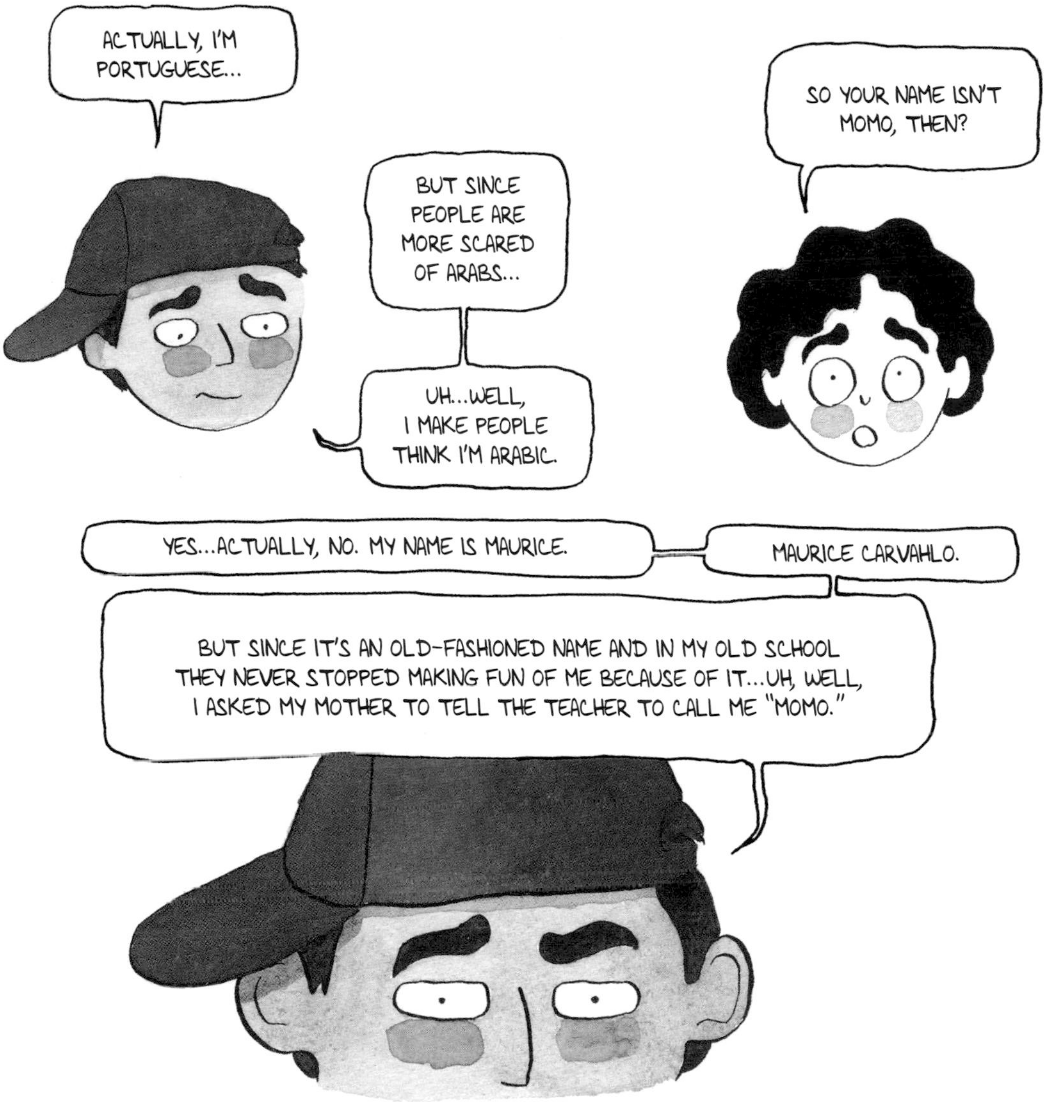
ACTUALLY, I'M PORTUGUESE...
BUT SINCE PEOPLE ARE MORE SCARED OF ARABS...
UH...WELL, I MAKE PEOPLE THINK I'M ARABIC.
SO YOUR NAME ISN'T MOMO, THEN?
YES...ACTUALLY, NO. MY NAME IS MAURICE.
MAURICE CARVAHLO.
BUT SINCE IT'S AN OLD-FASHIONED NAME AND IN MY OLD SCHOOL THEY NEVER STOPPED MAKING FUN OF ME BECAUSE OF IT...UH, WELL, I ASKED MY MOTHER TO TELL THE TEACHER TO CALL ME "MOMO."

I didn't know it yet, but that day I'd found a new friend and the guarantee that no one would ever make fun of me again.

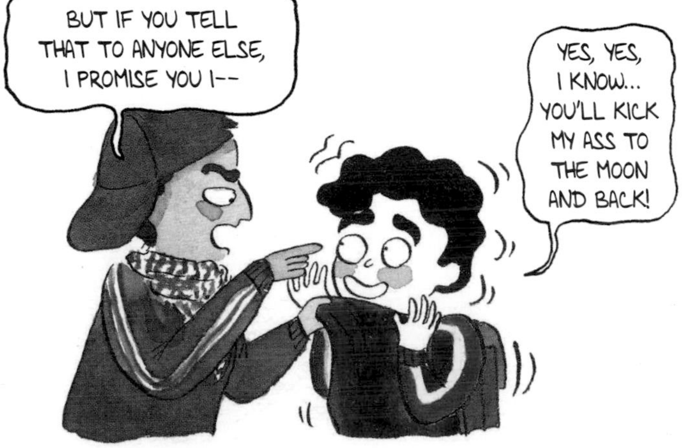
BUT IF YOU TELL THAT TO ANYONE ELSE, I PROMISE YOU I--
YES, YES, I KNOW... YOU'LL KICK MY ASS TO THE MOON AND BACK!

That is, until something happened that I never would've imagined possible in a civilized society...

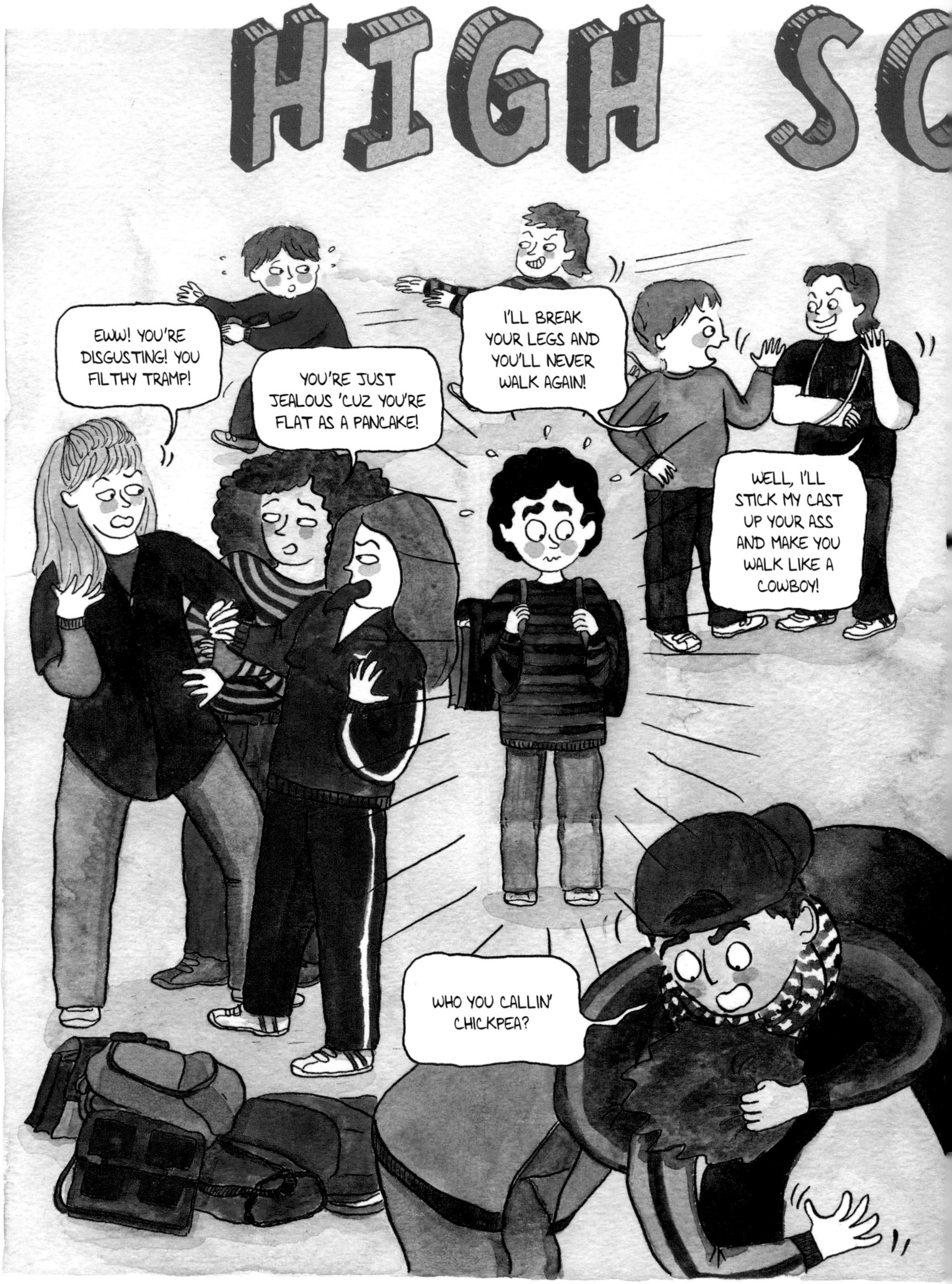
HIGH SC
EWW! YOU'RE DISGUSTING! YOU FILTHY TRAMP!
YOU'RE JUST JEALOUS 'CUZ YOU'RE FLAT AS A PANCAKE!
I'LL BREAK YOUR LEGS AND YOU'LL NEVER WALK AGAIN!
WELL, I'LL STICK MY CAST UP YOUR ASS AND MAKE YOU WALK LIKE A COWBOY!
WHO YOU CALLIN' CHICKPEA?

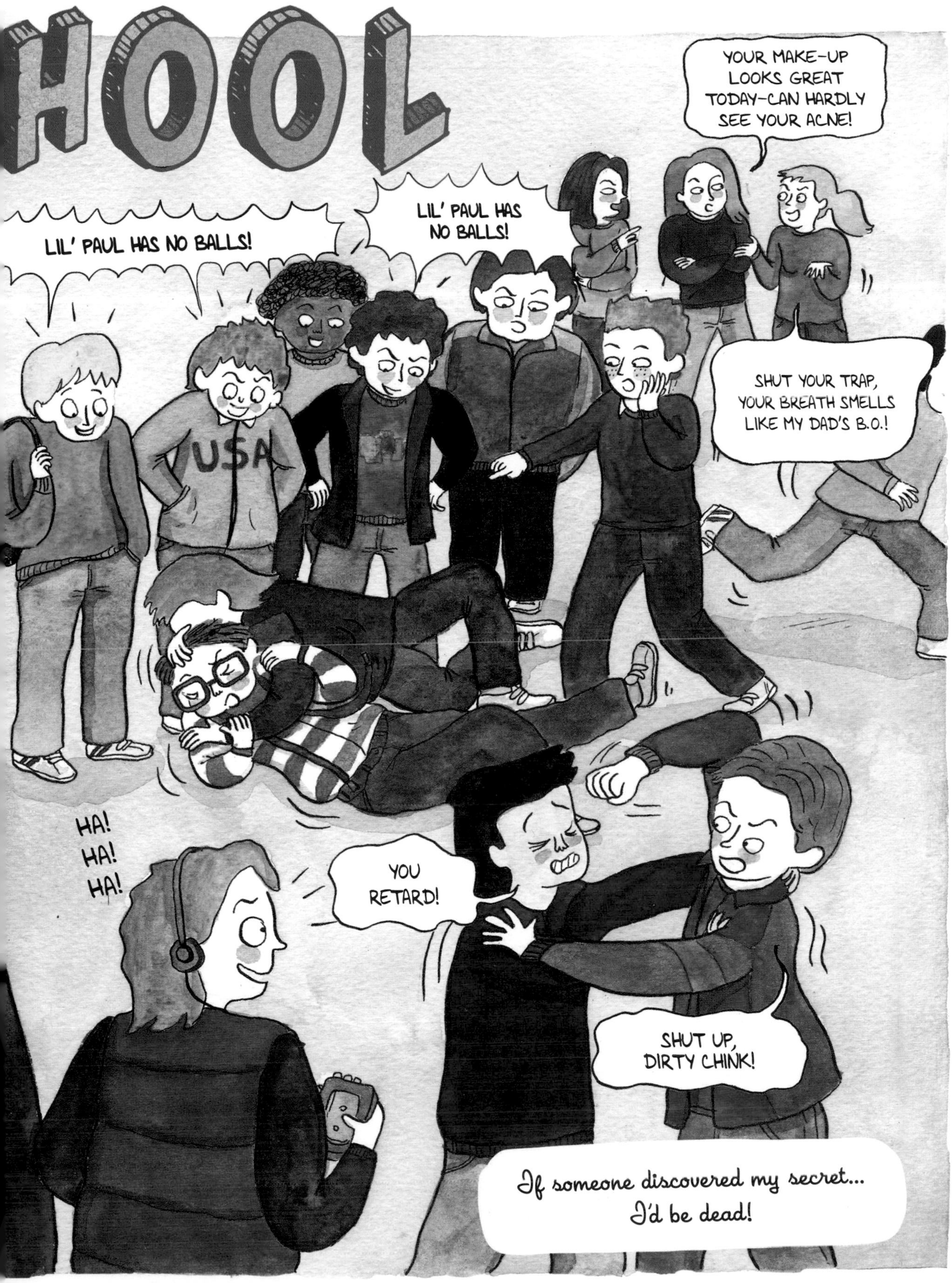
HOOL
YOUR MAKE-UP LOOKS GREAT TODAY—CAN HARDLY SEE YOUR ACNE!
LIL' PAUL HAS NO BALLS!
LIL' PAUL HAS NO BALLS!
SHUT YOUR TRAP, YOUR BREATH SMELLS LIKE MY DAD'S B.O.!
HA! HA! HA!
YOU RETARD!
SHUT UP, DIRTY CHINK!
If someone discovered my secret... I'd be dead!

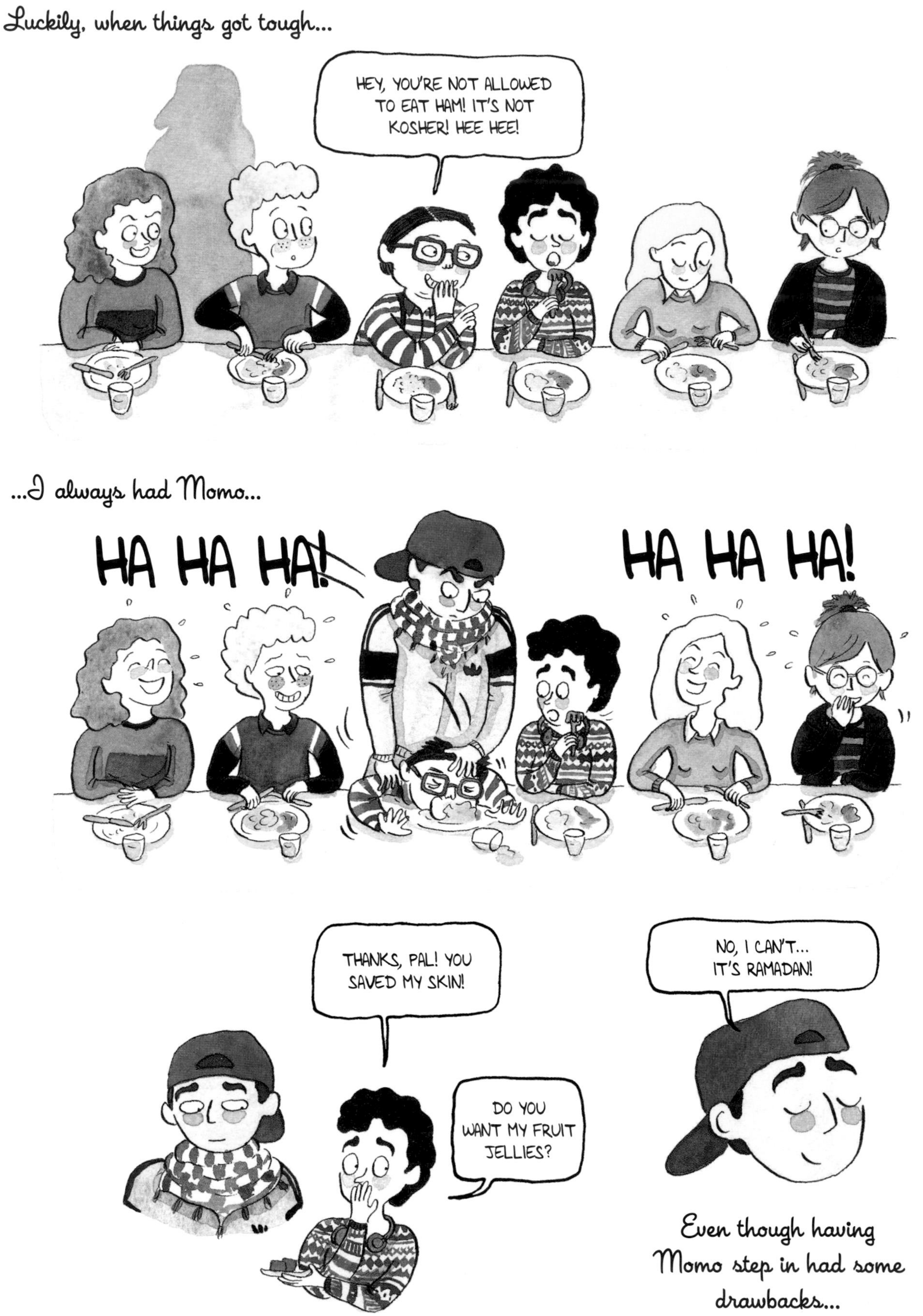
Luckily, when things got tough...
HEY, YOU'RE NOT ALLOWED TO EAT HAM! IT'S NOT KOSHER! HEE HEE!
...I always had Momo...
HA HA HA!
HA HA HA!
THANKS, PAL! YOU SAVED MY SKIN!
DO YOU WANT MY FRUIT JELLIES?
NO, I CAN'T... IT'S RAMADAN!
Even though having Momo step in had some drawbacks...

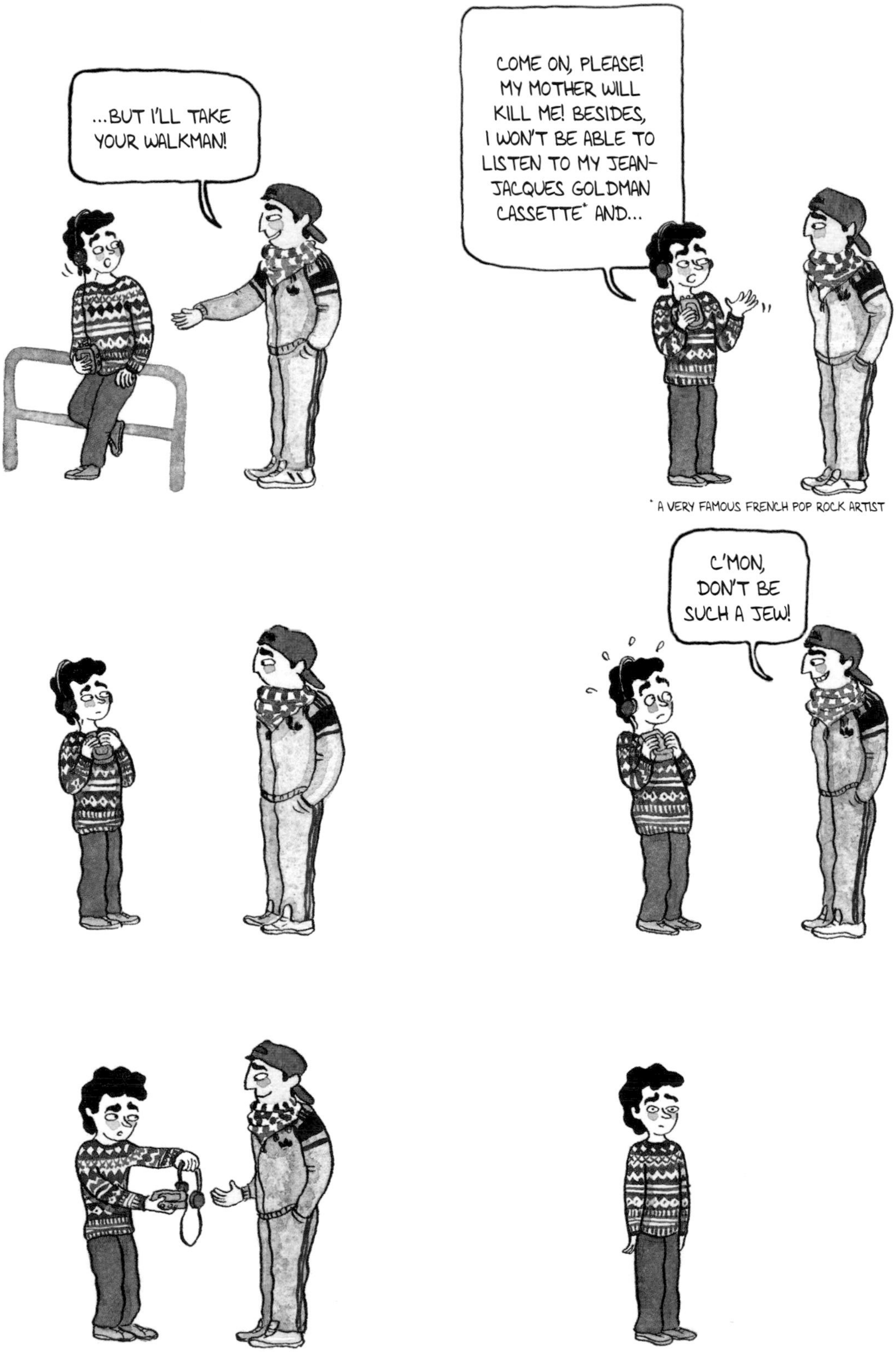
...BUT I'LL TAKE YOUR WALKMAN!
COME ON, PLEASE! MY MOTHER WILL KILL ME! BESIDES, I WON'T BE ABLE TO LISTEN TO MY JEAN-JACQUES GOLDMAN CASSETTE* AND...
* A VERY FAMOUS FRENCH POP ROCK ARTIST
C'MON, DON'T BE SUCH A JEW!

But all these drawbacks were nothing compared to a huge danger, a peril I had never been prepared for. And this time, I would have to face it alone...

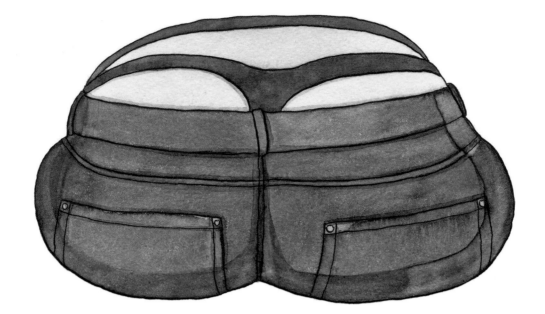

THAAANKS!

 Jasmine...!

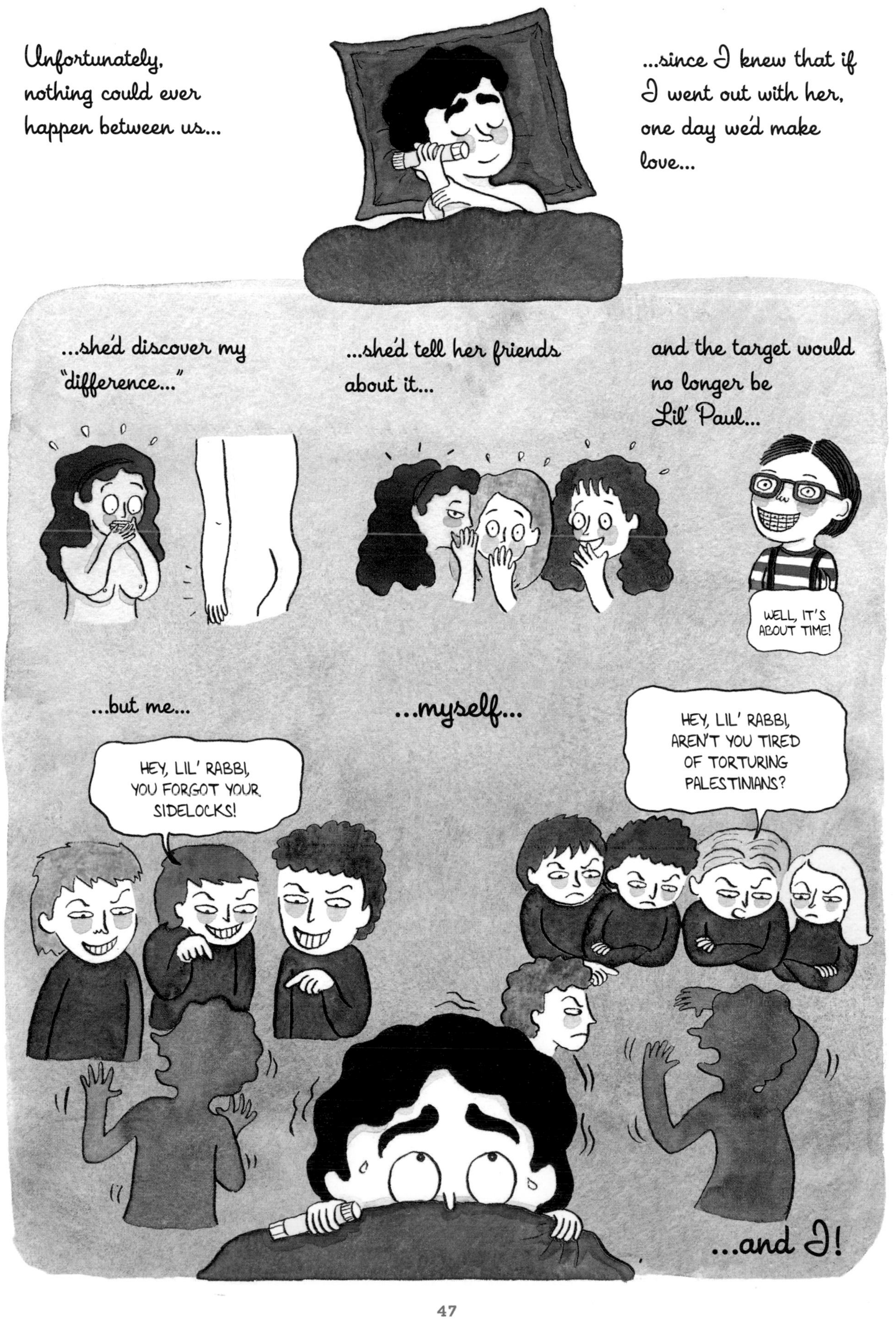
Unfortunately, nothing could ever happen between us...
...since I knew that if I went out with her, one day we'd make love...
...she'd discover my "difference..."
...she'd tell her friends about it...
and the target would no longer be Lil' Paul...
WELL, IT'S ABOUT TIME!
...but me...
...myself...
HEY, LIL' RABBI, YOU FORGOT YOUR SIDELOCKS!
HEY, LIL' RABBI, AREN'T YOU TIRED OF TORTURING PALESTINIANS?
...and I!

It was decided! Even though most of my buddies had taken the plunge...

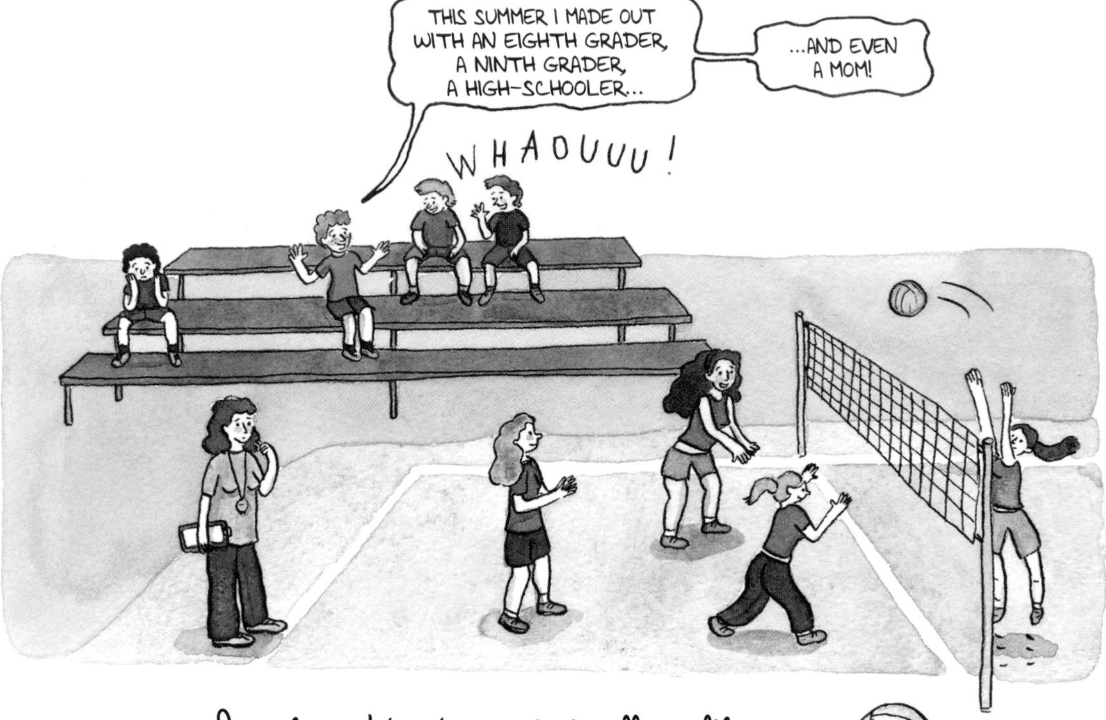
THIS SUMMER I MADE OUT WITH AN EIGHTH GRADER, A NINTH GRADER, A HIGH-SCHOOLER...
...AND EVEN A MOM!
WHAOUUU!

...I preferred to stay a virgin all my life...

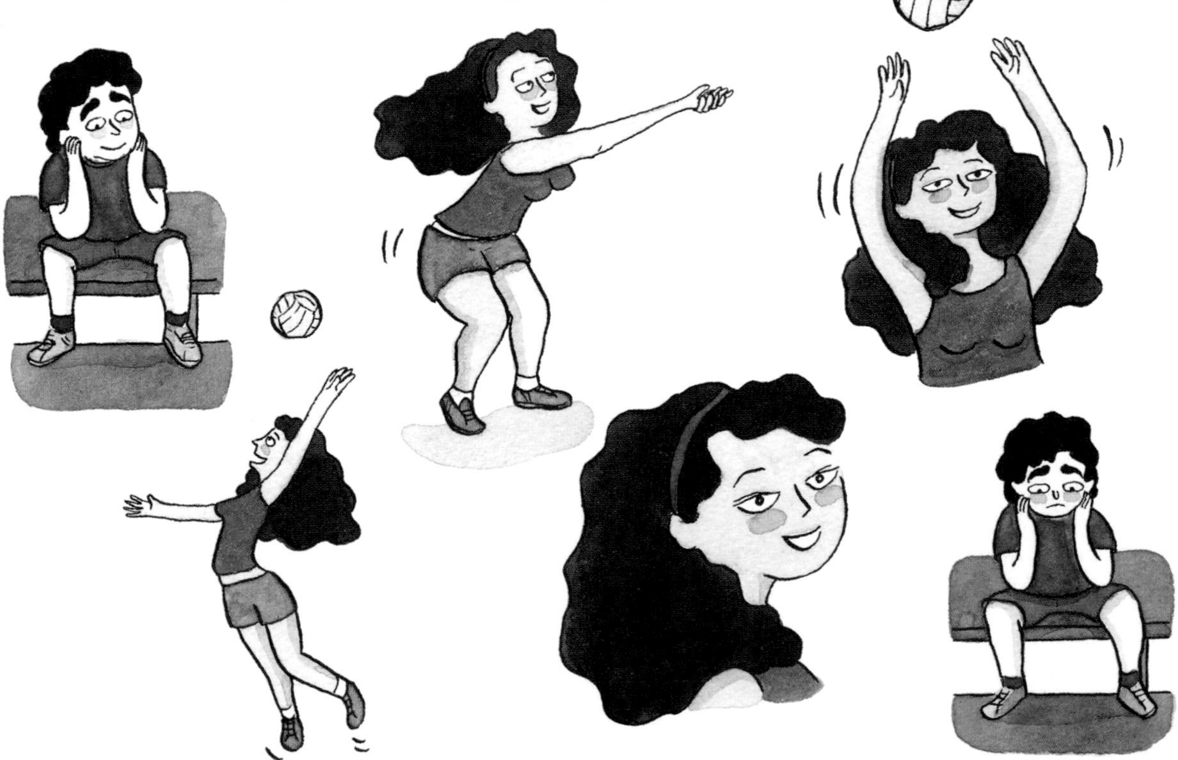

...rather than take the risk of being discovered.

And while at home, life went on as usual...

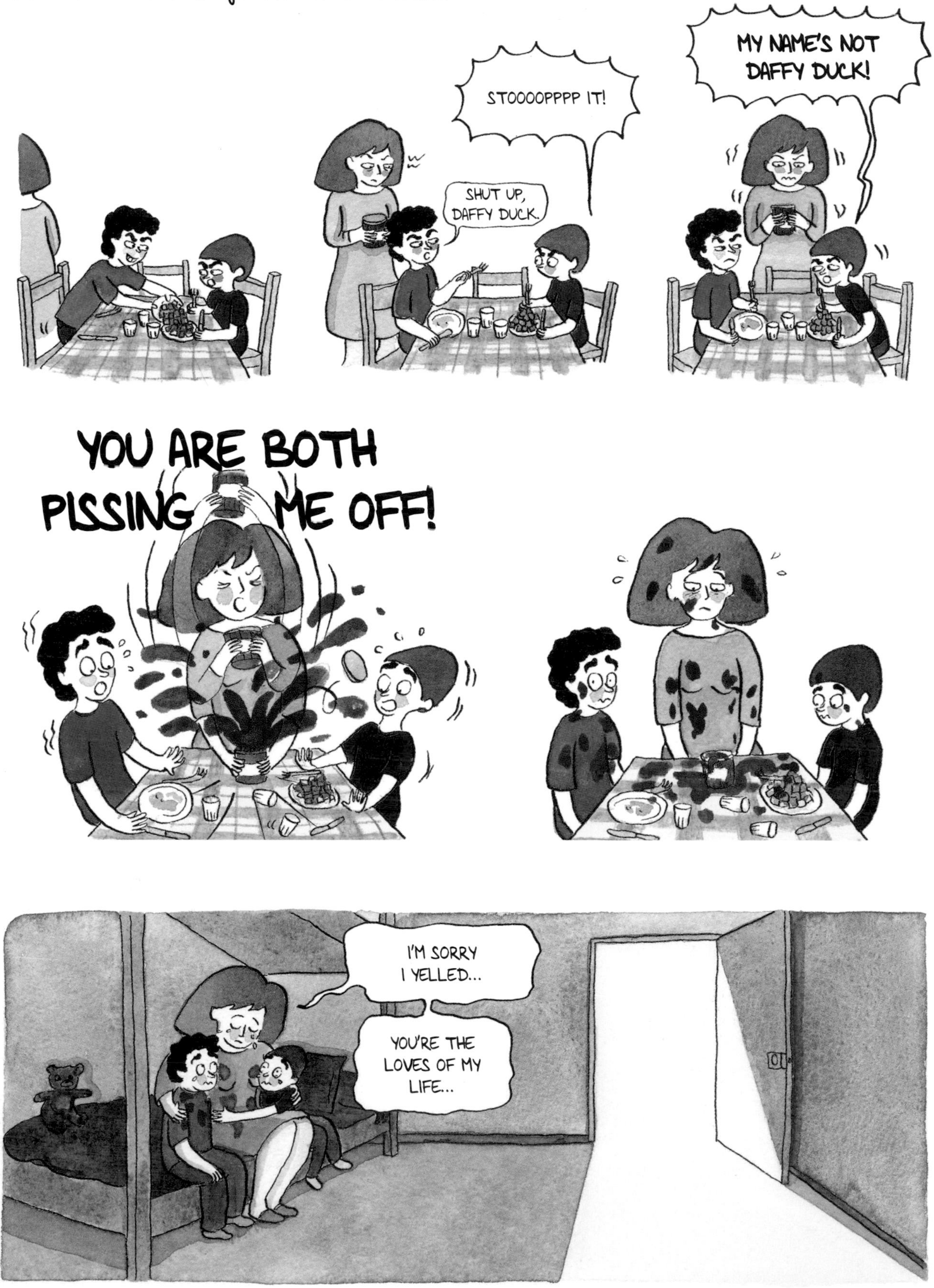
SHUT UP, DAFFY DUCK.
STOOOOPPPP IT!
MY NAME'S NOT DAFFY DUCK!
YOU ARE BOTH PISSING ME OFF!
I'M SORRY I YELLED...
YOU'RE THE LOVES OF MY LIFE...

I gradually became aware that the family I was so proud of in the past...was actually an embarrassing one.

Thus, I realized that my grandmother probably wasn't the great psychic I thought she was...

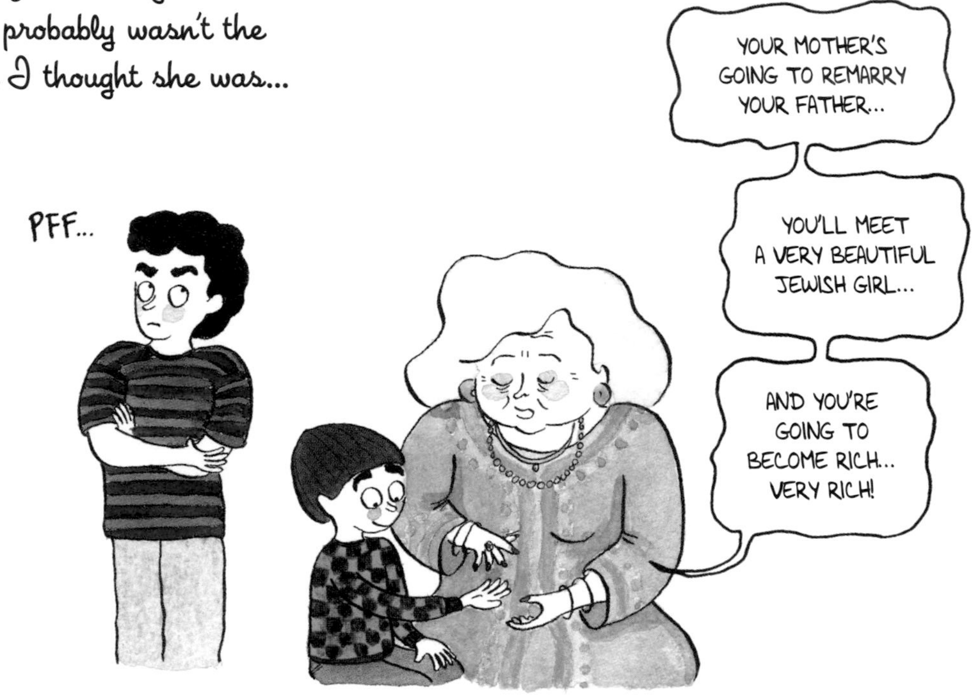

YOUR MOTHER'S GOING TO REMARRY YOUR FATHER...
PFF...
YOU'LL MEET A VERY BEAUTIFUL JEWISH GIRL...
AND YOU'RE GOING TO BECOME RICH... VERY RICH!

...that my uncle Yves' extraordinary achievements were probably less Superman inspired and more...

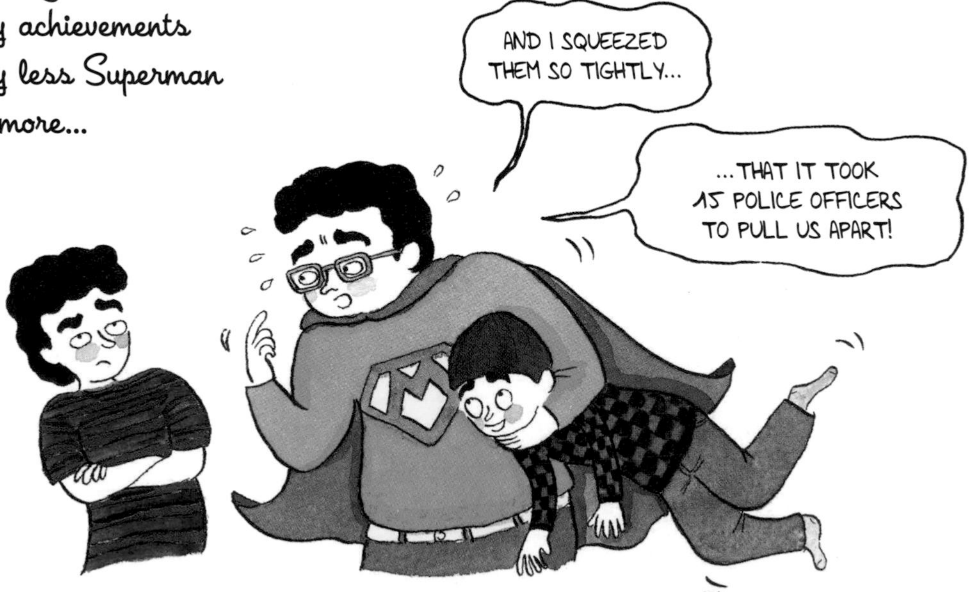

AND I SQUEEZED THEM SO TIGHTLY...
...THAT IT TOOK 15 POLICE OFFICERS TO PULL US APART!

..."Myth-Man" based.

...and that my uncle's brother's great-nephew didn't personally know the first cousin once removed of the President's aunt by marriage at all, but simply had managed to get...

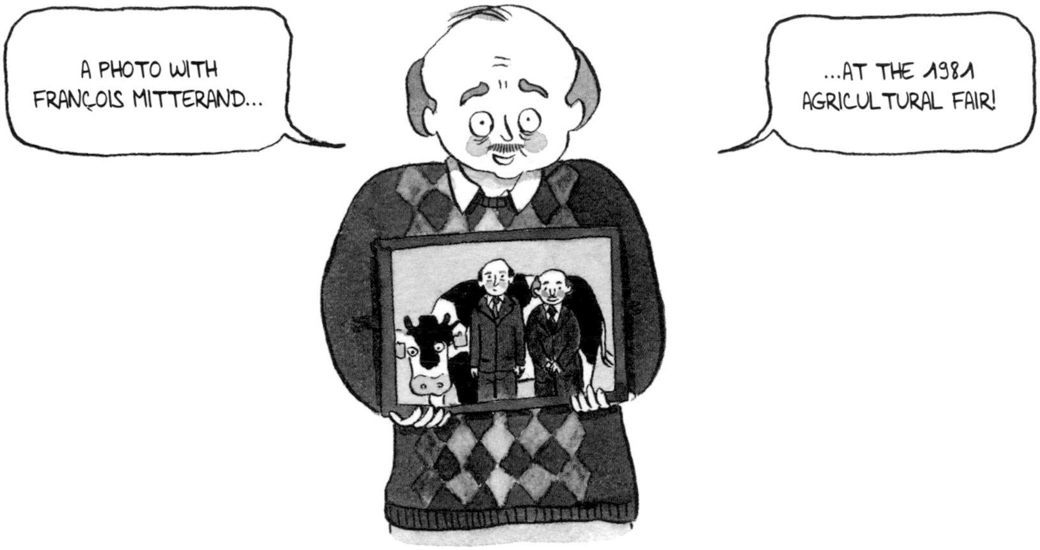
A PHOTO WITH FRANÇOIS MITTERAND...
...AT THE 1981 AGRICULTURAL FAIR!

I no longer even wanted any dafina, which my grandmother spent hours making for us.

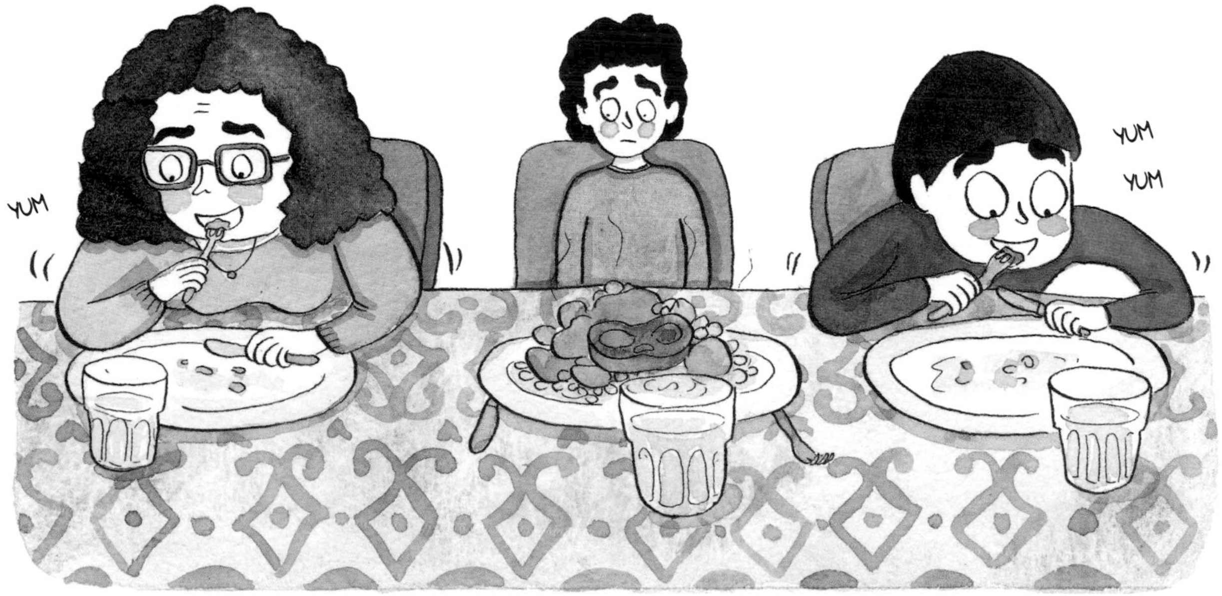
YUM
YUM
YUM

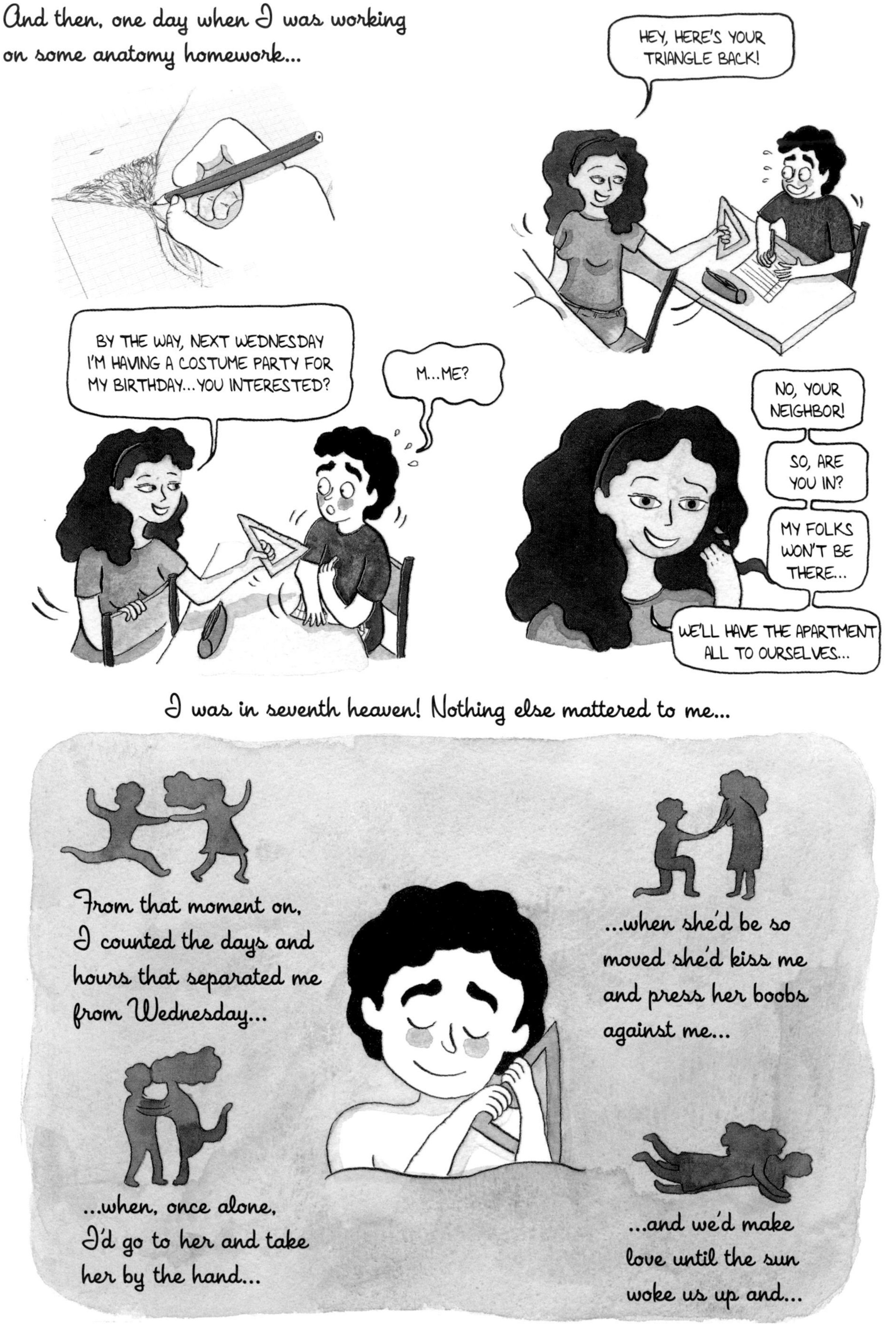
And then, one day when I was working on some anatomy homework...
HEY, HERE'S YOUR TRIANGLE BACK!
BY THE WAY, NEXT WEDNESDAY I'M HAVING A COSTUME PARTY FOR MY BIRTHDAY... YOU INTERESTED?
M...ME?
NO, YOUR NEIGHBOR!
SO, ARE YOU IN?
MY FOLKS WON'T BE THERE...
WE'LL HAVE THE APARTMENT ALL TO OURSELVES...
I was in seventh heaven! Nothing else mattered to me...
From that moment on, I counted the days and hours that separated me from Wednesday...
...when, once alone, I'd go to her and take her by the hand...
...when she'd be so moved she'd kiss me and press her boobs against me...
...and we'd make love until the sun woke us up and...

GET UP, KIDS!

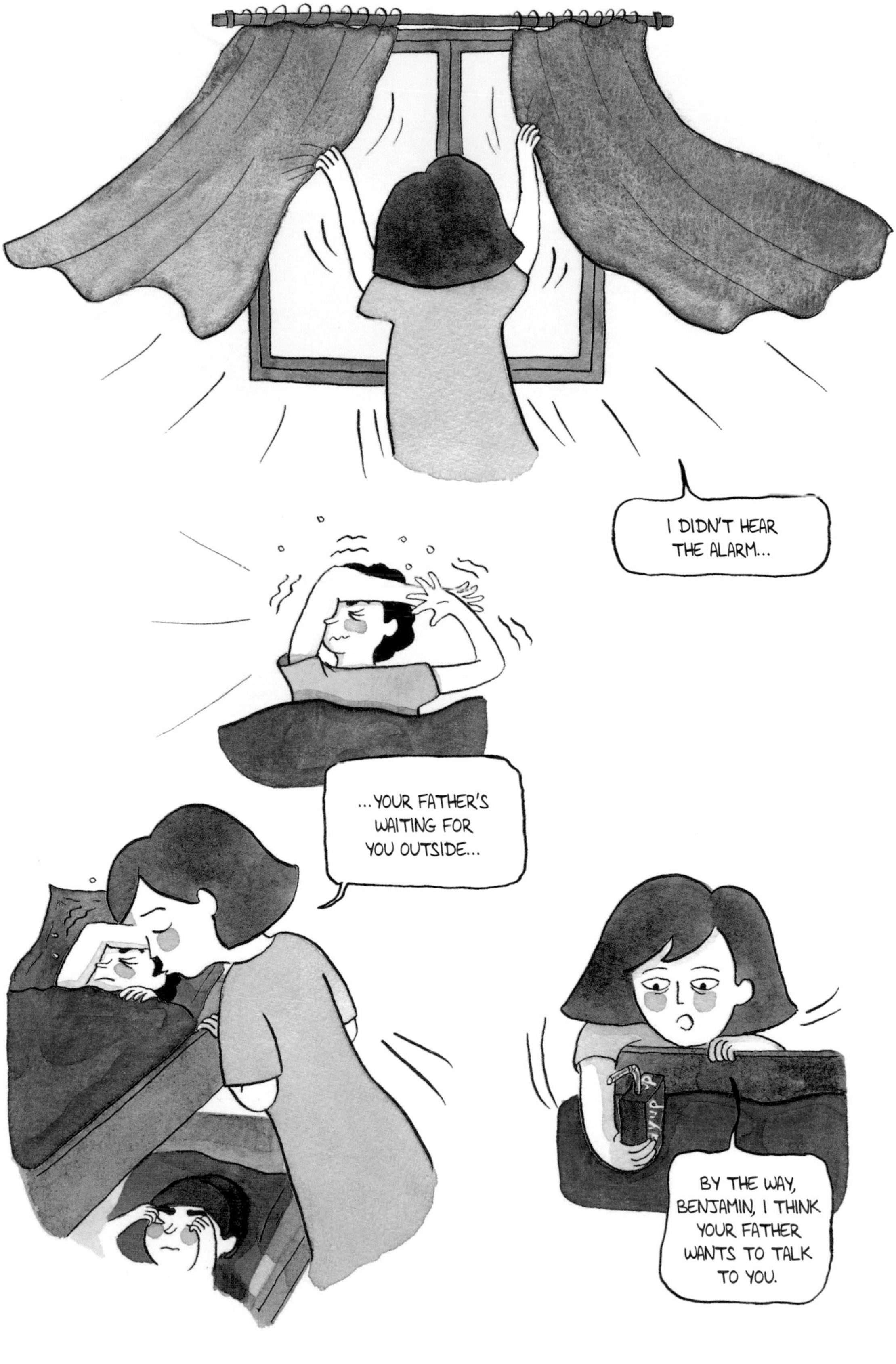

I DIDN'T HEAR THE ALARM...
...YOUR FATHER'S WAITING FOR YOU OUTSIDE...
BY THE WAY, BENJAMIN, I THINK YOUR FATHER WANTS TO TALK TO YOU.

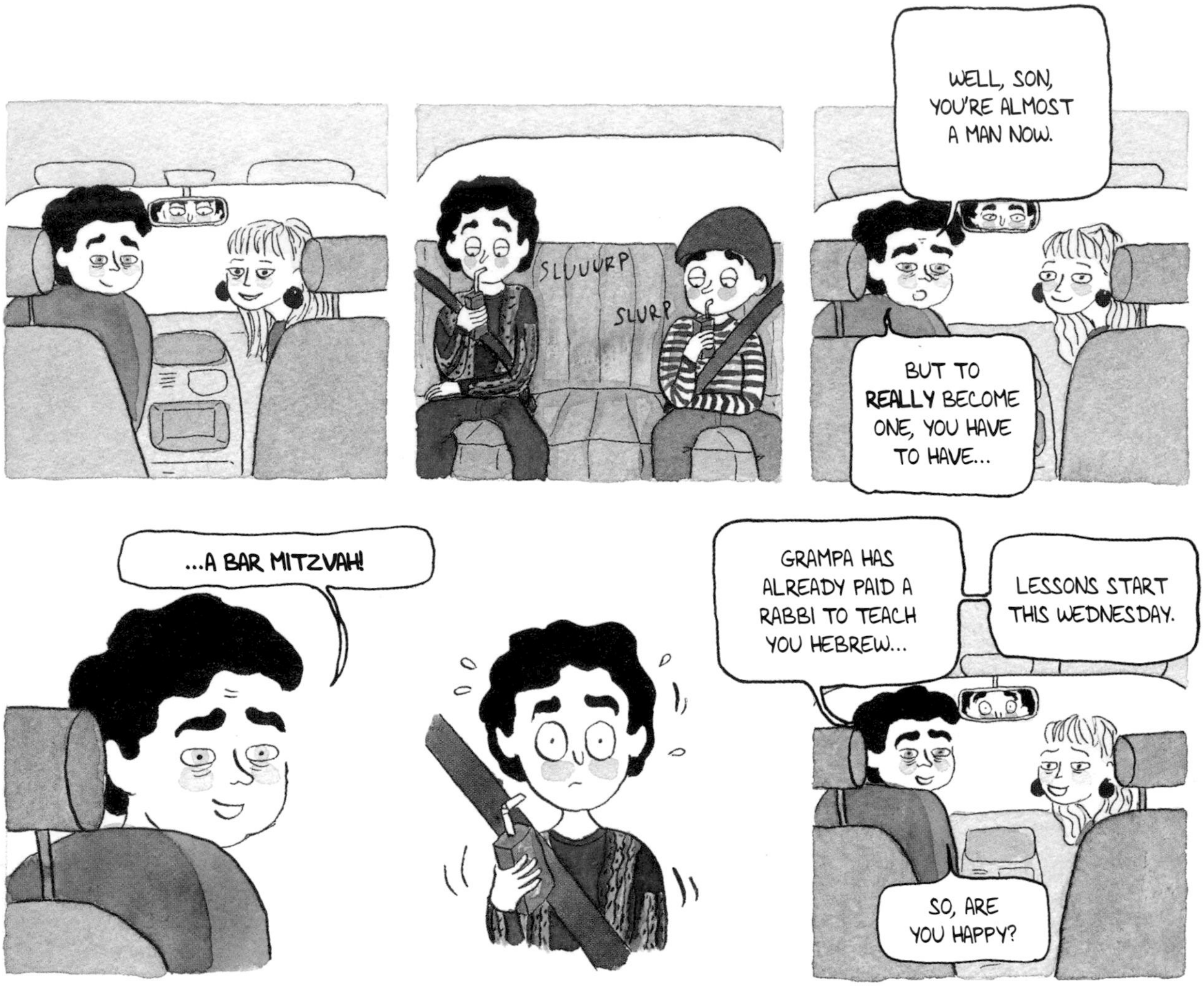
SLUUURP
SLURP
WELL, SON, YOU'RE ALMOST A MAN NOW.
BUT TO **REALLY** BECOME ONE, YOU HAVE TO HAVE...
...A BAR MITZVAH!
GRAMPA HAS ALREADY PAID A RABBI TO TEACH YOU HEBREW...
LESSONS START THIS WEDNESDAY.
SO, ARE YOU HAPPY?

Yes, you heard right: **that** Wednesday!
The day of Jasmine's costume party! So, of
course, I could've told him:

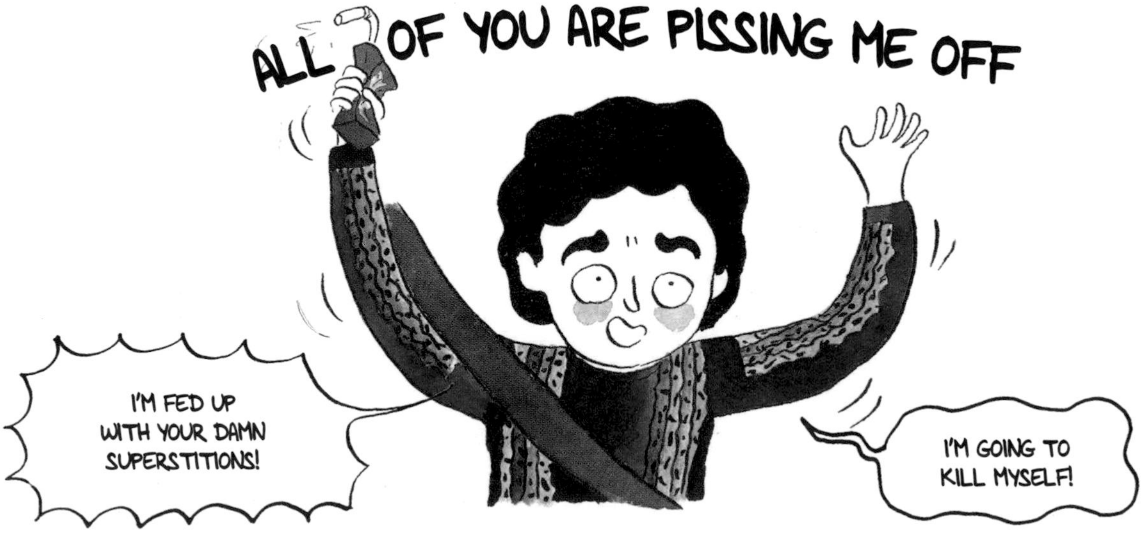
ALL OF YOU ARE PISSING ME OFF
I'M FED UP WITH YOUR DAMN SUPERSTITIONS!
I'M GOING TO KILL MYSELF!

Then he would've probably answered me.

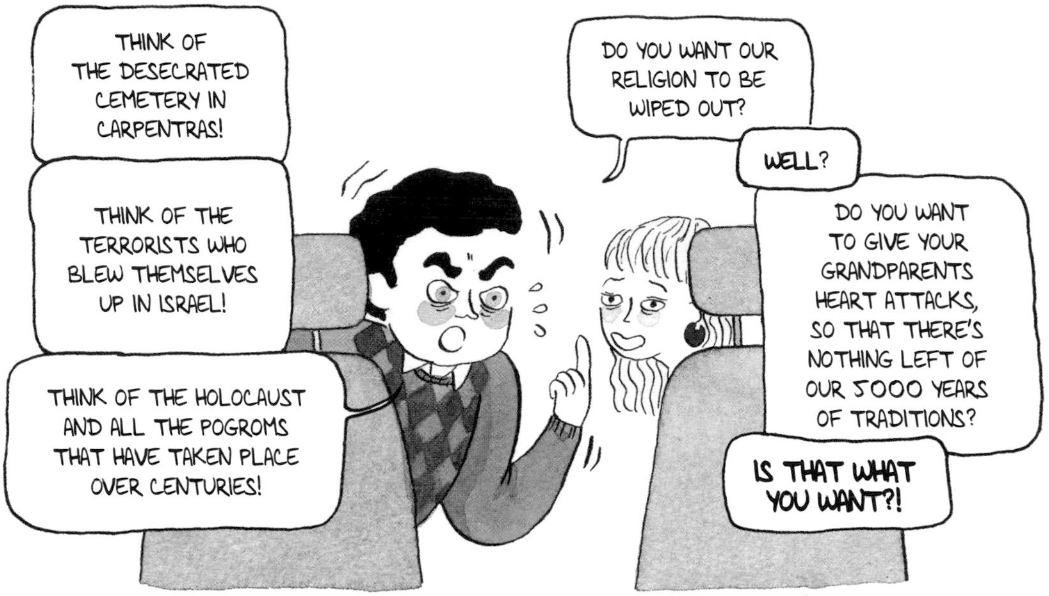
THINK OF THE DESECRATED CEMETERY IN CARPENTRAS!
THINK OF THE TERRORISTS WHO BLEW THEMSELVES UP IN ISRAEL!
THINK OF THE HOLOCAUST AND ALL THE POGROMS THAT HAVE TAKEN PLACE OVER CENTURIES!
DO YOU WANT OUR RELIGION TO BE WIPED OUT?
WELL?
DO YOU WANT TO GIVE YOUR GRANDPARENTS HEART ATTACKS, SO THAT THERE'S NOTHING LEFT OF OUR 5000 YEARS OF TRADITIONS?
IS THAT WHAT YOU WANT?!

So, instead, I looked him right in the eyes and said,

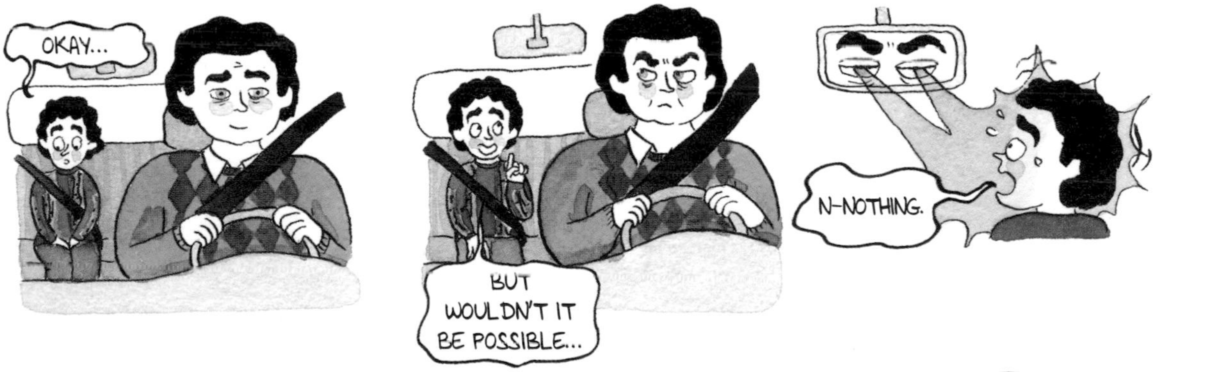
OKAY...
BUT WOULDN'T IT BE POSSIBLE...
N-NOTHING.

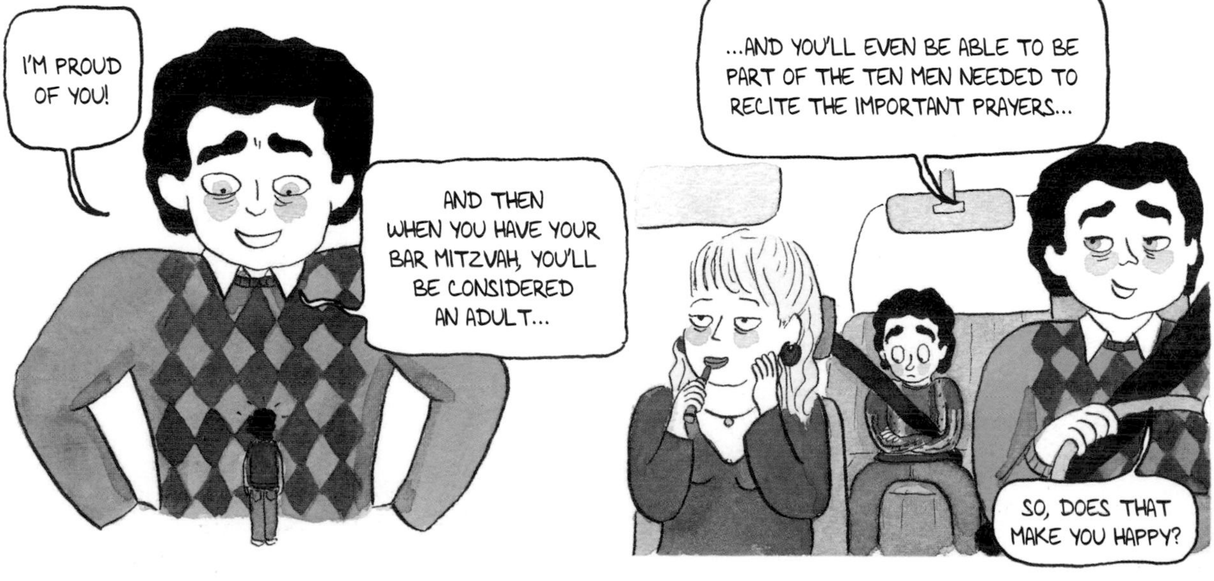
I'M PROUD OF YOU!
AND THEN WHEN YOU HAVE YOUR BAR MITZVAH, YOU'LL BE CONSIDERED AN ADULT...
...AND YOU'LL EVEN BE ABLE TO BE PART OF THE TEN MEN NEEDED TO RECITE THE IMPORTANT PRAYERS...
SO, DOES THAT MAKE YOU HAPPY?

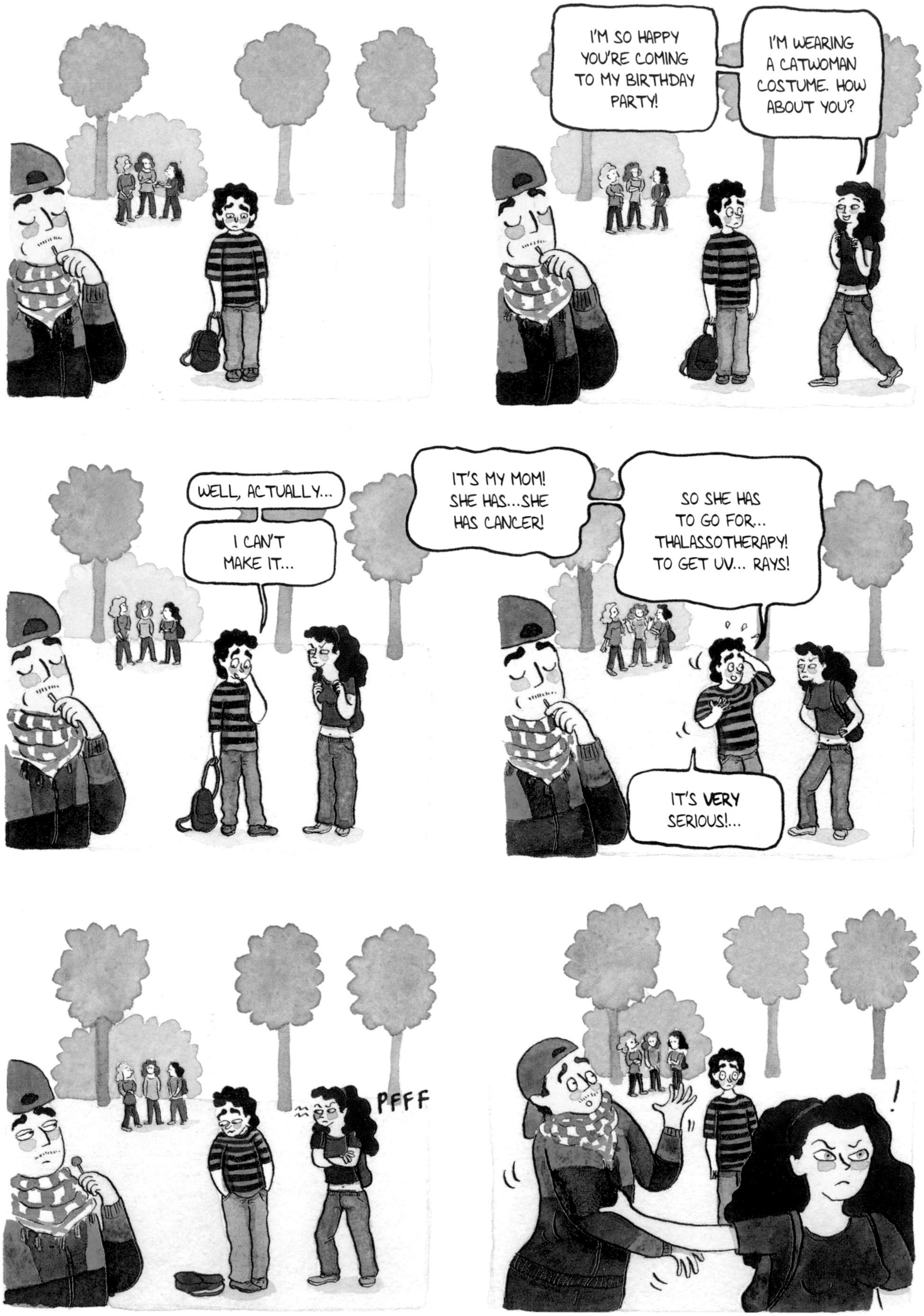

I'M SO HAPPY YOU'RE COMING TO MY BIRTHDAY PARTY!
I'M WEARING A CATWOMAN COSTUME. HOW ABOUT YOU?
WELL, ACTUALLY...
I CAN'T MAKE IT...
IT'S MY MOM! SHE HAS...SHE HAS CANCER!
SO SHE HAS TO GO FOR... THALASSOTHERAPY! TO GET UV... RAYS!
IT'S **VERY** SERIOUS!...
PFFF
!

So while a rabbi tried to teach me a smattering of Hebrew every Wednesday for 200 francs per hour*...

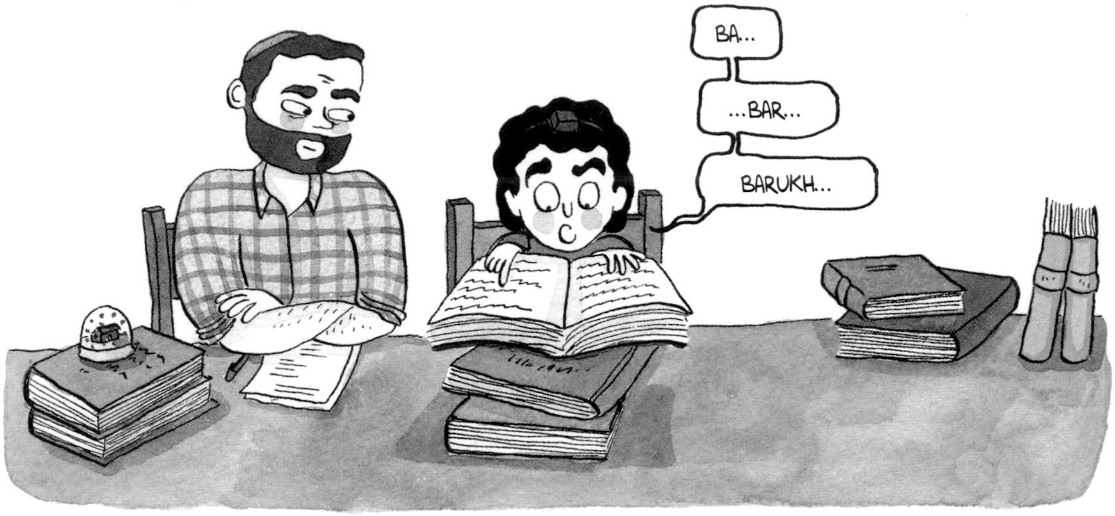
BA...
...BAR...
BARUKH...

* THAT'S ABOUT $35

...and to teach me the "essential" rules of Judaism...

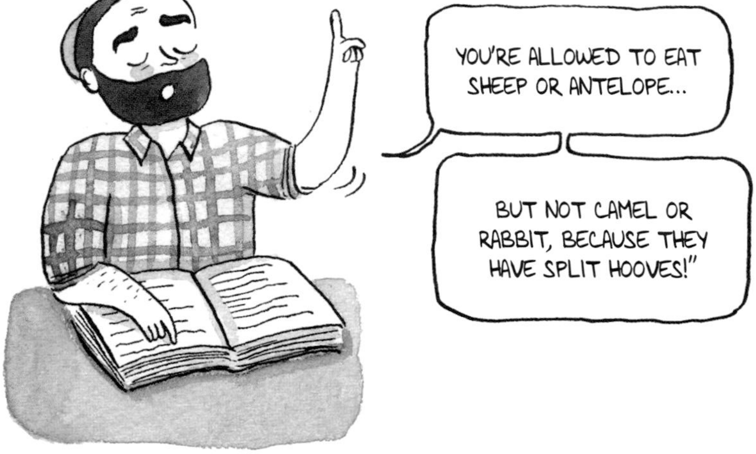
YOU'RE ALLOWED TO EAT SHEEP OR ANTELOPE...
BUT NOT CAMEL OR RABBIT, BECAUSE THEY HAVE SPLIT HOOVES!"

...I looked for a way to escape the grip of this "cult" that had simultaneously achieved the feat of killing the god of the Christians and oppressing all the Muslims in the world, and who, in it's insatiable quest for power, had even managed to make me miss...

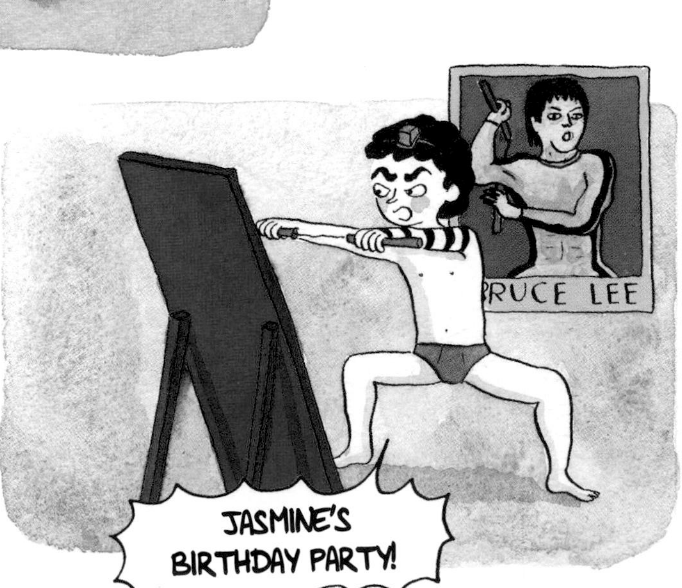
RUCE LEE
JASMINE'S BIRTHDAY PARTY!

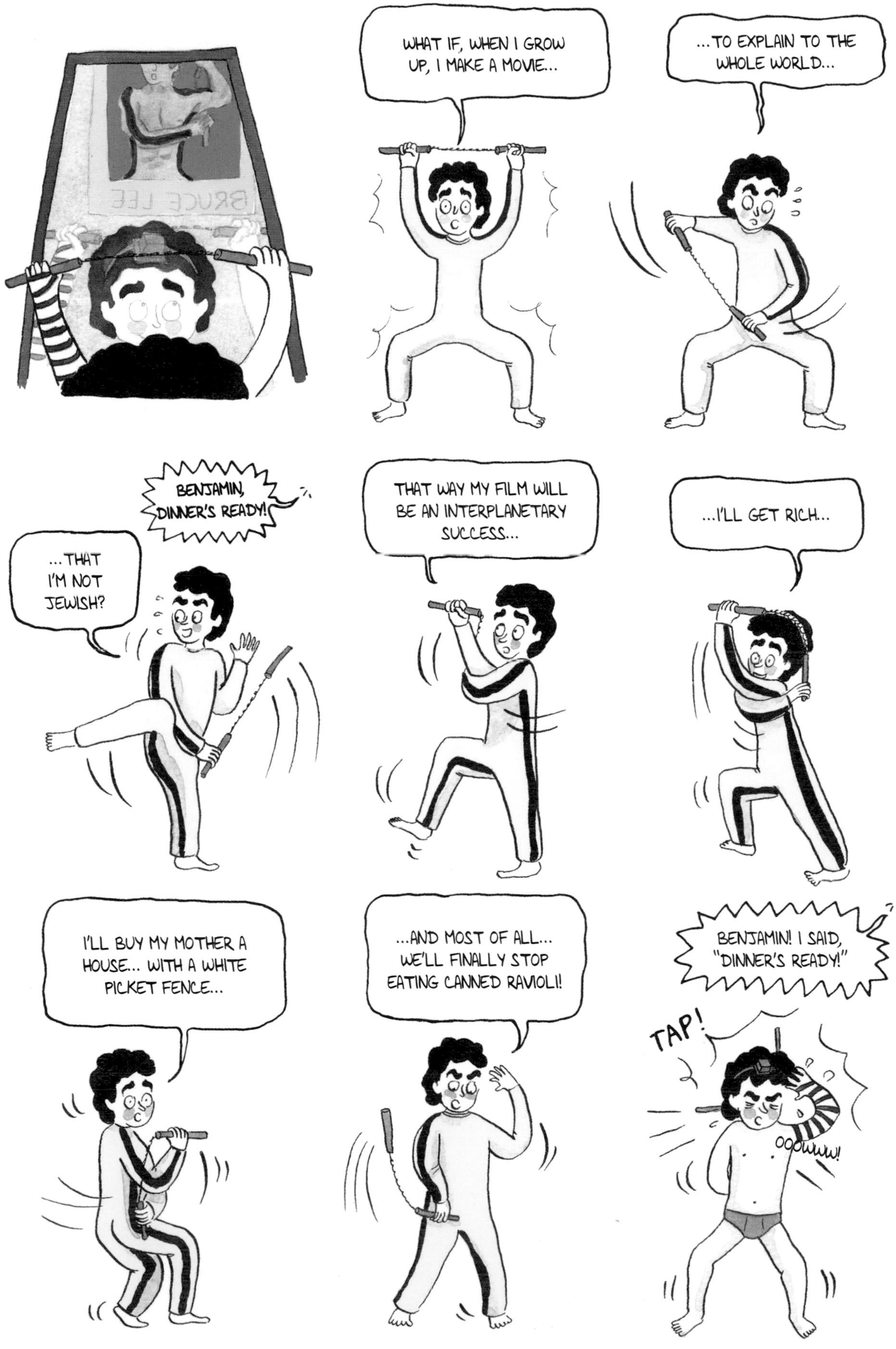
BRUCE LEE
WHAT IF, WHEN I GROW UP, I MAKE A MOVIE...
...TO EXPLAIN TO THE WHOLE WORLD...
BENJAMIN, DINNER'S READY!
...THAT I'M NOT JEWISH?
THAT WAY MY FILM WILL BE AN INTERPLANETARY SUCCESS...
...I'LL GET RICH...
I'LL BUY MY MOTHER A HOUSE... WITH A WHITE PICKET FENCE...
...AND MOST OF ALL... WE'LL FINALLY STOP EATING CANNED RAVIOLI!
BENJAMIN! I SAID, "DINNER'S READY!"
TAP!
OOOWWW!

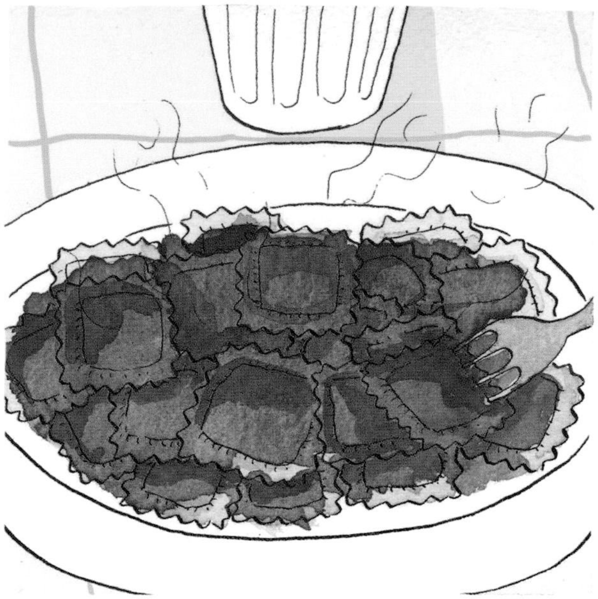

Okay, maybe that's all a bit too ambitious...

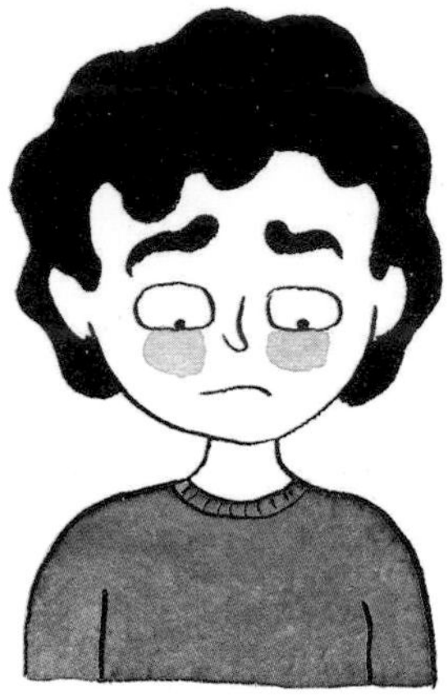

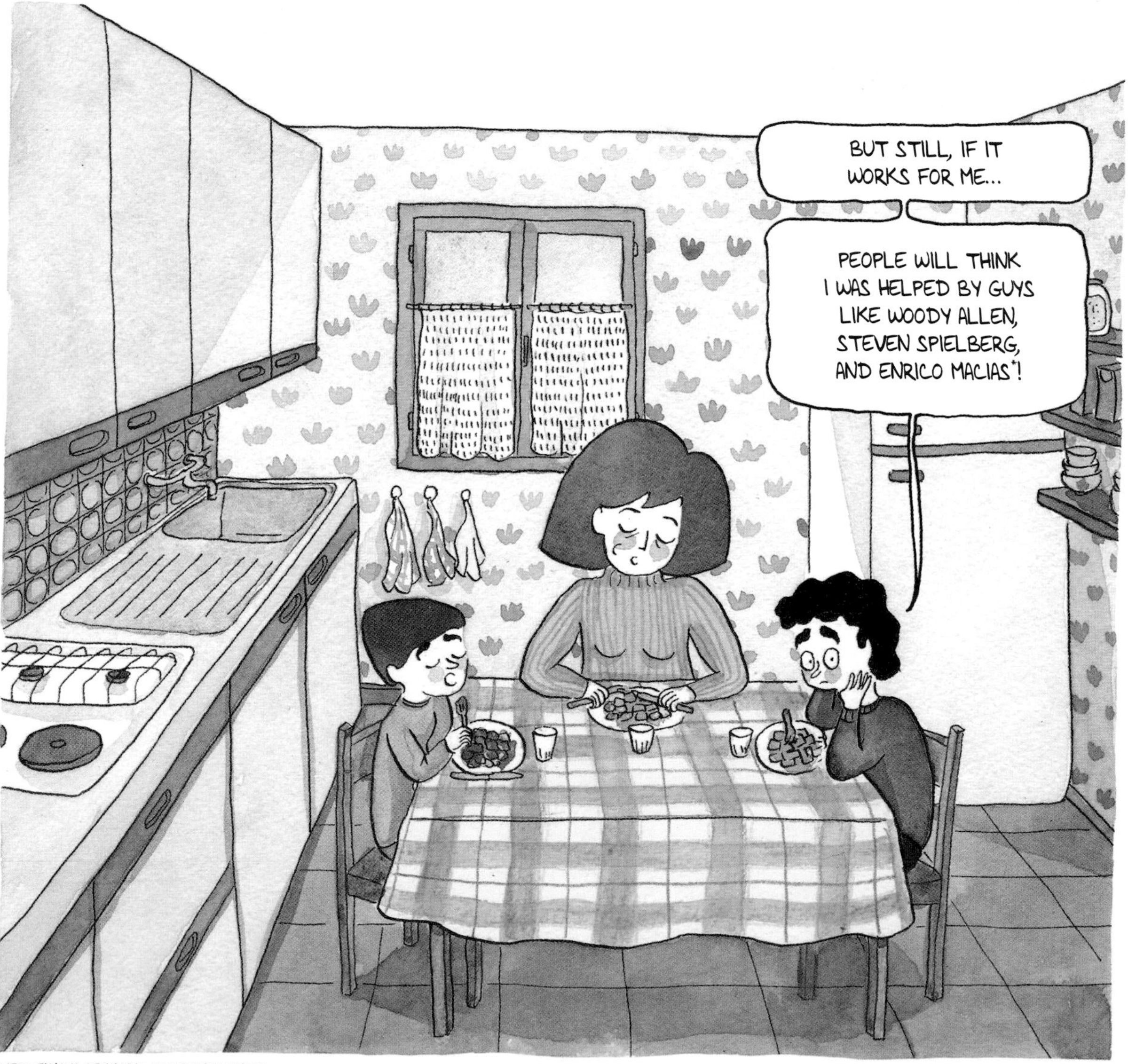
BUT STILL, IF IT WORKS FOR ME...
PEOPLE WILL THINK I WAS HELPED BY GUYS LIKE WOODY ALLEN, STEVEN SPIELBERG, AND ENRICO MACIAS*!

* VERY FAMOUS SEPHARDIC POP FRENCH SINGER

So on January 26, 1990 at 8:54 in the morning...

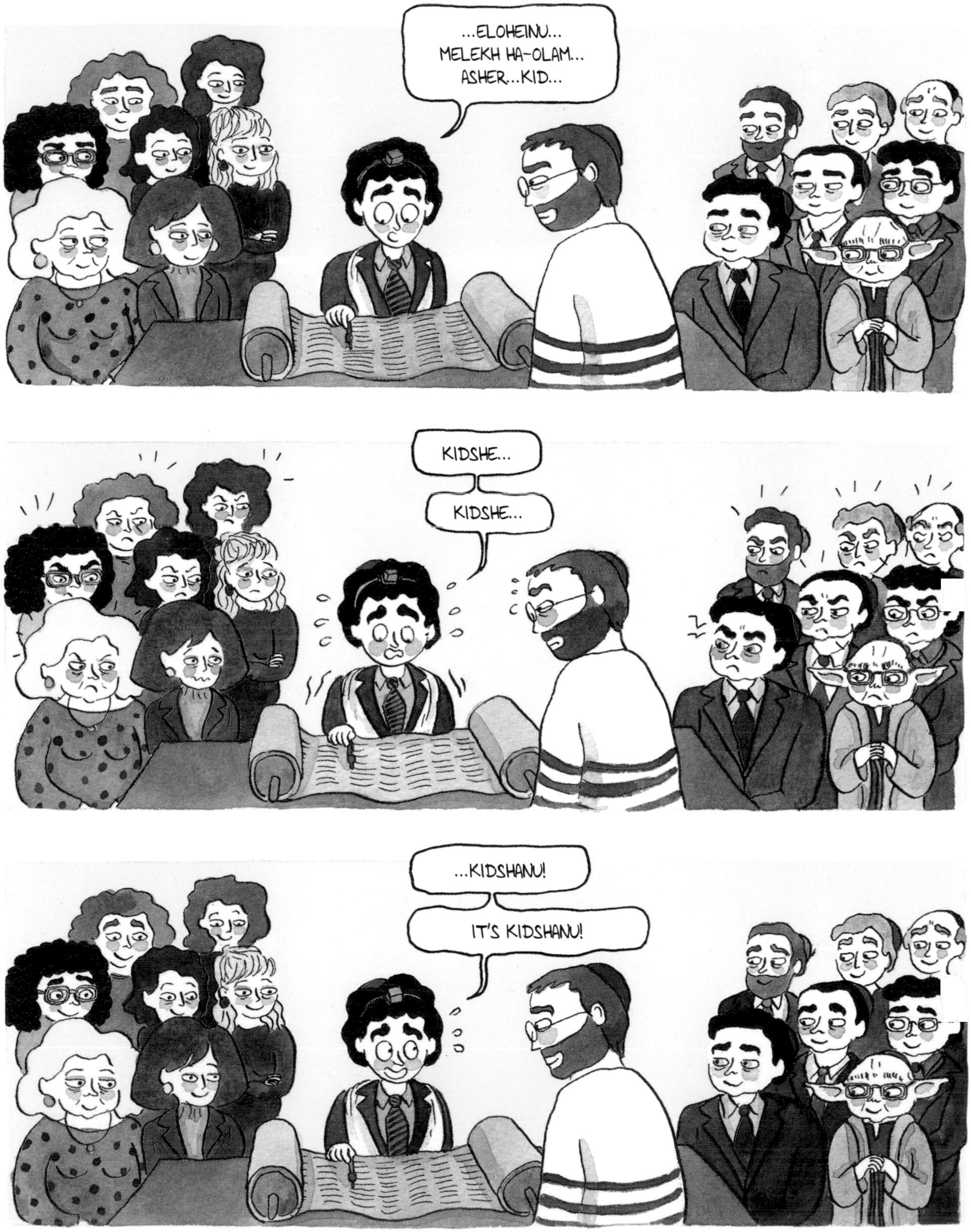
...ELOHEINU...
MELEKH HA-OLAM...
ASHER...KID...
KIDSHE...
KIDSHE...
...KIDSHANU!
IT'S KIDSHANU!

This event felt like a true injustice. And unfortunately, it was just the first on a very long list...

My brother grew taller than me...

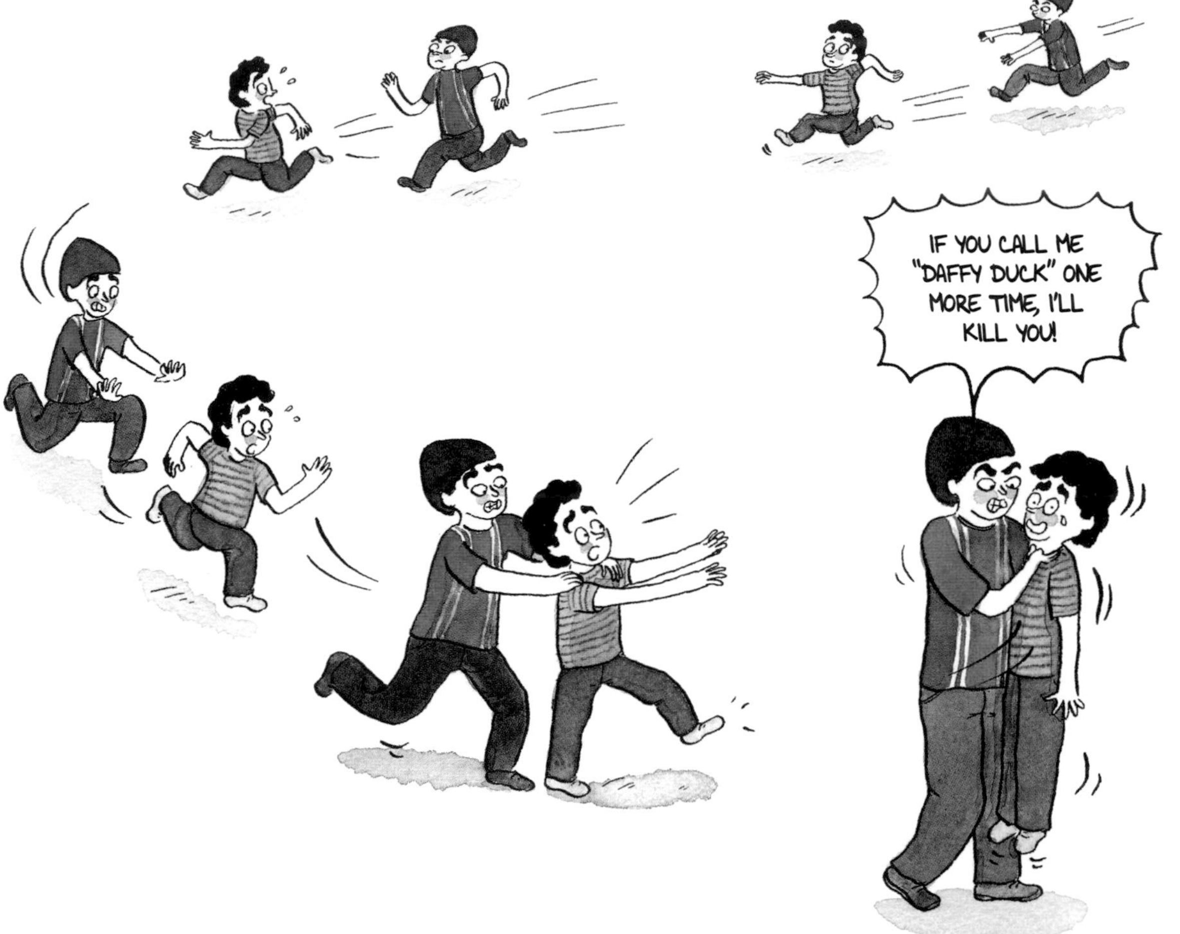

IF YOU CALL ME "DAFFY DUCK" ONE MORE TIME, I'LL KILL YOU!

...Jasmine started ignoring me completely...

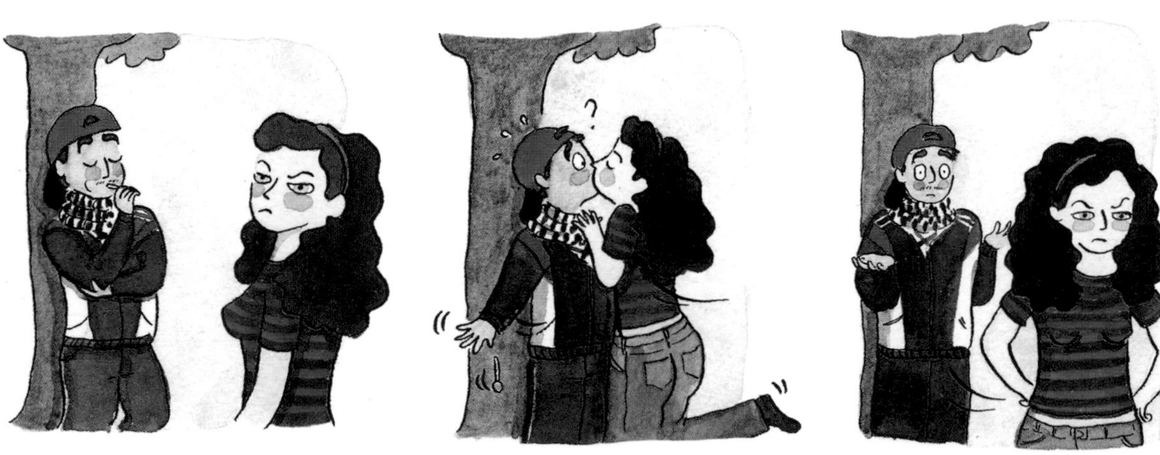

...and while I wanted to go to a college prep school...

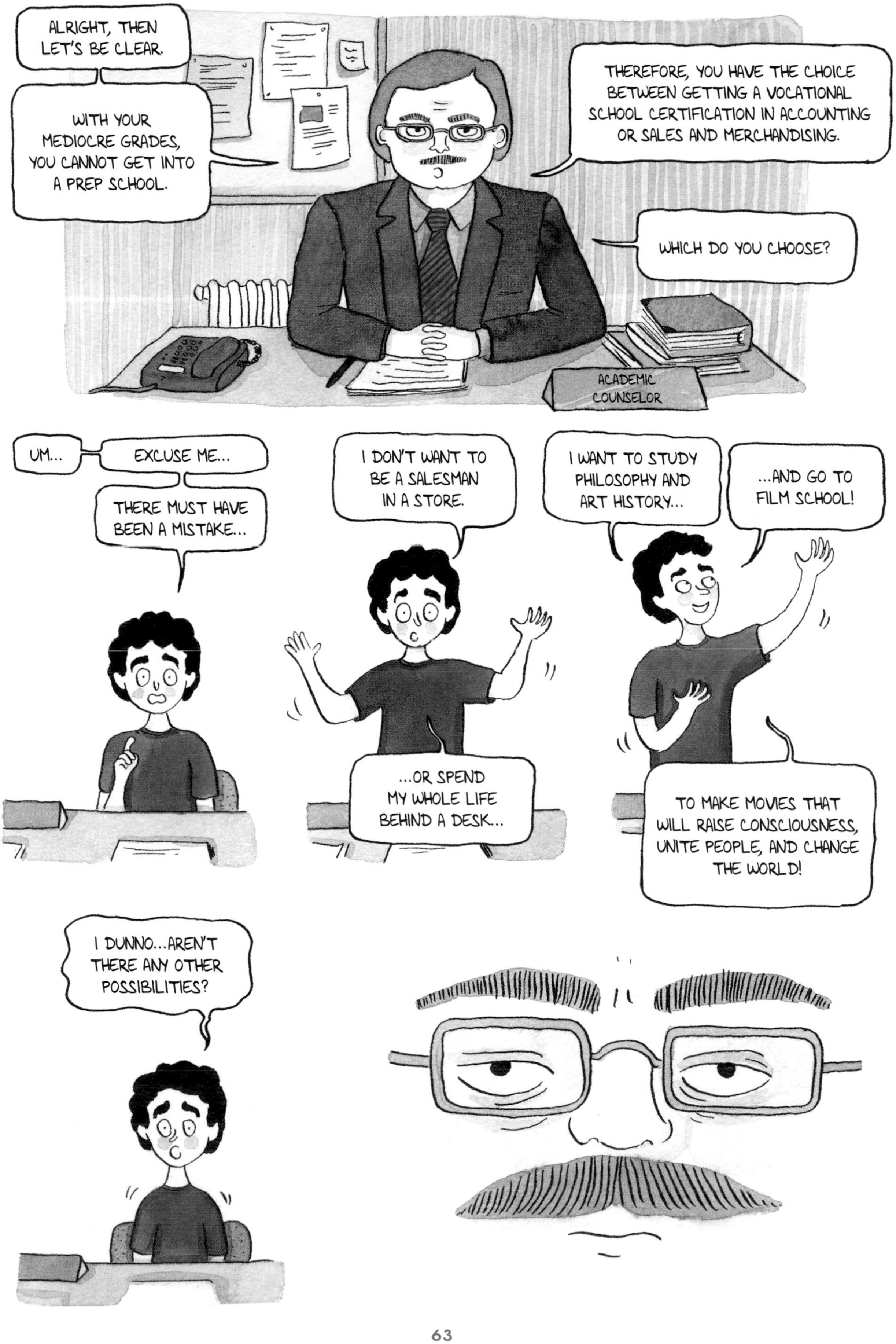
ALRIGHT, THEN LET'S BE CLEAR.
WITH YOUR MEDIOCRE GRADES, YOU CANNOT GET INTO A PREP SCHOOL.
THEREFORE, YOU HAVE THE CHOICE BETWEEN GETTING A VOCATIONAL SCHOOL CERTIFICATION IN ACCOUNTING OR SALES AND MERCHANDISING.
WHICH DO YOU CHOOSE?
ACADEMIC COUNSELOR
UM...
EXCUSE ME...
THERE MUST HAVE BEEN A MISTAKE...
I DON'T WANT TO BE A SALESMAN IN A STORE.
...OR SPEND MY WHOLE LIFE BEHIND A DESK...
I WANT TO STUDY PHILOSOPHY AND ART HISTORY...
...AND GO TO FILM SCHOOL!
TO MAKE MOVIES THAT WILL RAISE CONSCIOUSNESS, UNITE PEOPLE, AND CHANGE THE WORLD!
I DUNNO...AREN'T THERE ANY OTHER POSSIBILITIES?

So while my buddy Momo left school to go work with his father in construction...Steve, Jasmine, and I found ourselves at the...

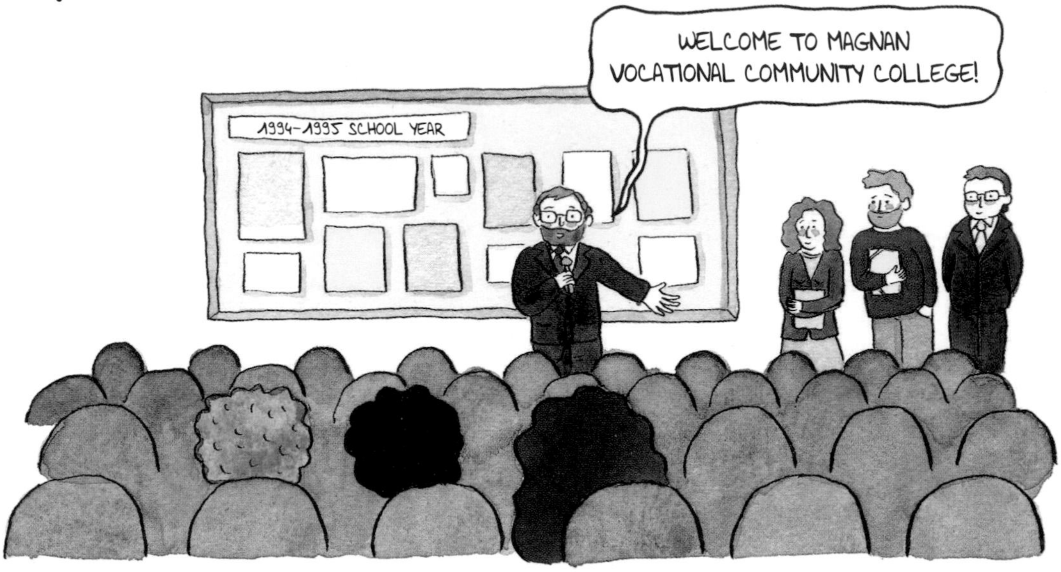
WELCOME TO MAGNAN VOCATIONAL COMMUNITY COLLEGE!
1994-1995 SCHOOL YEAR

I had to acknowledge that I would never be President, a great filmmaker, or the savior of humanity.

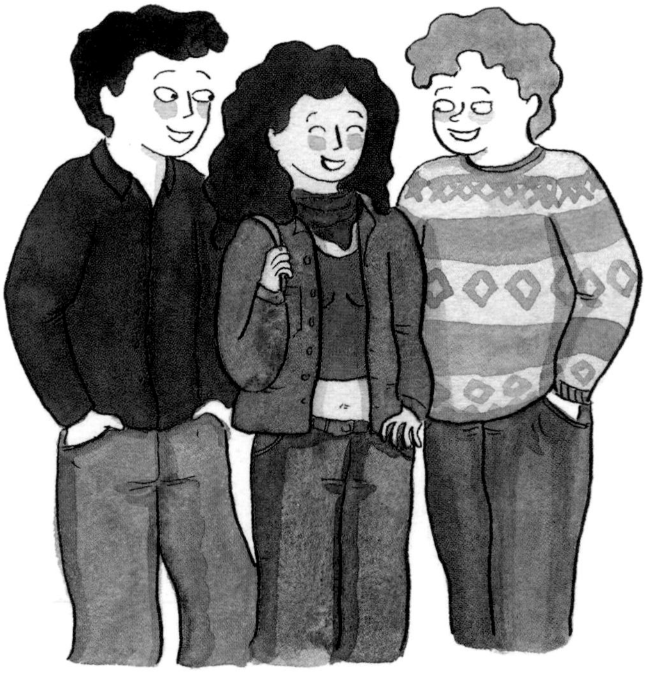

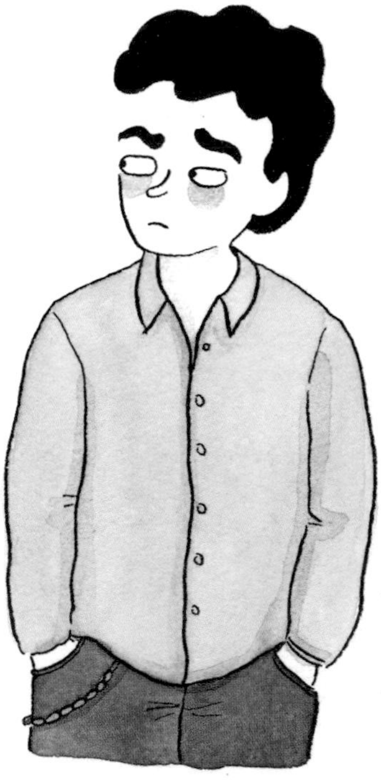

I also would never be with Jasmine again either...

But at least there was one advantage to this school: the color of your skin, your religion, blood type or political opinions didn't matter at all. All that counted was:

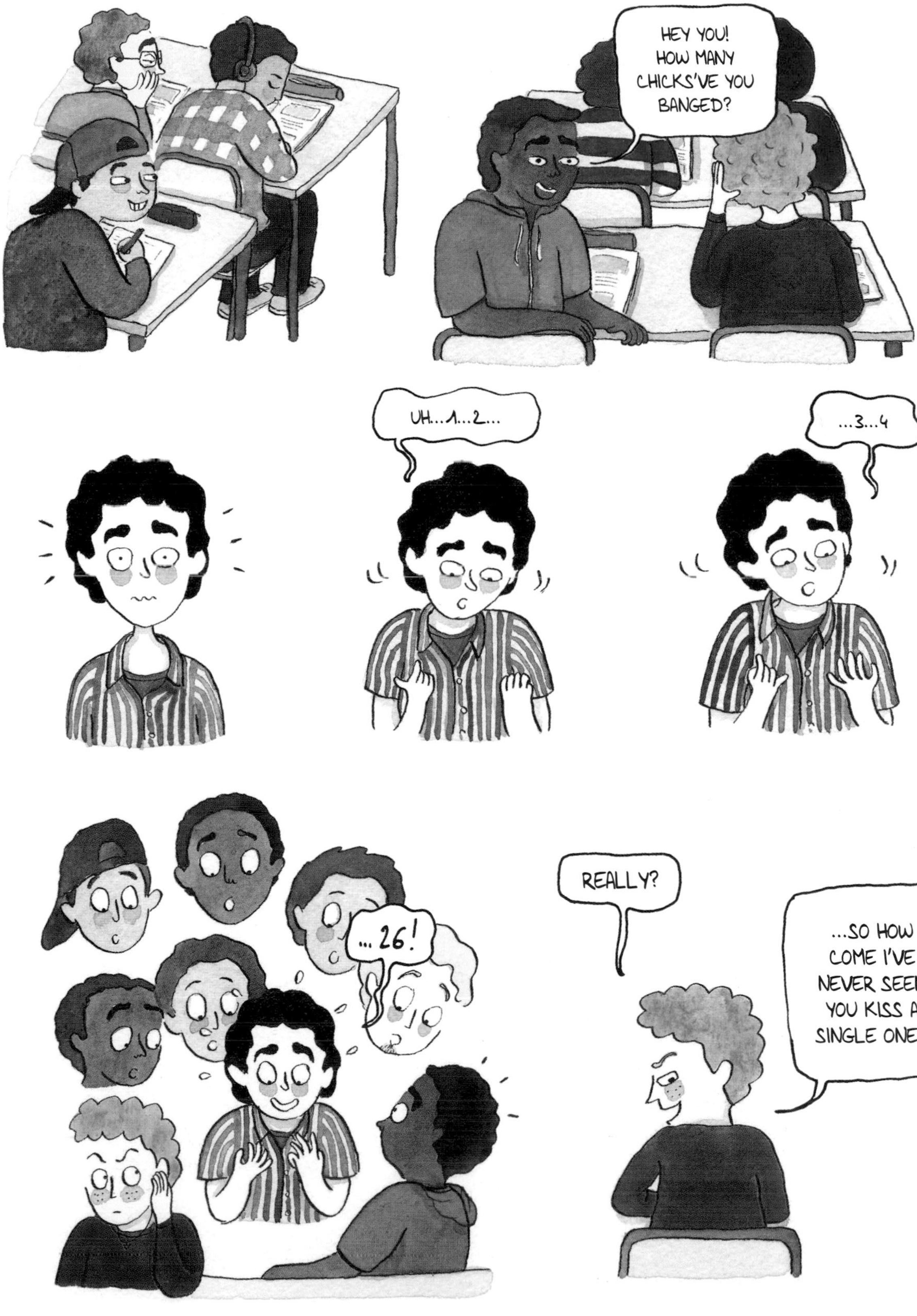
HEY YOU! HOW MANY CHICKS'VE YOU BANGED?
UH...1...2...
...3...4
...26!
REALLY?
...SO HOW COME I'VE NEVER SEEN YOU KISS A SINGLE ONE?

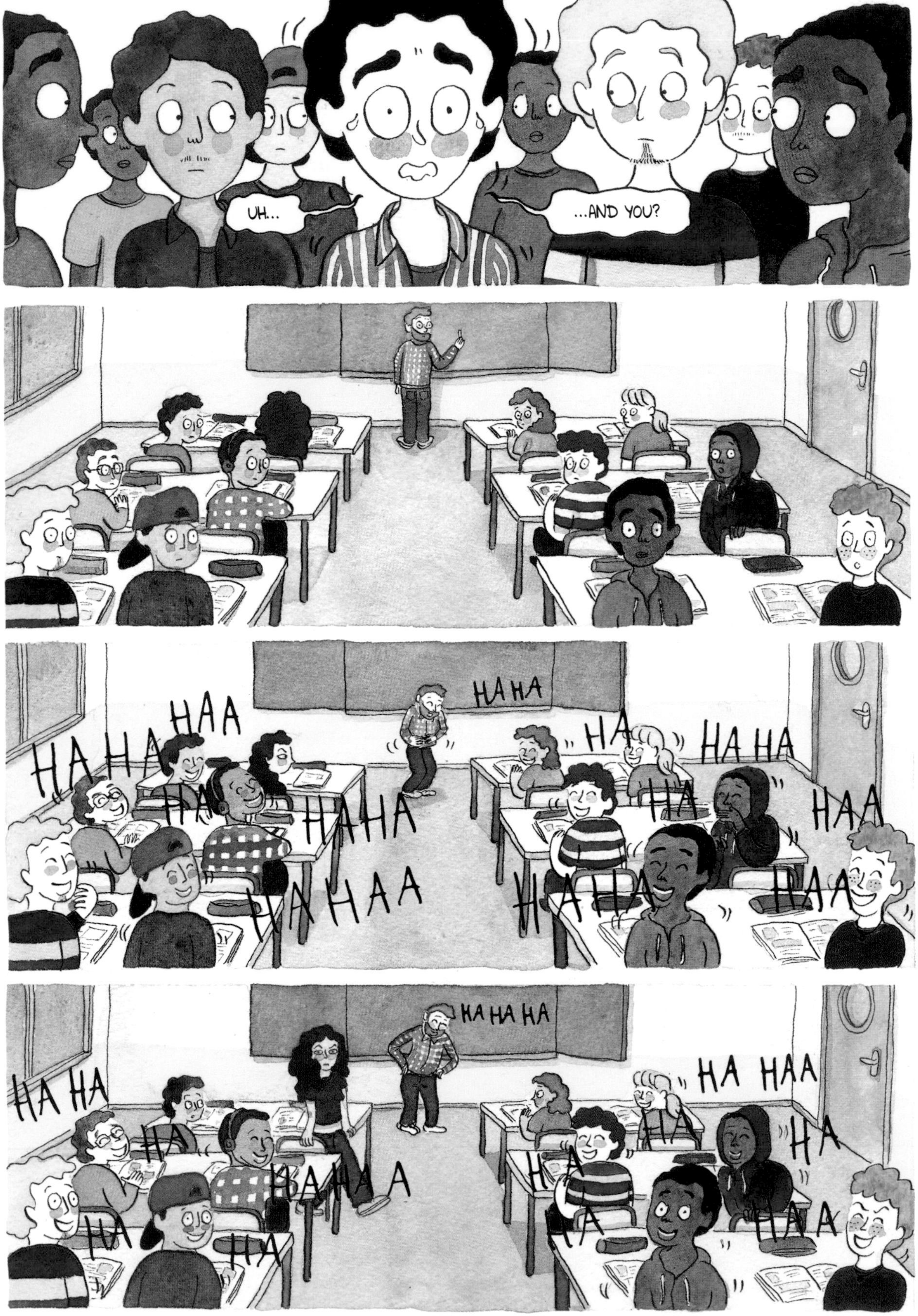
UH...
...AND YOU?
HAHA
HAA
HAHA
HA
HAHA
HAHAA
HAHA
HA
HAHA
HA
HAA
HAHA
HAA
HAHAHA
HAHA
HA HAA
HA
HA
HAHAA
HA
HA
HA
HA
HAA

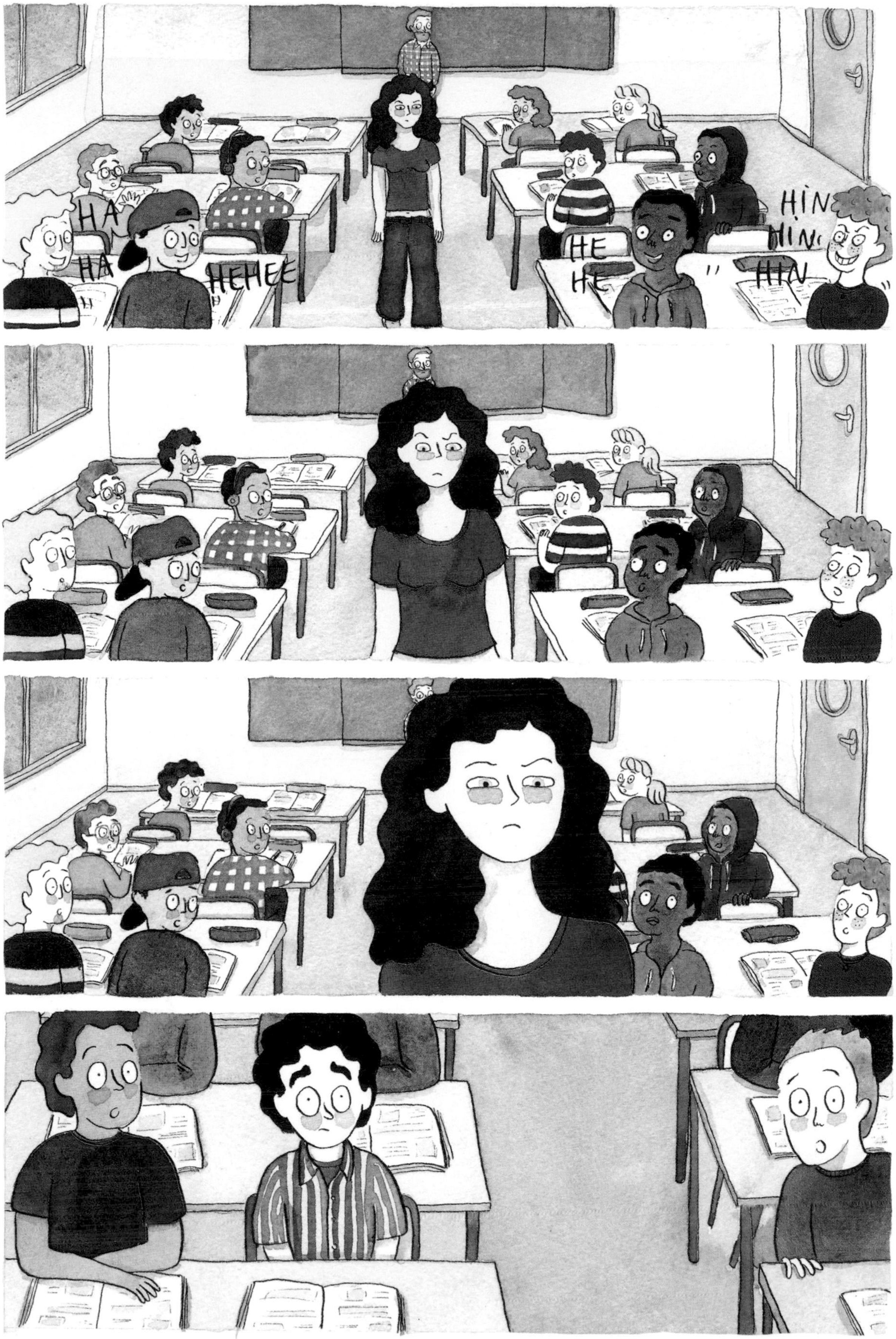
HA
HA
HEHEE
HE
HE
HIN
HIN
HIN

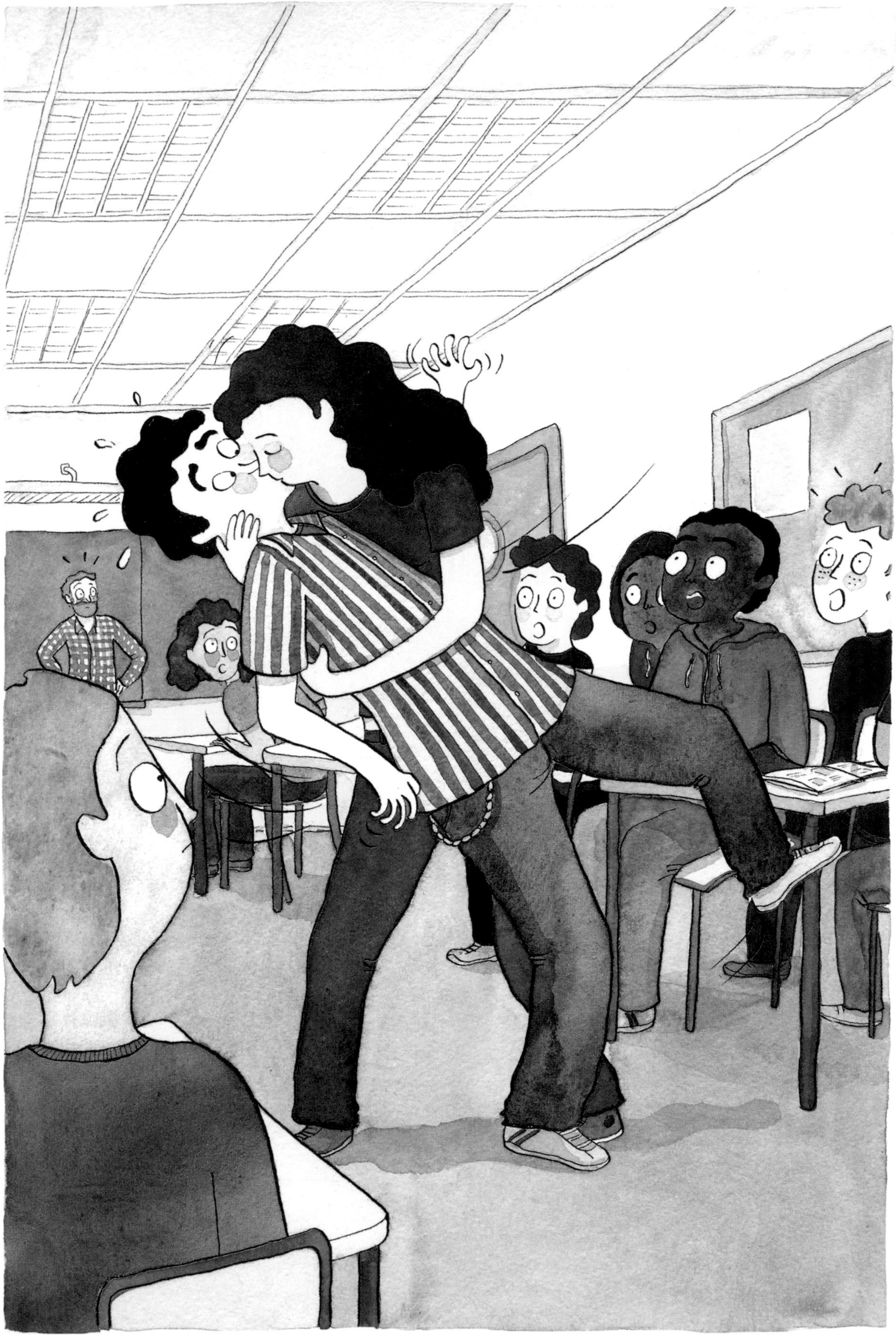

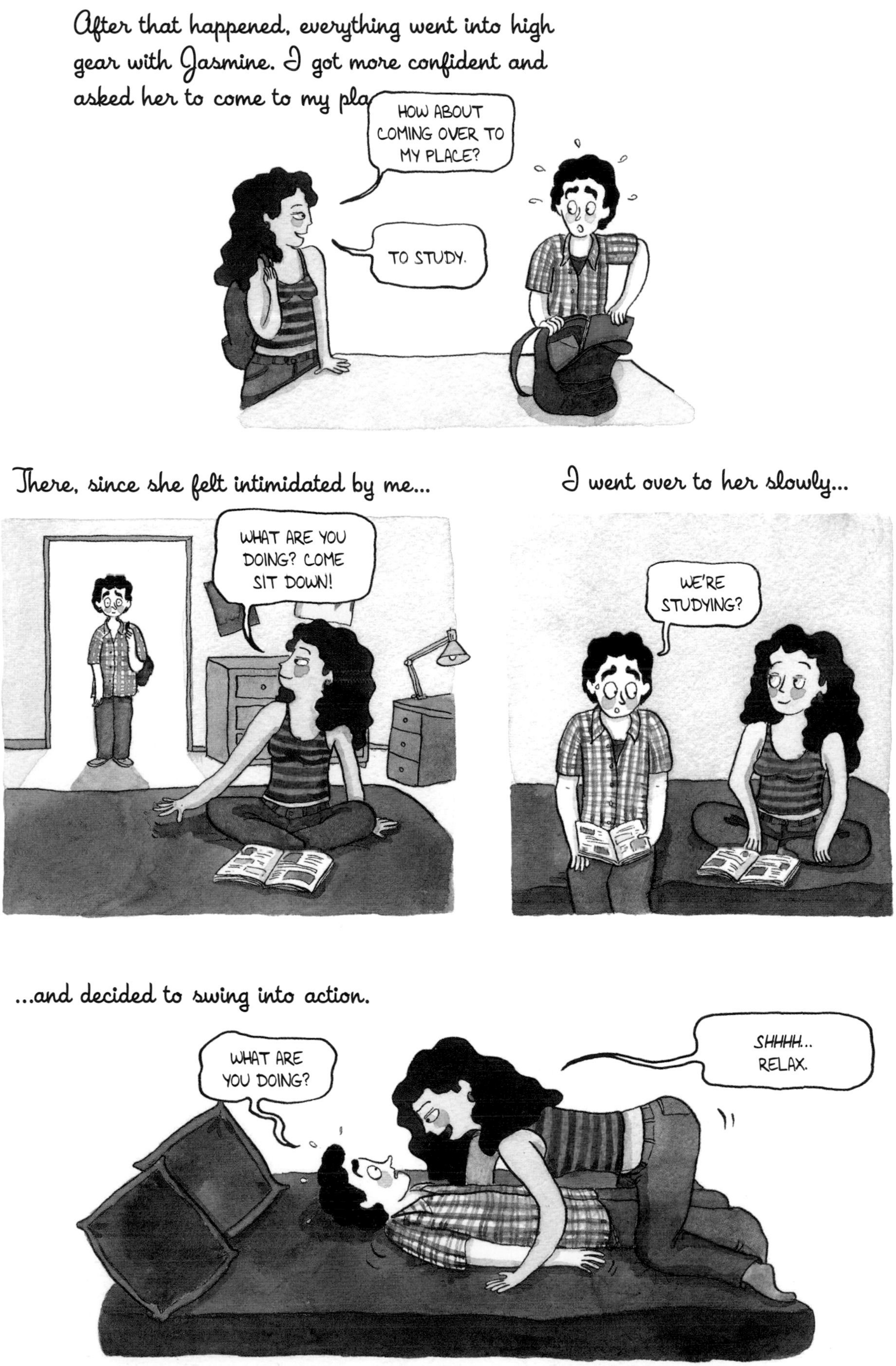
After that happened, everything went into high gear with Jasmine. I got more confident and asked her to come to my pla
HOW ABOUT COMING OVER TO MY PLACE?
TO STUDY.
There, since she felt intimidated by me...
WHAT ARE YOU DOING? COME SIT DOWN!
I went over to her slowly...
WE'RE STUDYING?
...and decided to swing into action.
WHAT ARE YOU DOING?
SHHHH.. RELAX.

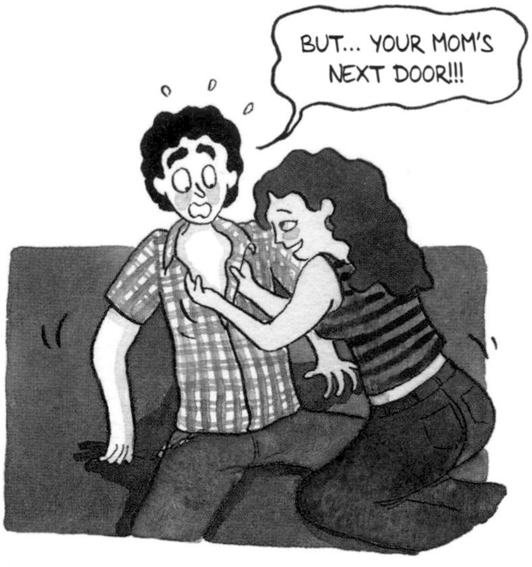
BUT... YOUR MOM'S NEXT DOOR!!!

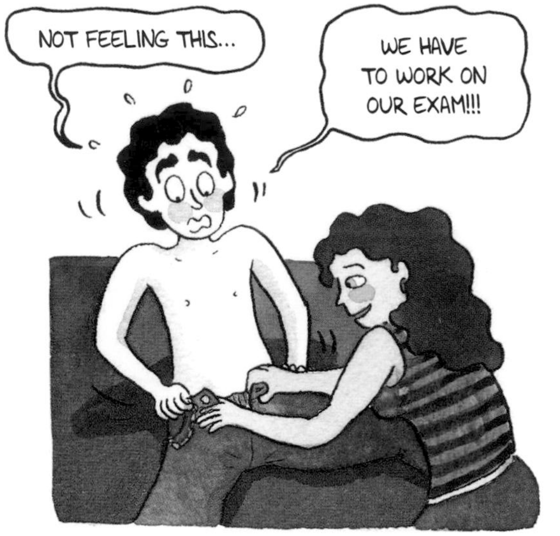
NOT FEELING THIS...
WE HAVE TO WORK ON OUR EXAM!!!

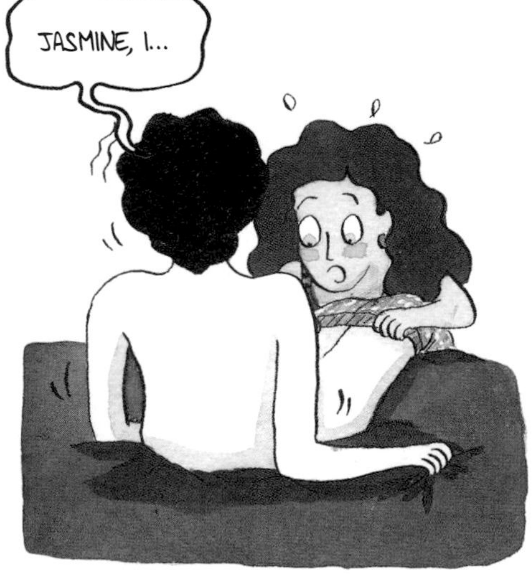
JASMINE, I...

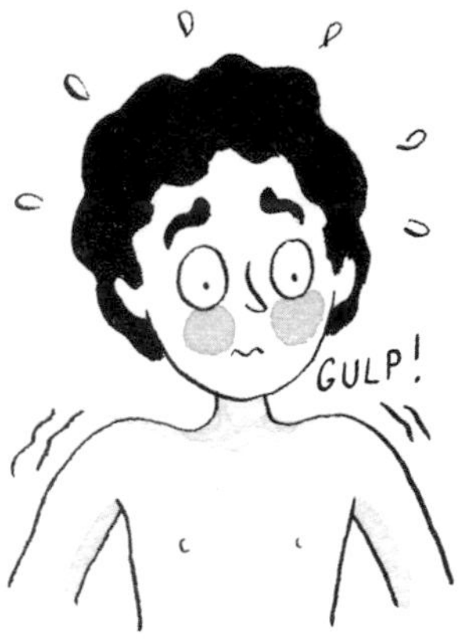
GULP!

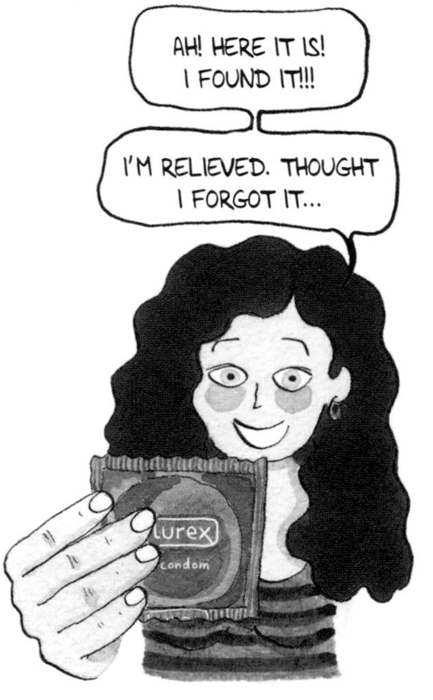
AH! HERE IT IS! I FOUND IT!!!
I'M RELIEVED. THOUGHT I FORGOT IT...
condom

Not to brag, but I can definitely say that this moment was...unforgettable!

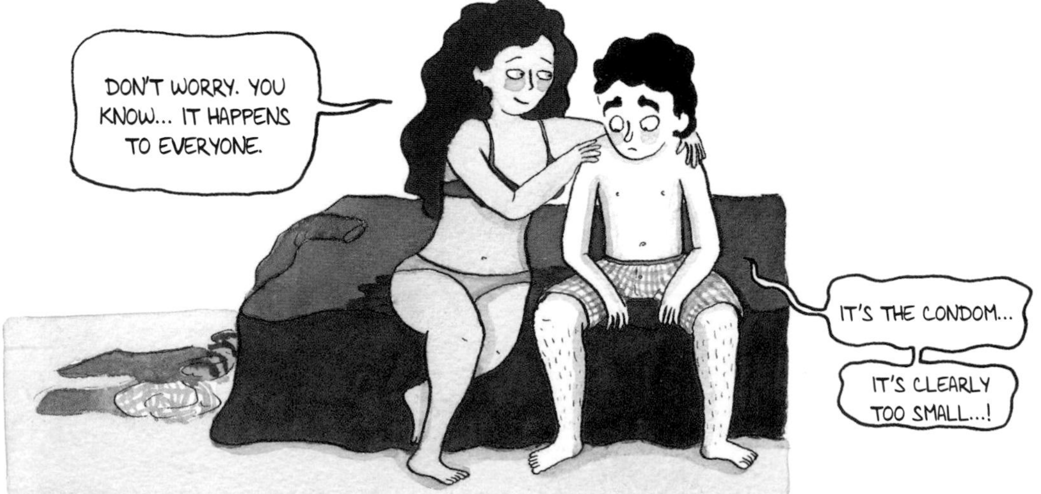
DON'T WORRY. YOU KNOW... IT HAPPENS TO EVERYONE.
IT'S THE CONDOM...
IT'S CLEARLY TOO SMALL...!

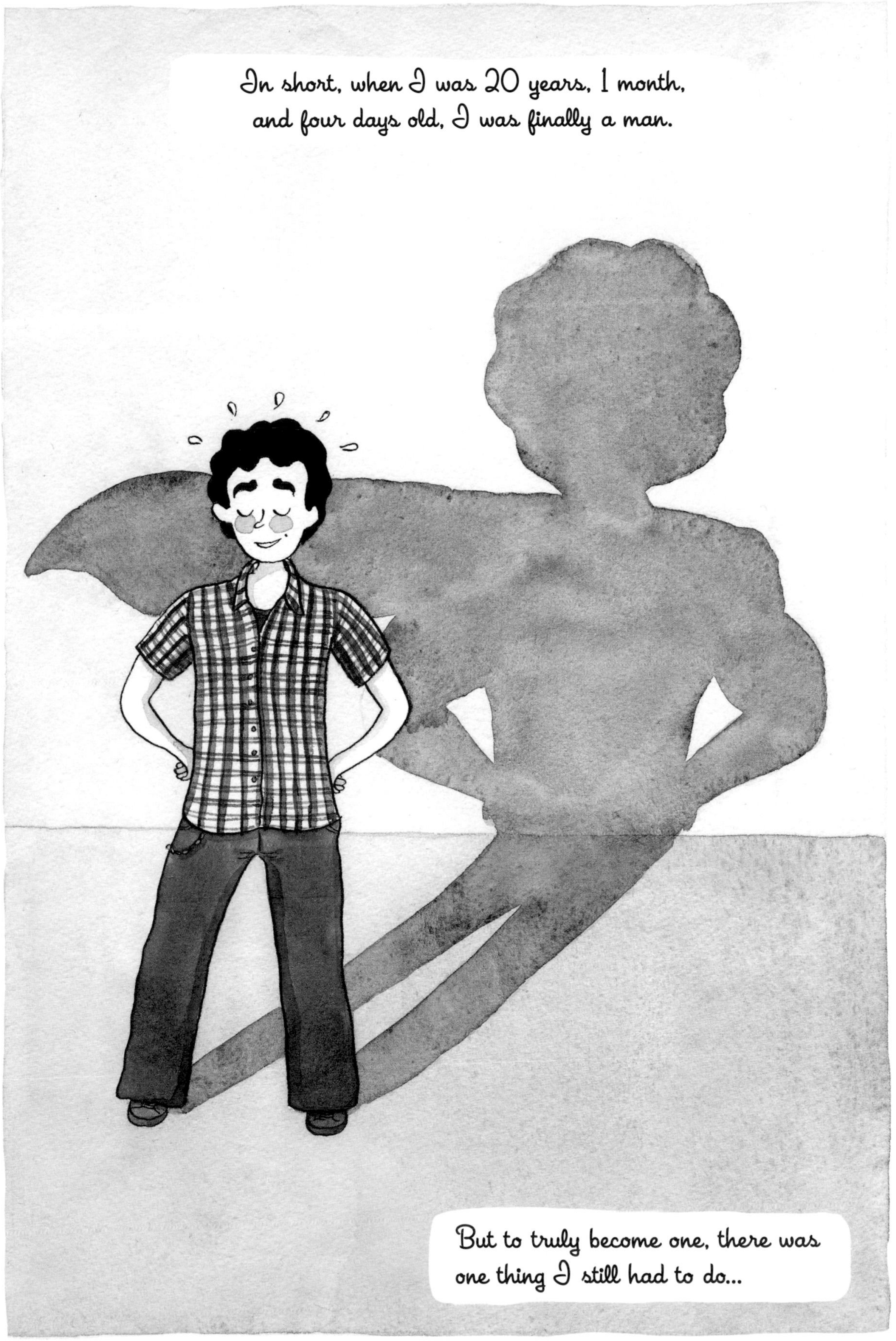
In short, when I was 20 years, 1 month, and four days old, I was finally a man.
But to truly become one, there was one thing I still had to do...

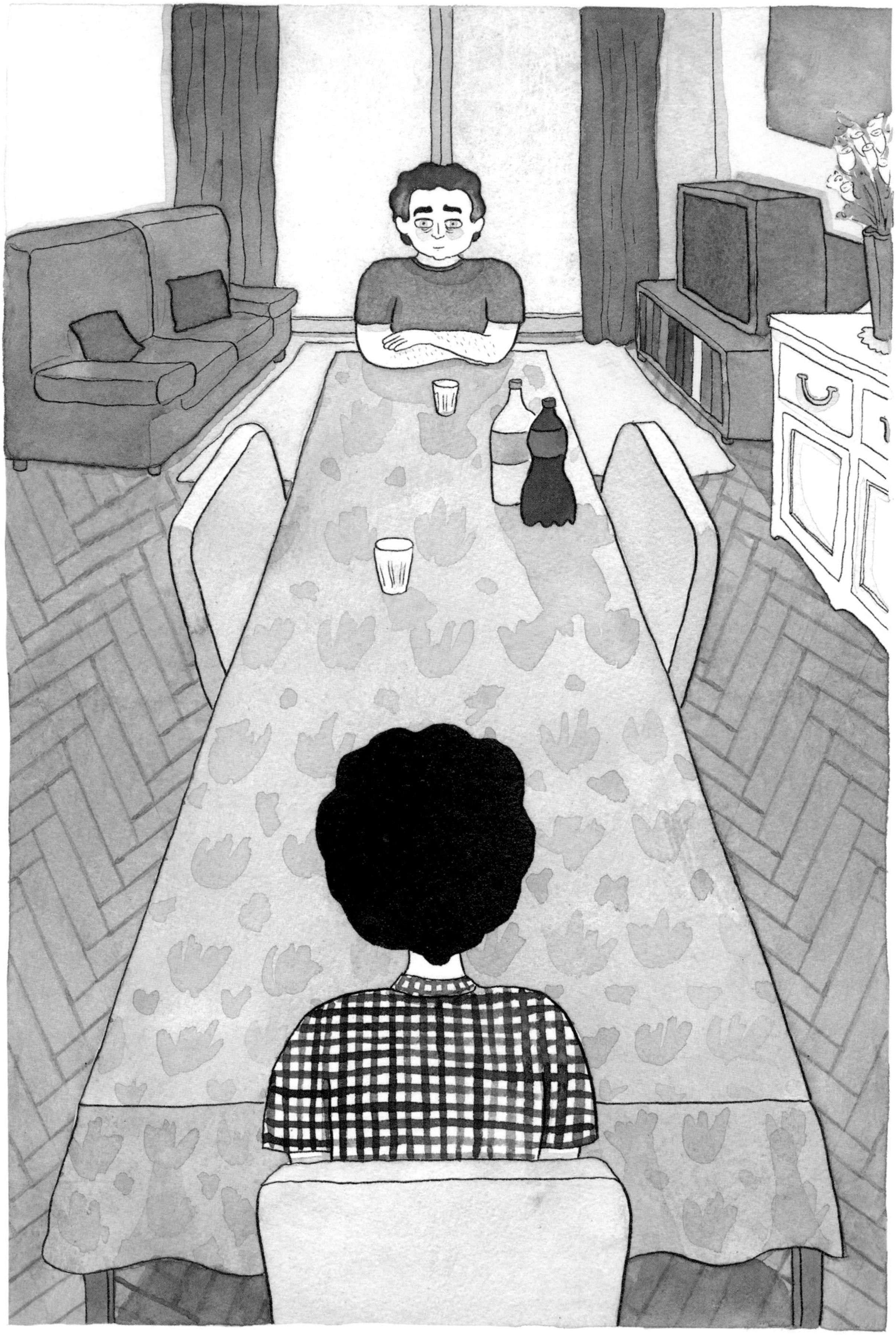

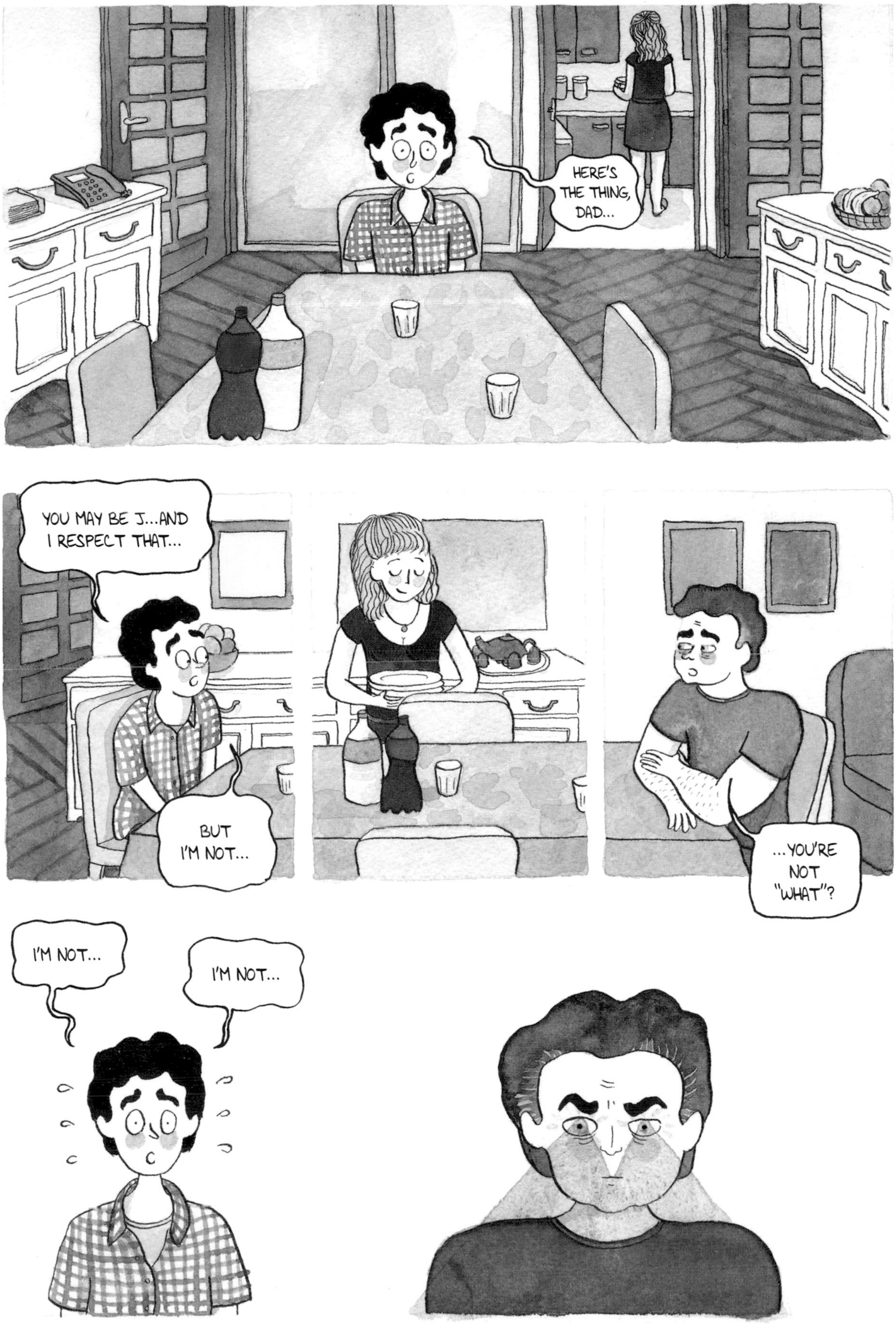
HERE'S THE THING, DAD...
YOU MAY BE J...AND I RESPECT THAT...
BUT I'M NOT...
...YOU'RE NOT "WHAT"?
I'M NOT...
I'M NOT...

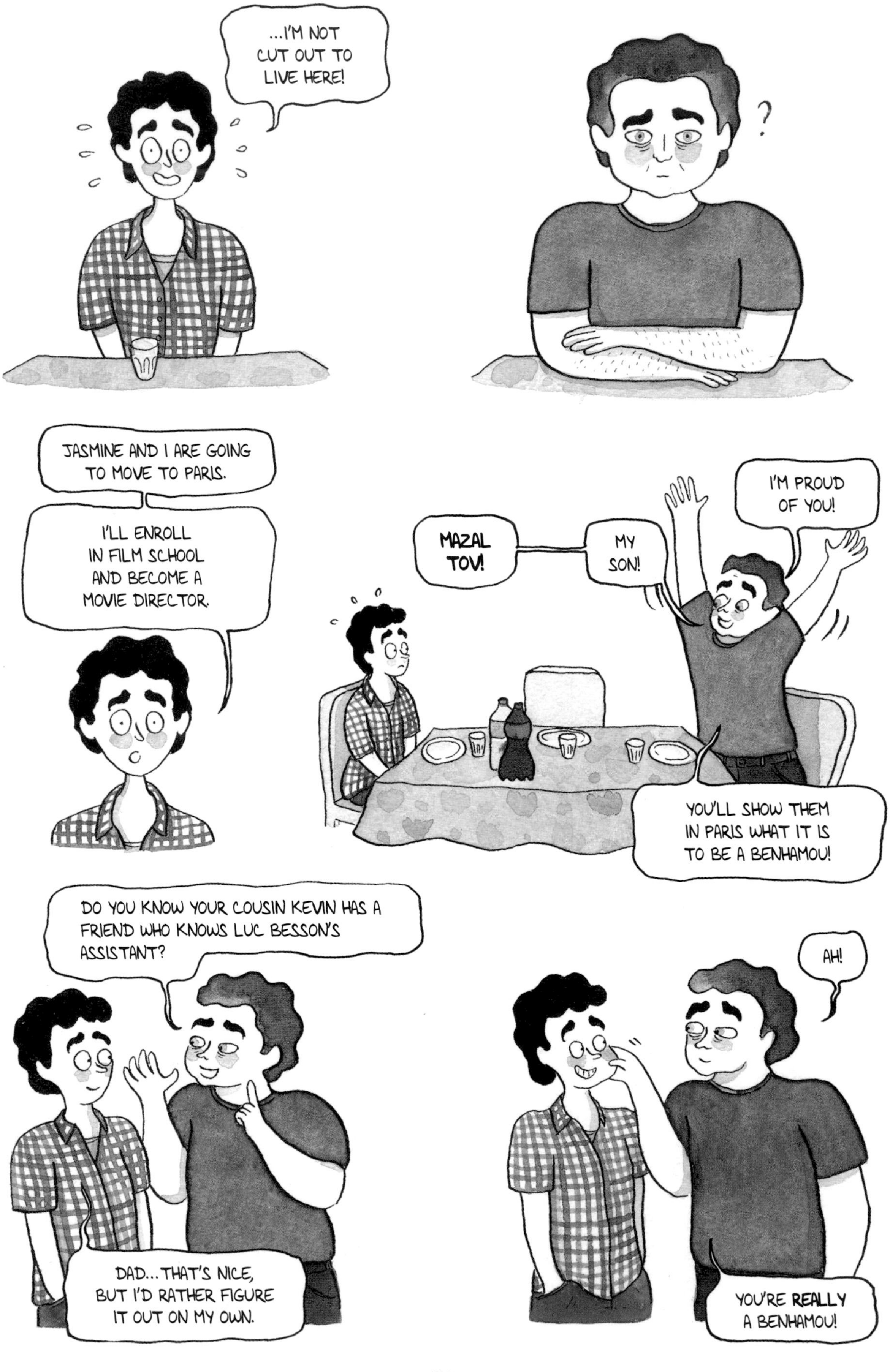
...I'M NOT CUT OUT TO LIVE HERE!
?
JASMINE AND I ARE GOING TO MOVE TO PARIS.
I'LL ENROLL IN FILM SCHOOL AND BECOME A MOVIE DIRECTOR.
MAZAL TOV!
MY SON!
I'M PROUD OF YOU!
YOU'LL SHOW THEM IN PARIS WHAT IT IS TO BE A BENHAMOU!
DO YOU KNOW YOUR COUSIN KEVIN HAS A FRIEND WHO KNOWS LUC BESSON'S ASSISTANT?
DAD...THAT'S NICE, BUT I'D RATHER FIGURE IT OUT ON MY OWN.
AH!
YOU'RE **REALLY** A BENHAMOU!

There, in the immense megalopolis that is Paris, I not only discovered that being different could be a richness that everyone cultivates...

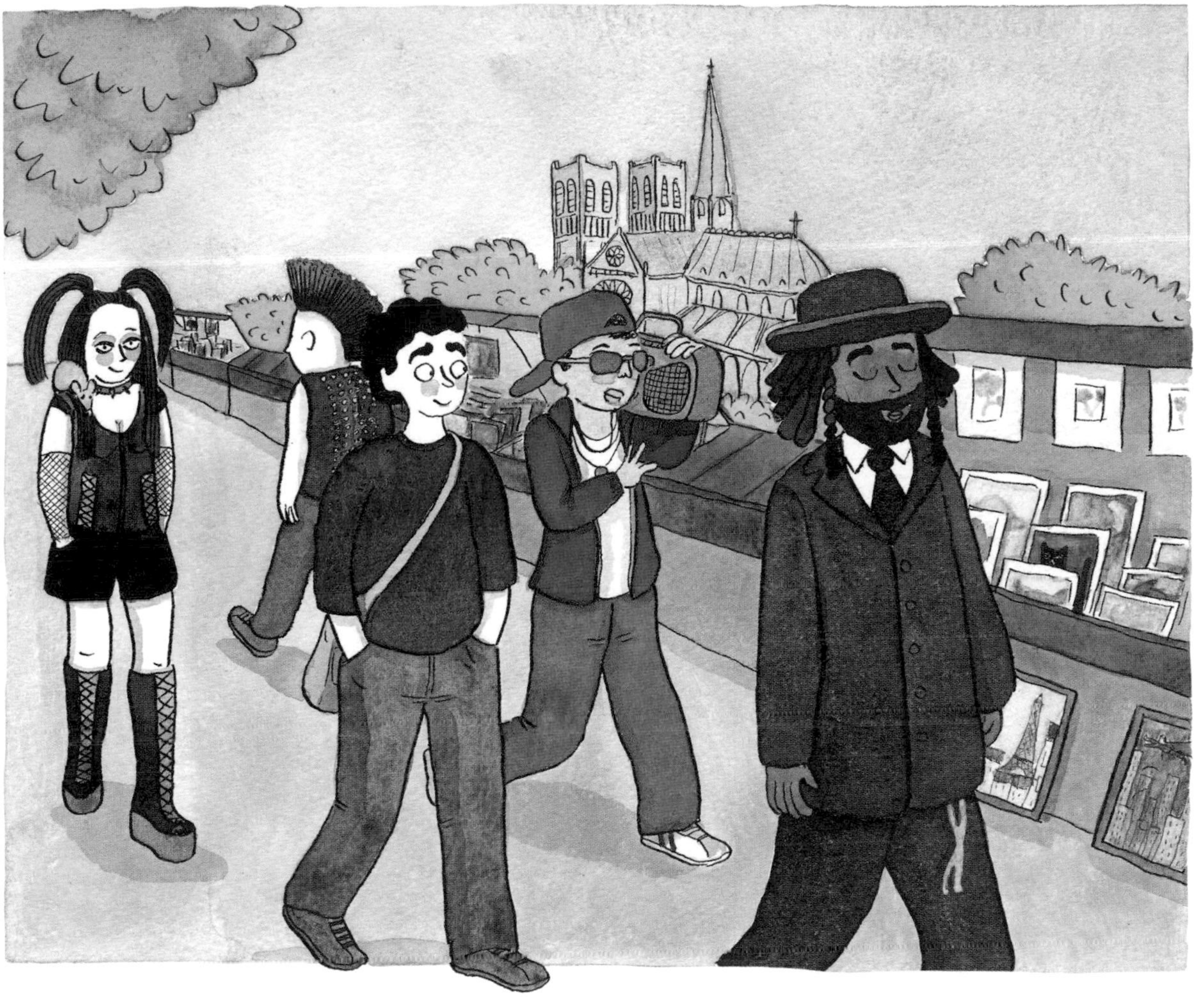

...but also that having suffered for your differences could be a way to increase your status...

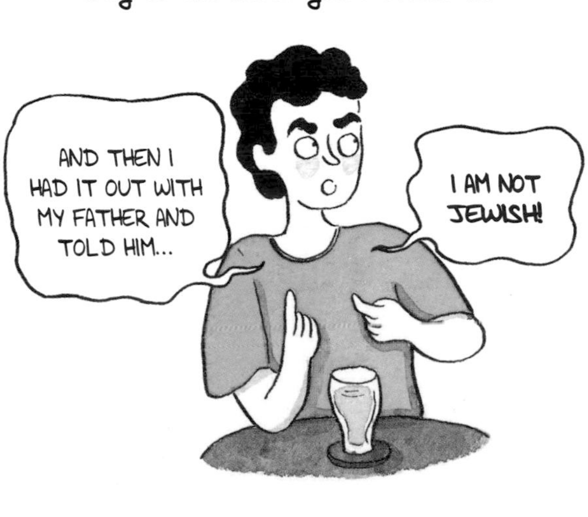
AND THEN I HAD IT OUT WITH MY FATHER AND TOLD HIM...
I AM NOT JEWISH!

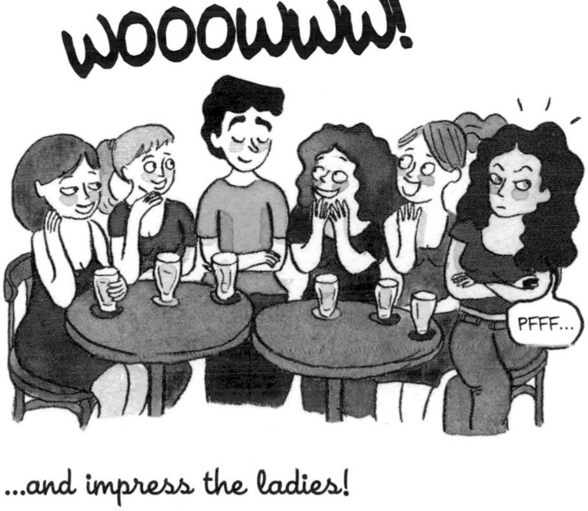
WOOOWWW!
PFFF...

...and impress the ladies!

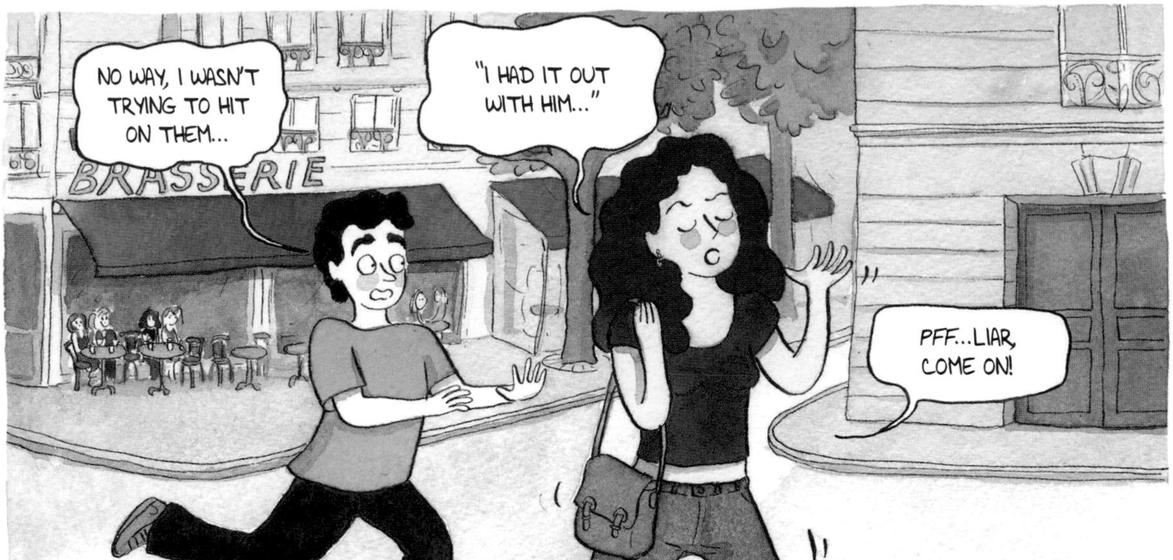
NO WAY, I WASN'T TRYING TO HIT ON THEM...
"I HAD IT OUT WITH HIM..."
PFF...LIAR, COME ON!
BRASSERIE

And several years later, when I filmed a short movie that was aired at 12:40 a.m. on the local channel...

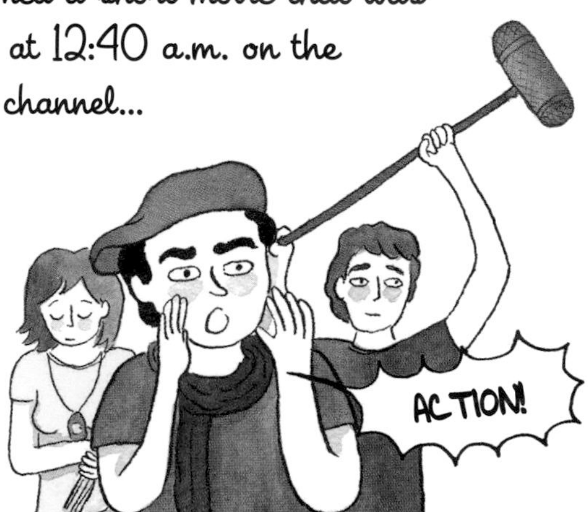
ACTION!

...I became a legend, in the eyes of my family:

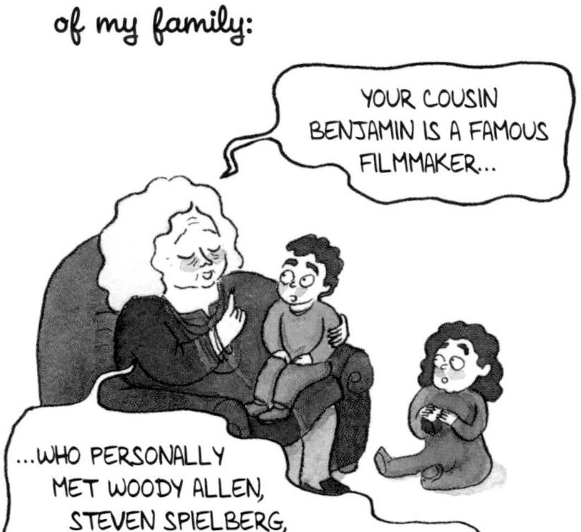
YOUR COUSIN BENJAMIN IS A FAMOUS FILMMAKER...
...WHO PERSONALLY MET WOODY ALLEN, STEVEN SPIELBERG, AND BOB DYLAN!

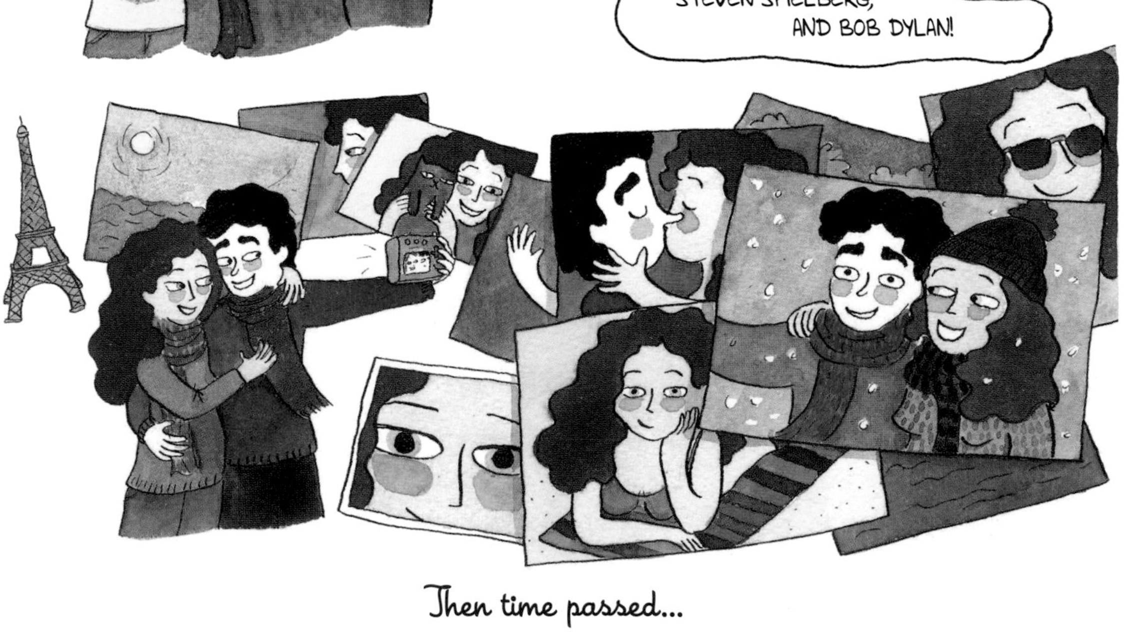

Then time passed...

In Nice, my second cousins had all grown up and family gatherings "where my father ate on the sly" began to taper off and then gradually disappeared...

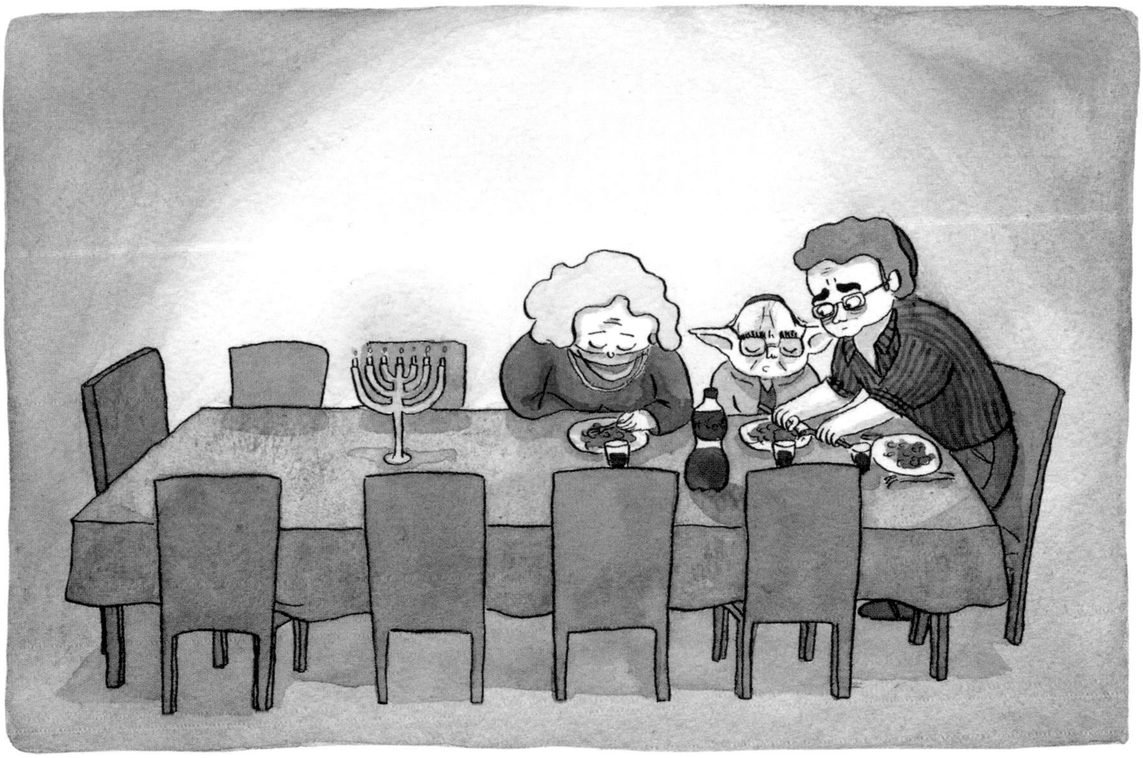

One morning when Jasmine was helping me find inspiration...

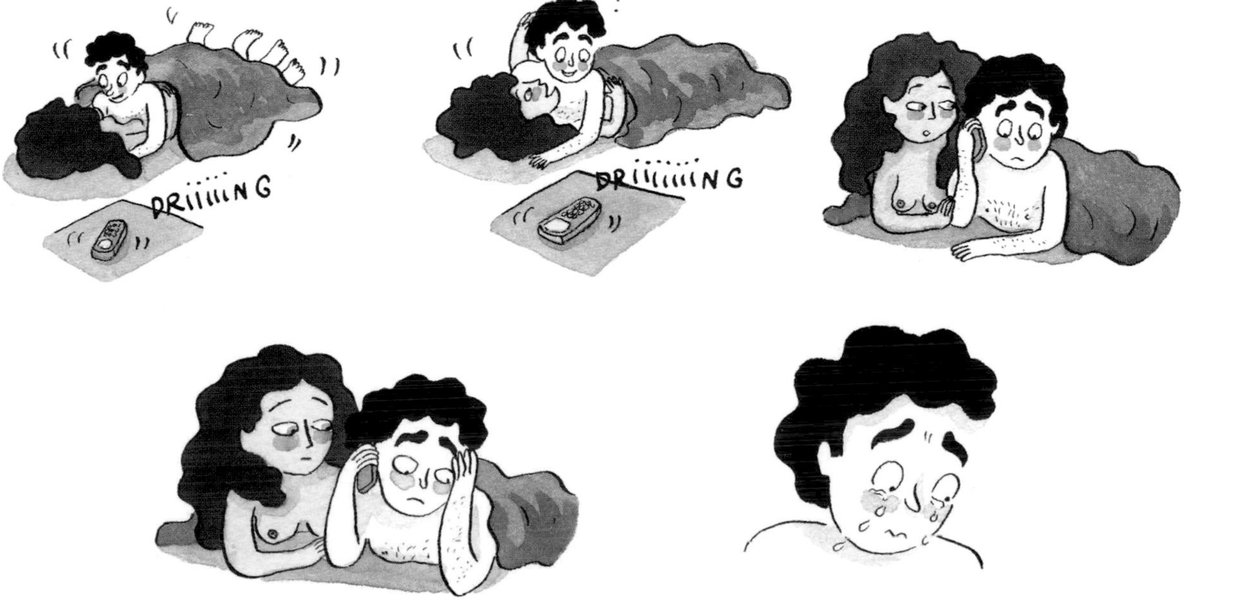
DRiiiiiNG
?
DRiiiiiiiiNG

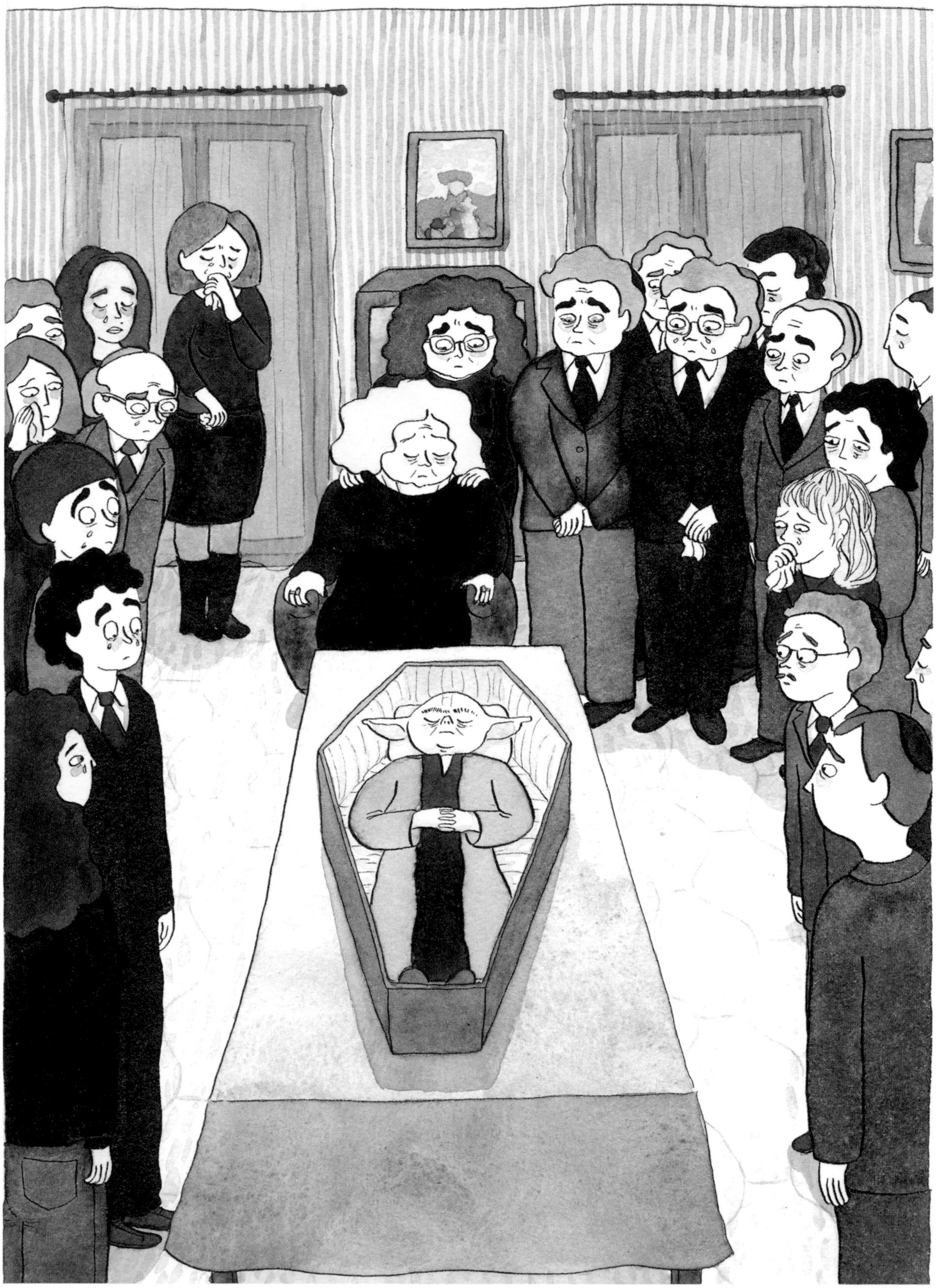

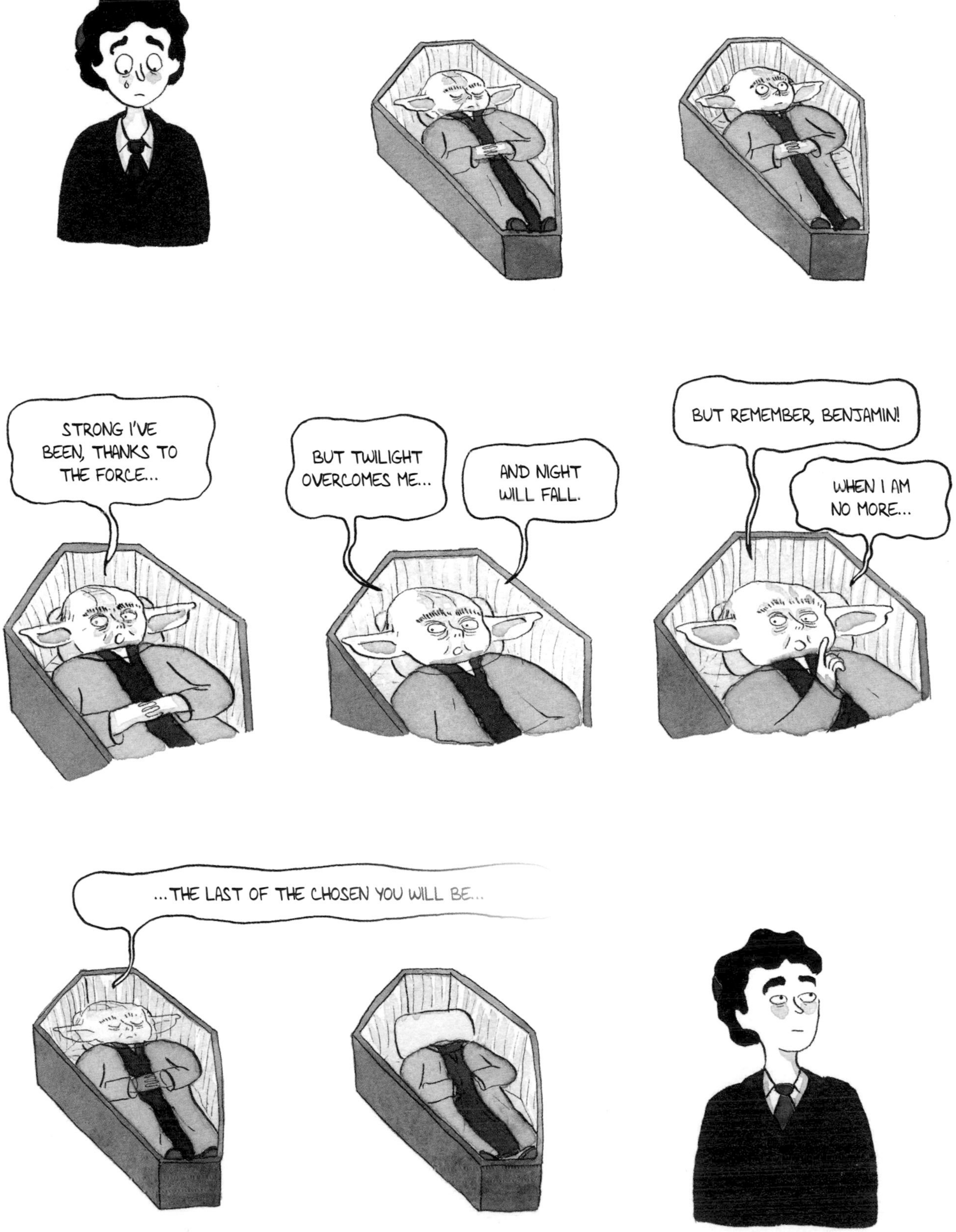
STRONG I'VE BEEN, THANKS TO THE FORCE...
BUT TWILIGHT OVERCOMES ME...
AND NIGHT WILL FALL.
BUT REMEMBER, BENJAMIN!
WHEN I AM NO MORE...
...THE LAST OF THE CHOSEN YOU WILL BE...

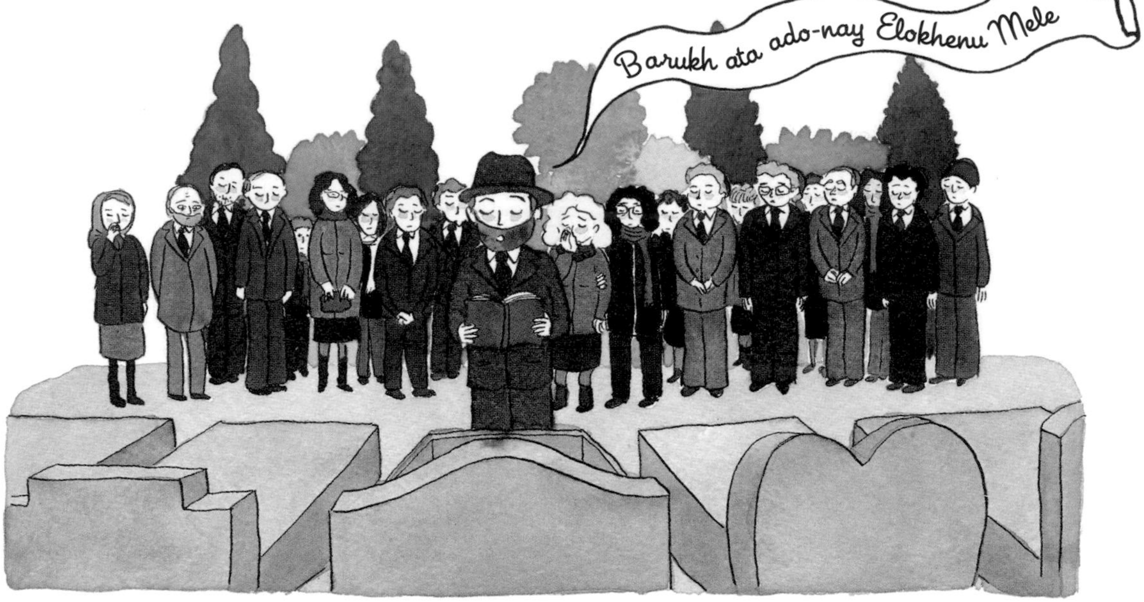
Barukh ata ado-nay Elokhenu Mele

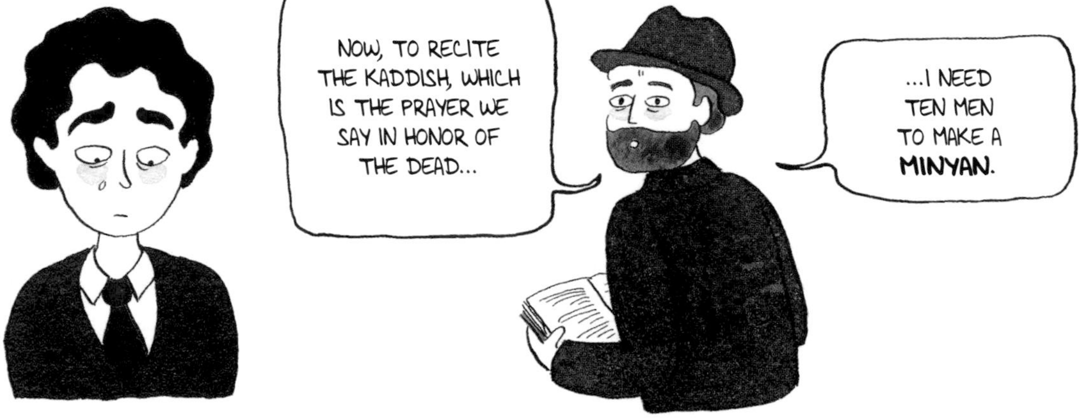
NOW, TO RECITE THE KADDISH, WHICH IS THE PRAYER WE SAY IN HONOR OF THE DEAD...
...I NEED TEN MEN TO MAKE A **MINYAN**.

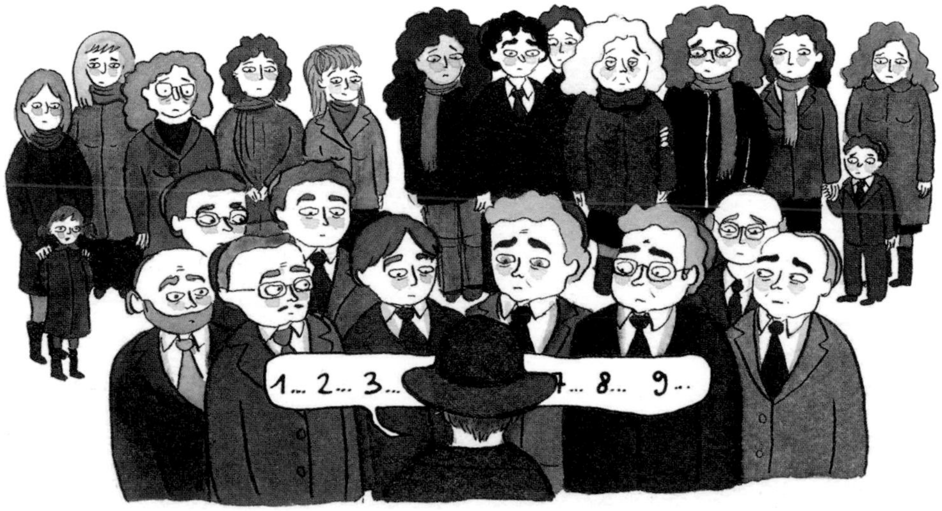
1... 2... 3...
7... 8... 9...

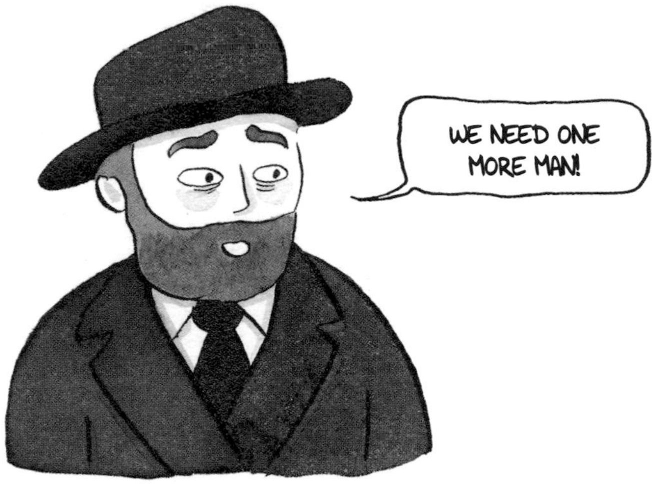
WE NEED ONE MORE MAN!

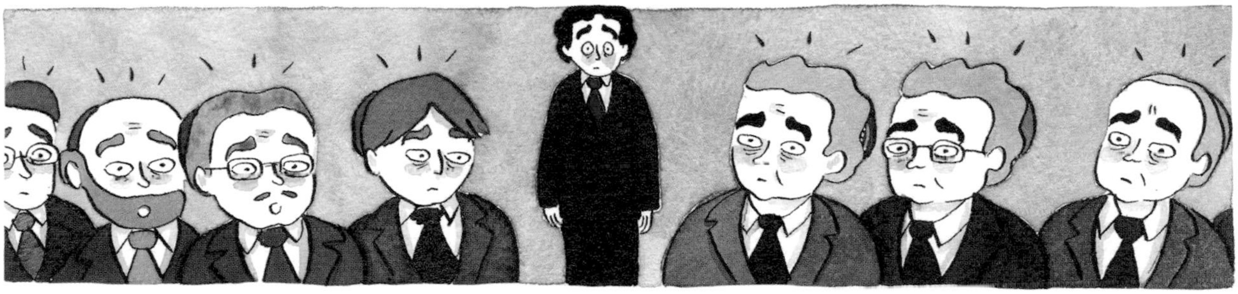

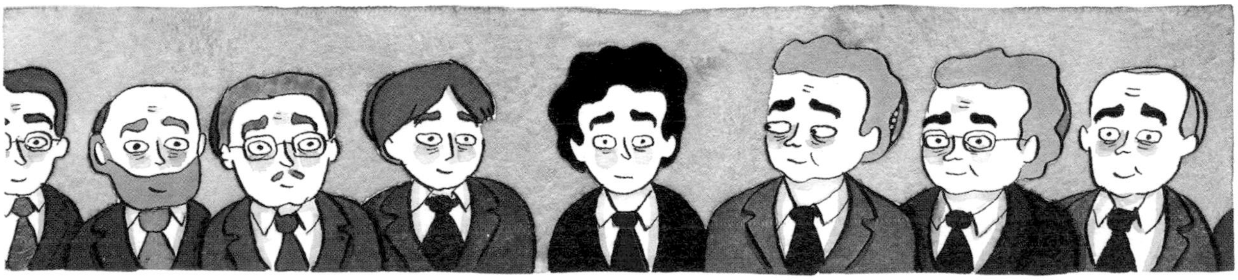

In that moment, and for the first time in my life, I felt the meaning of what my father had wanted to pass on to me.

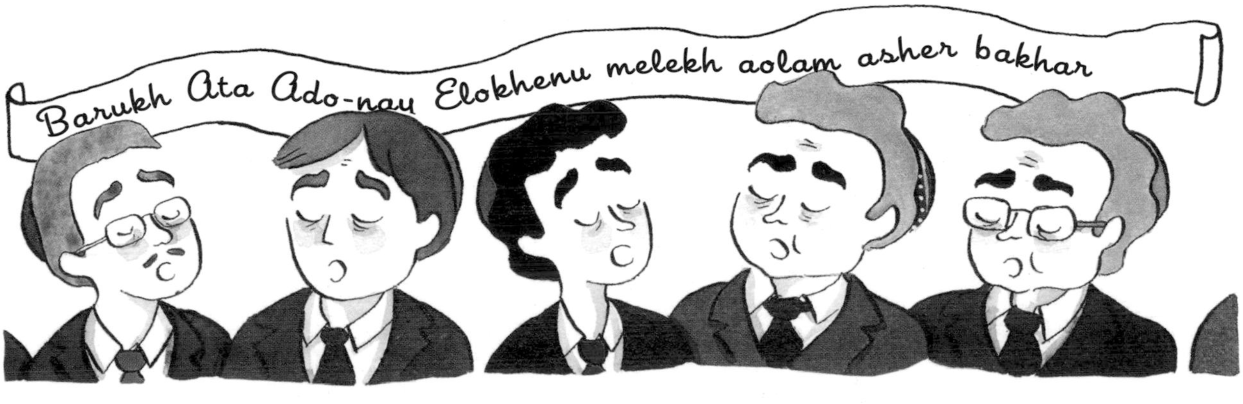
Barukh Ata Ado-nau Elokhenu melekh aolam asher bakhar

And even though I did not feel that I belonged to that religion, I realized that this family, which I had rejected so greatly...was my family.

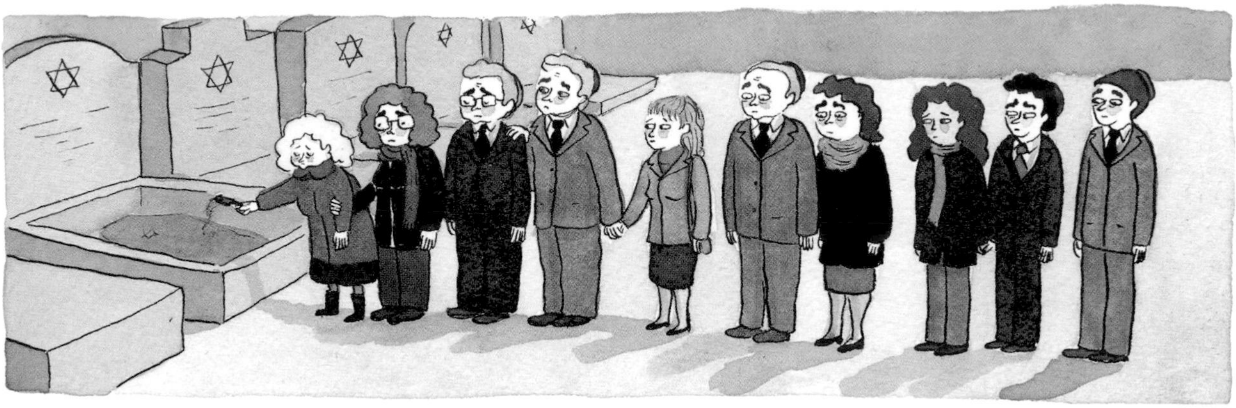

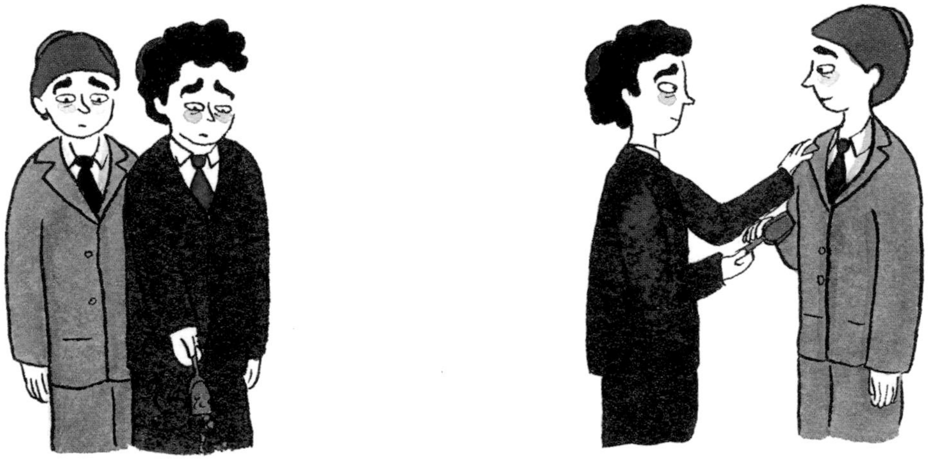

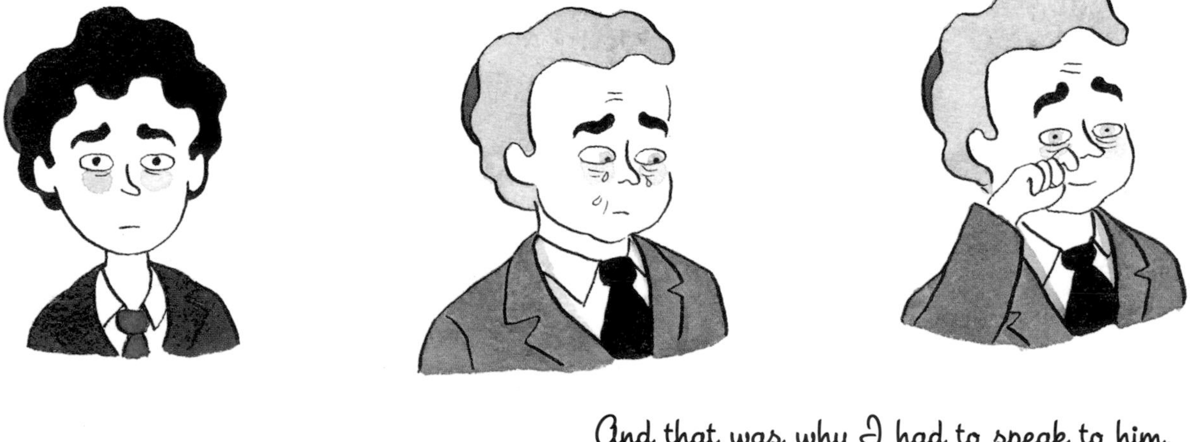

And that was why I had to speak to him.

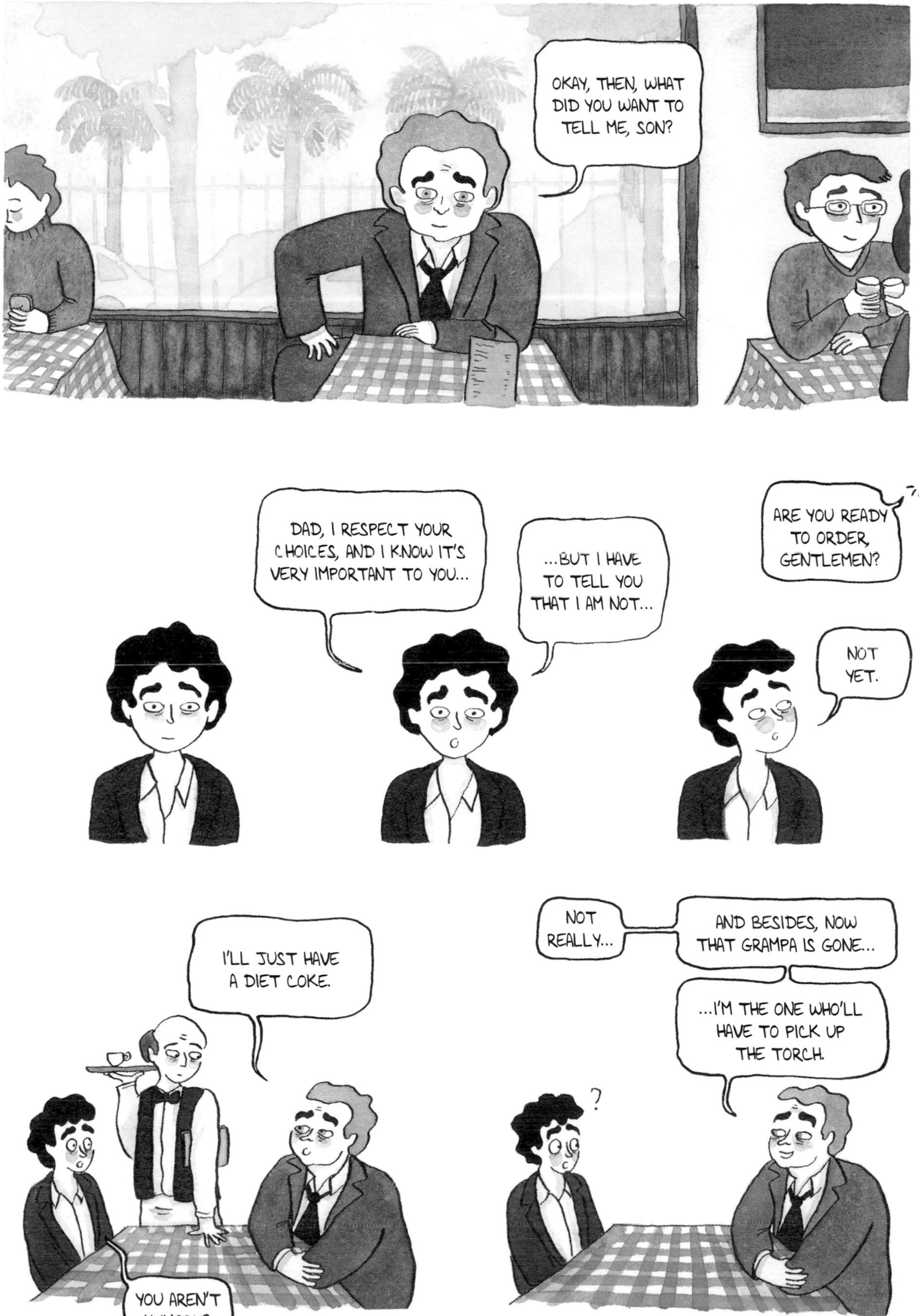
OKAY, THEN, WHAT DID YOU WANT TO TELL ME, SON?
DAD, I RESPECT YOUR CHOICES, AND I KNOW IT'S VERY IMPORTANT TO YOU...
...BUT I HAVE TO TELL YOU THAT I AM NOT...
ARE YOU READY TO ORDER, GENTLEMEN?
NOT YET.
I'LL JUST HAVE A DIET COKE.
YOU AREN'T HUNGRY?
NOT REALLY...
AND BESIDES, NOW THAT GRAMPA IS GONE...
...I'M THE ONE WHO'LL HAVE TO PICK UP THE TORCH.
?

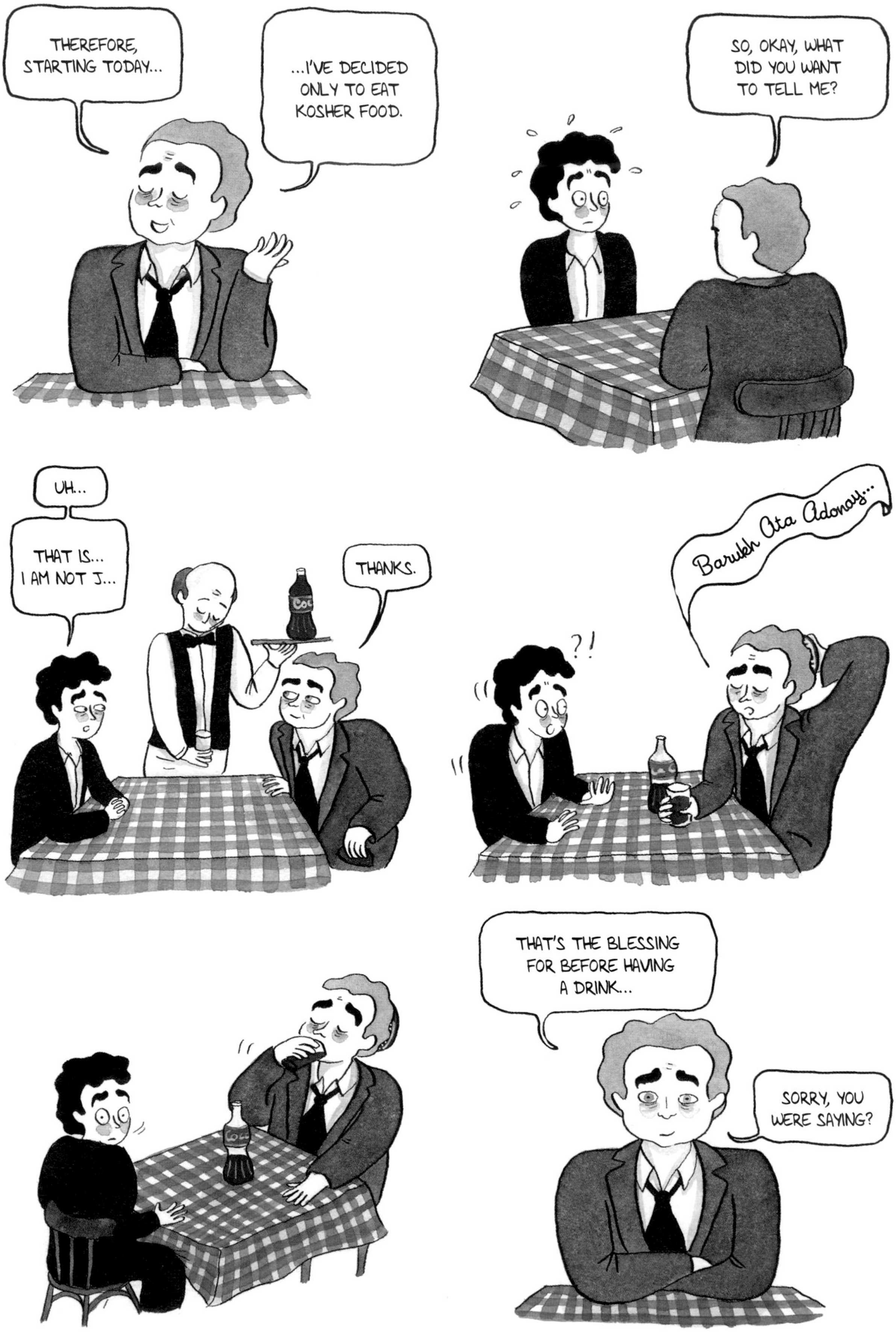
THEREFORE, STARTING TODAY...
...I'VE DECIDED ONLY TO EAT KOSHER FOOD.
SO, OKAY, WHAT DID YOU WANT TO TELL ME?
UH...
THAT IS... I AM NOT J...
THANKS.
Barukh Ata Adonay...
?!
THAT'S THE BLESSING FOR BEFORE HAVING A DRINK...
SORRY, YOU WERE SAYING?

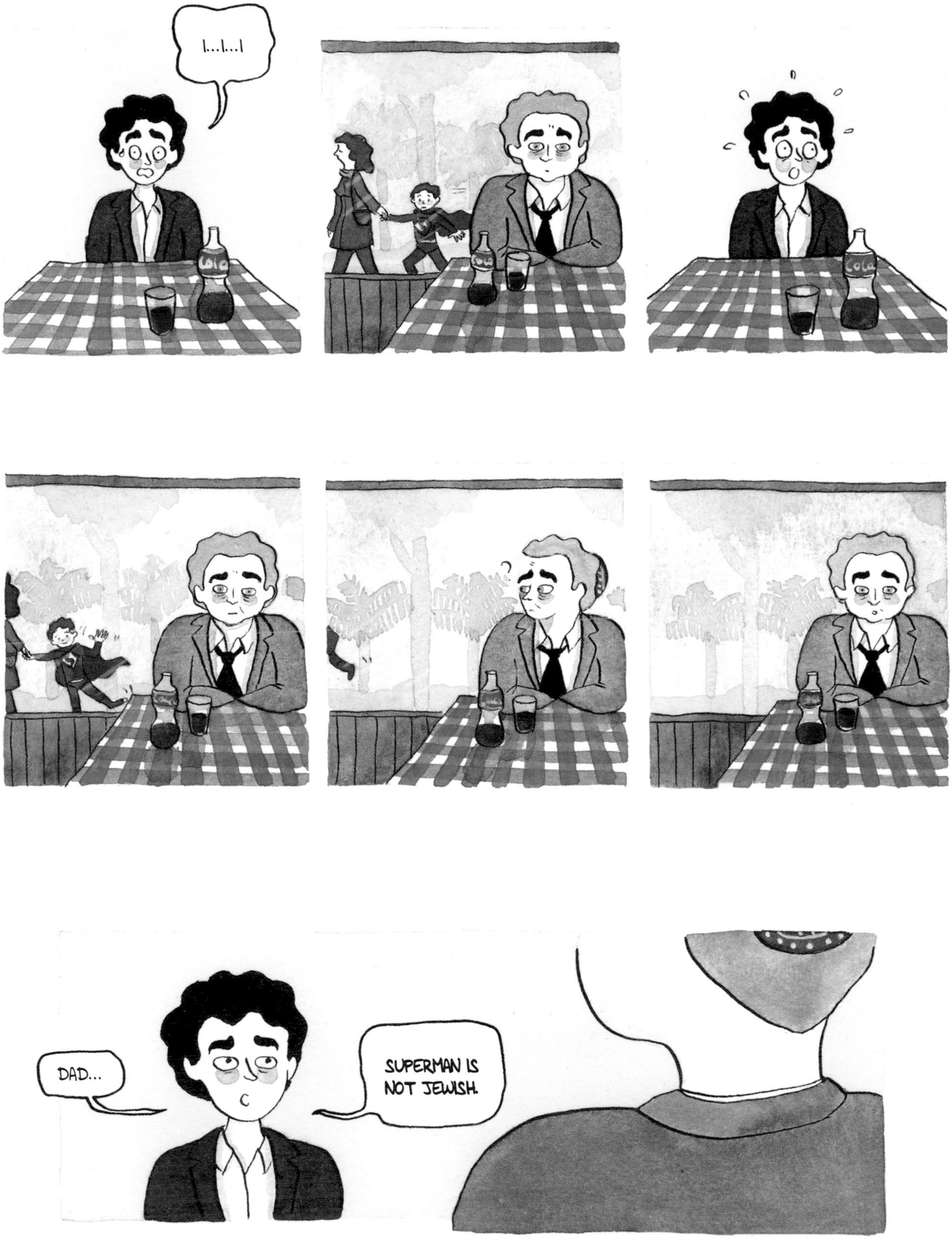
I...I...I
DAD...
SUPERMAN IS NOT JEWISH.

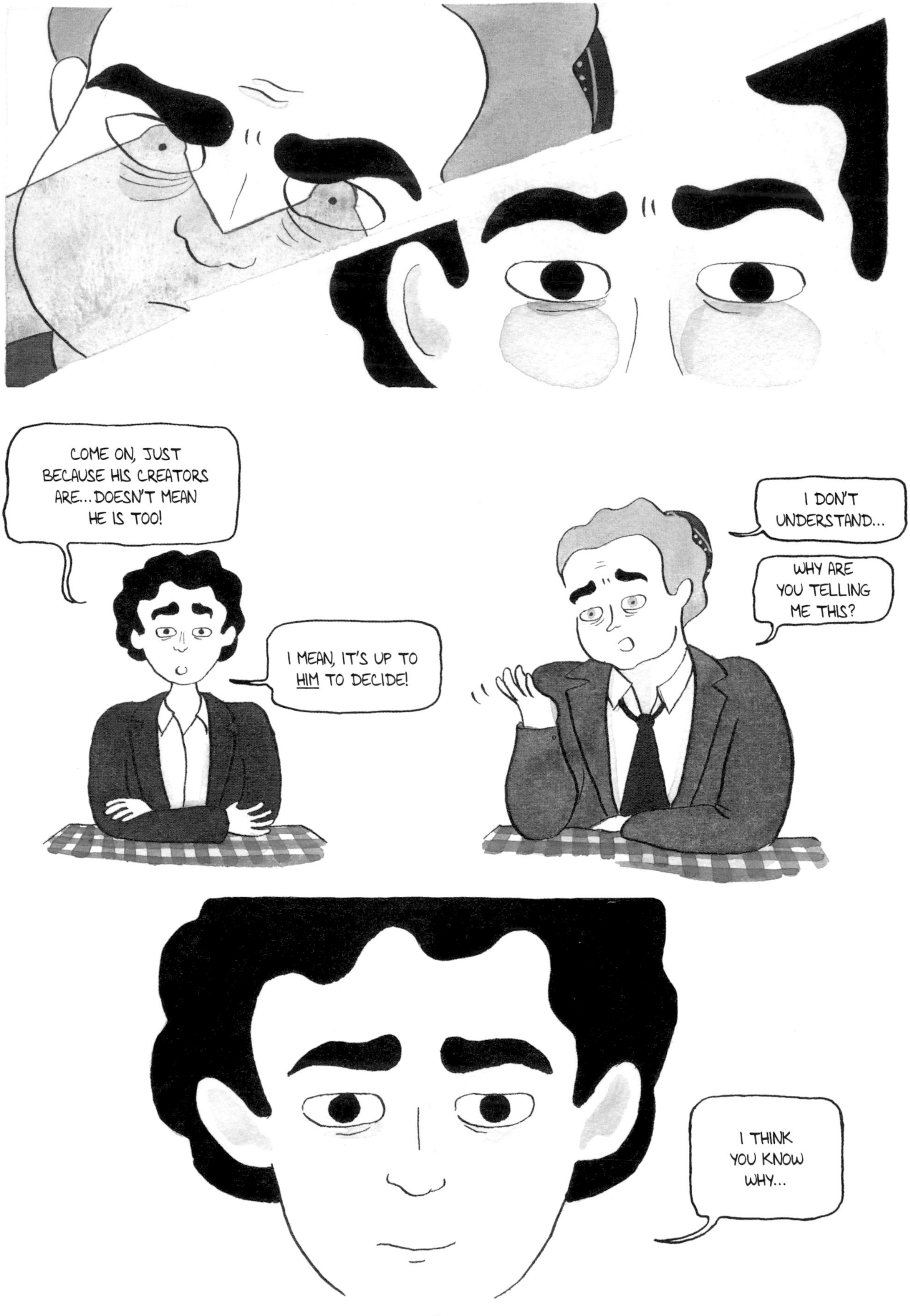
COME ON, JUST BECAUSE HIS CREATORS ARE... DOESN'T MEAN HE IS TOO!
I MEAN, IT'S UP TO HIM TO DECIDE!
I DON'T UNDERSTAND...
WHY ARE YOU TELLING ME THIS?
I THINK YOU KNOW WHY...

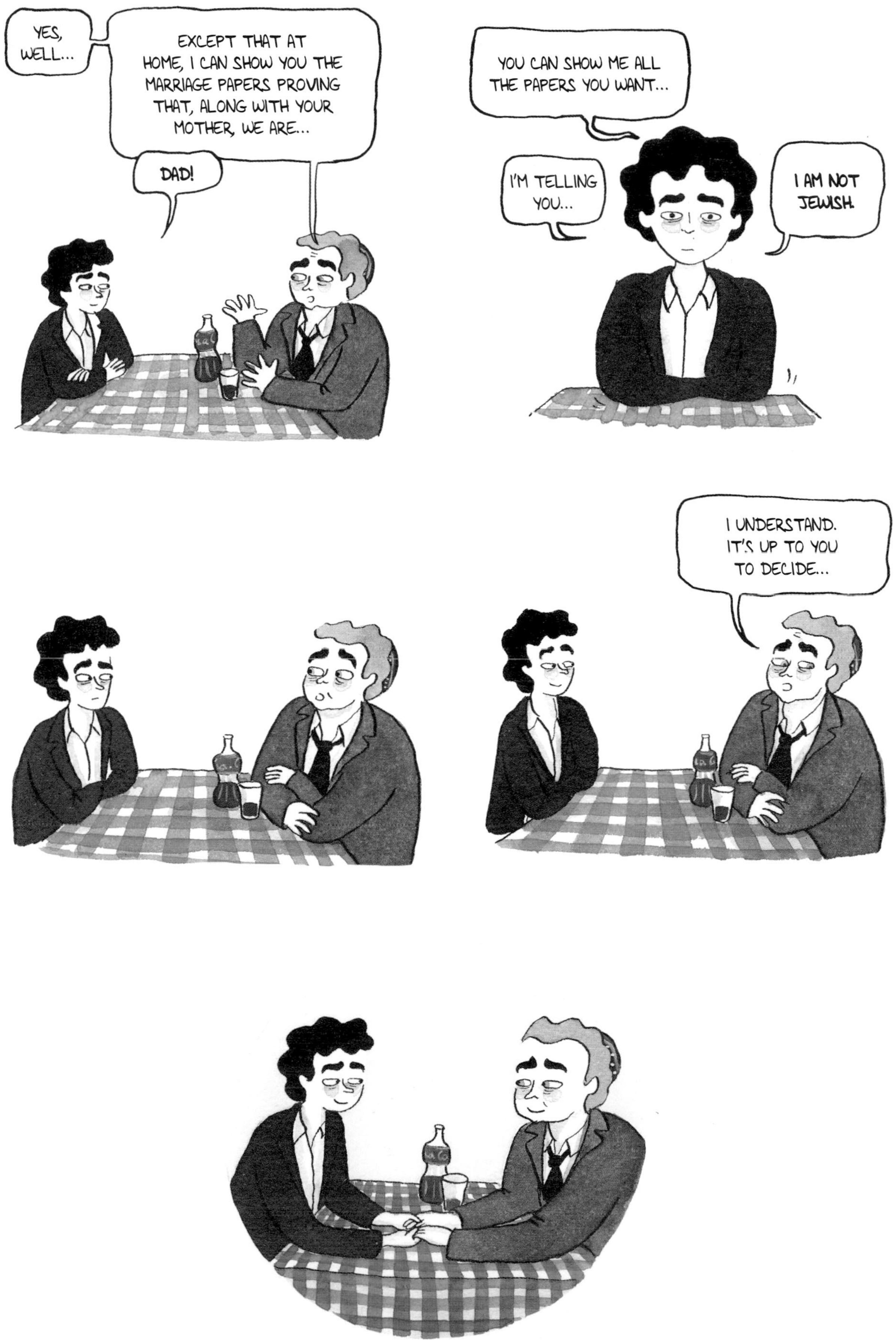
YES, WELL...
EXCEPT THAT AT HOME, I CAN SHOW YOU THE MARRIAGE PAPERS PROVING THAT, ALONG WITH YOUR MOTHER, WE ARE...
DAD!
YOU CAN SHOW ME ALL THE PAPERS YOU WANT...
I'M TELLING YOU...
I AM NOT JEWISH.
I UNDERSTAND. IT'S UP TO YOU TO DECIDE...

Okay, in reality, his reaction was a little different...

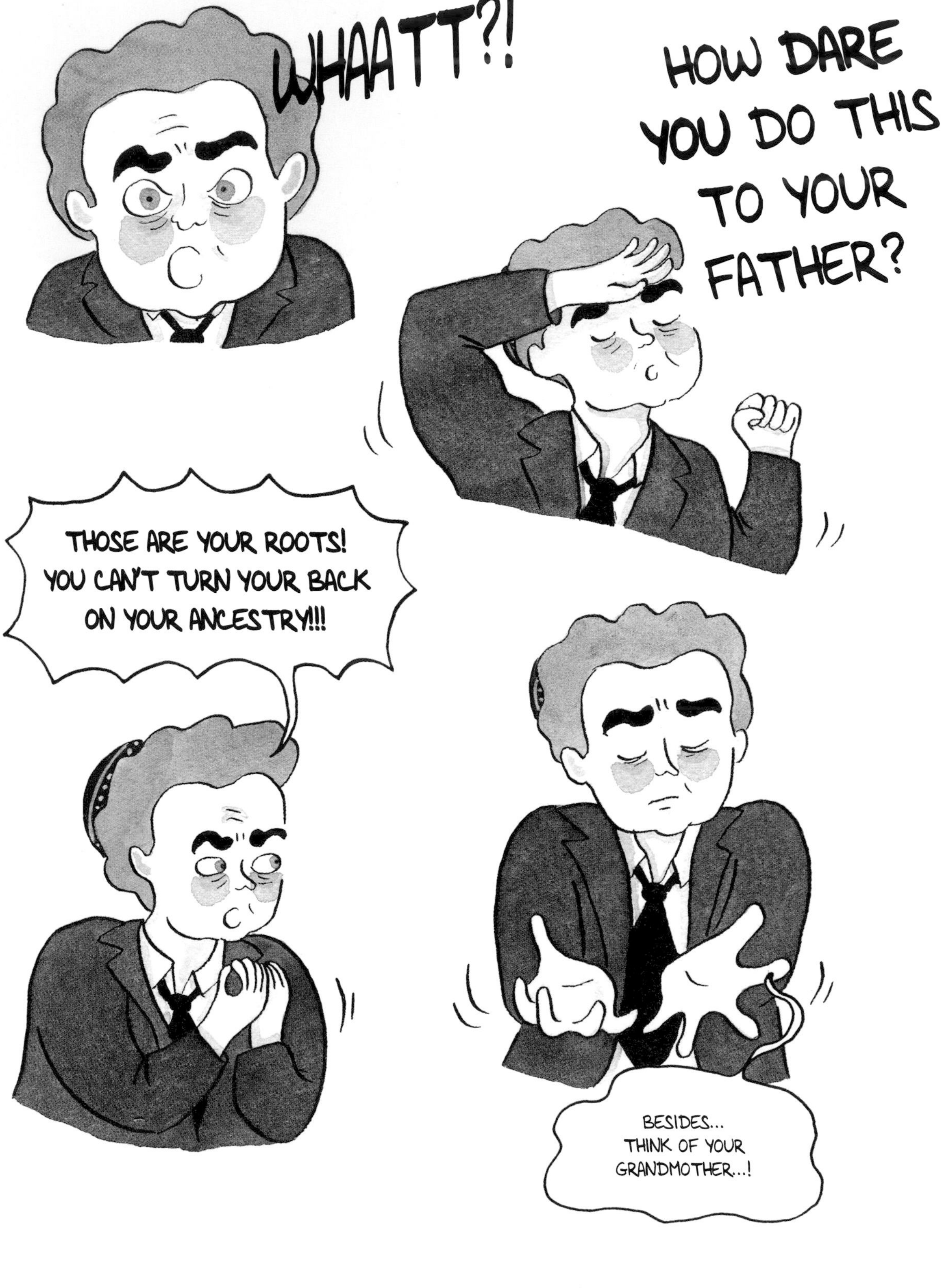

WHAATT?!
HOW DARE YOU DO THIS TO YOUR FATHER?
THOSE ARE YOUR ROOTS! YOU CAN'T TURN YOUR BACK ON YOUR ANCESTRY!!!
BESIDES... THINK OF YOUR GRANDMOTHER...!

But what's important to remember is that that day,
his only choice was to accept <u>mine</u>.

BOOM...   BOOM...   BOOM...

Since then, I made up my mind...

BOOM...   BOOM...   BOOM...

...and it changed my life...

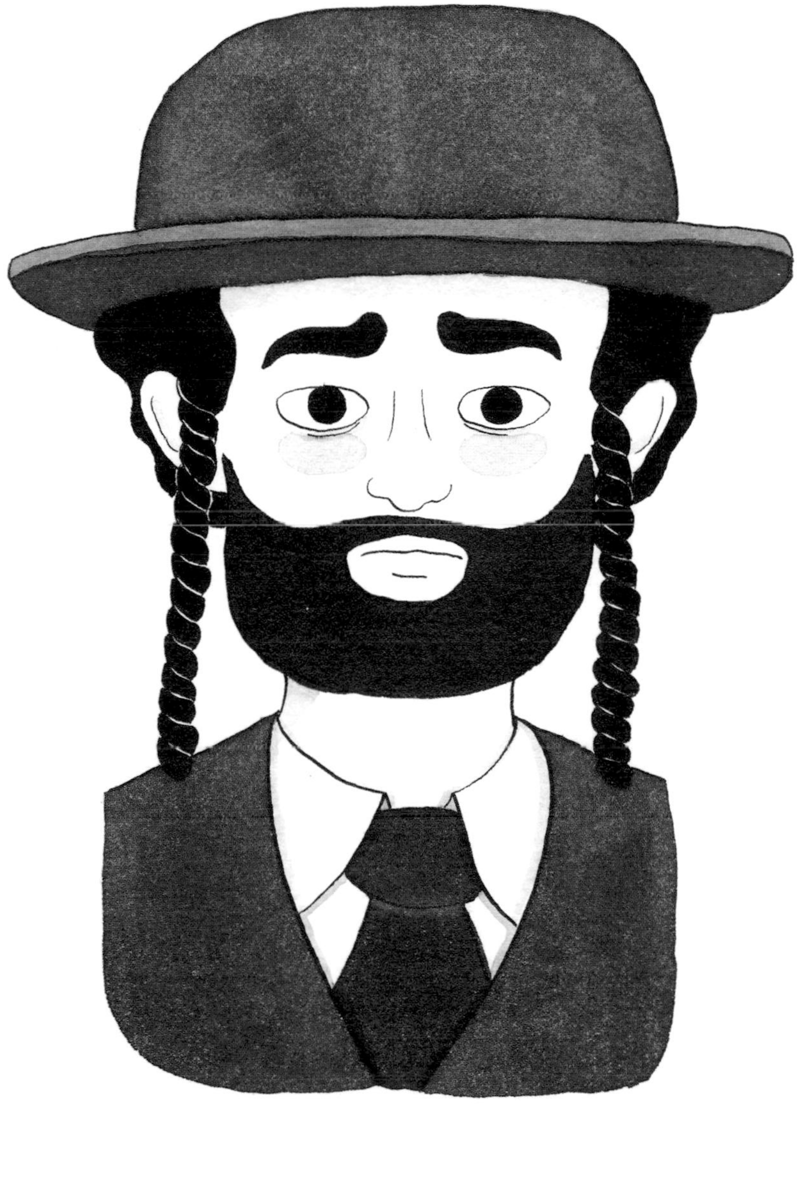
BOOM...
BOOM...

BOOM...   BOOM...   BOOM...

Whatever people say about me...

BOOM...  BOOM...

BOOM...   BOOM...   BOOM...   BOOM...

...never, and I do say never...

BOOM...   BOOM...   BOOM...   BOOM...

BOOM...   BOOM...   BOOM...   BOOM...

...will I torture myself to figure out...

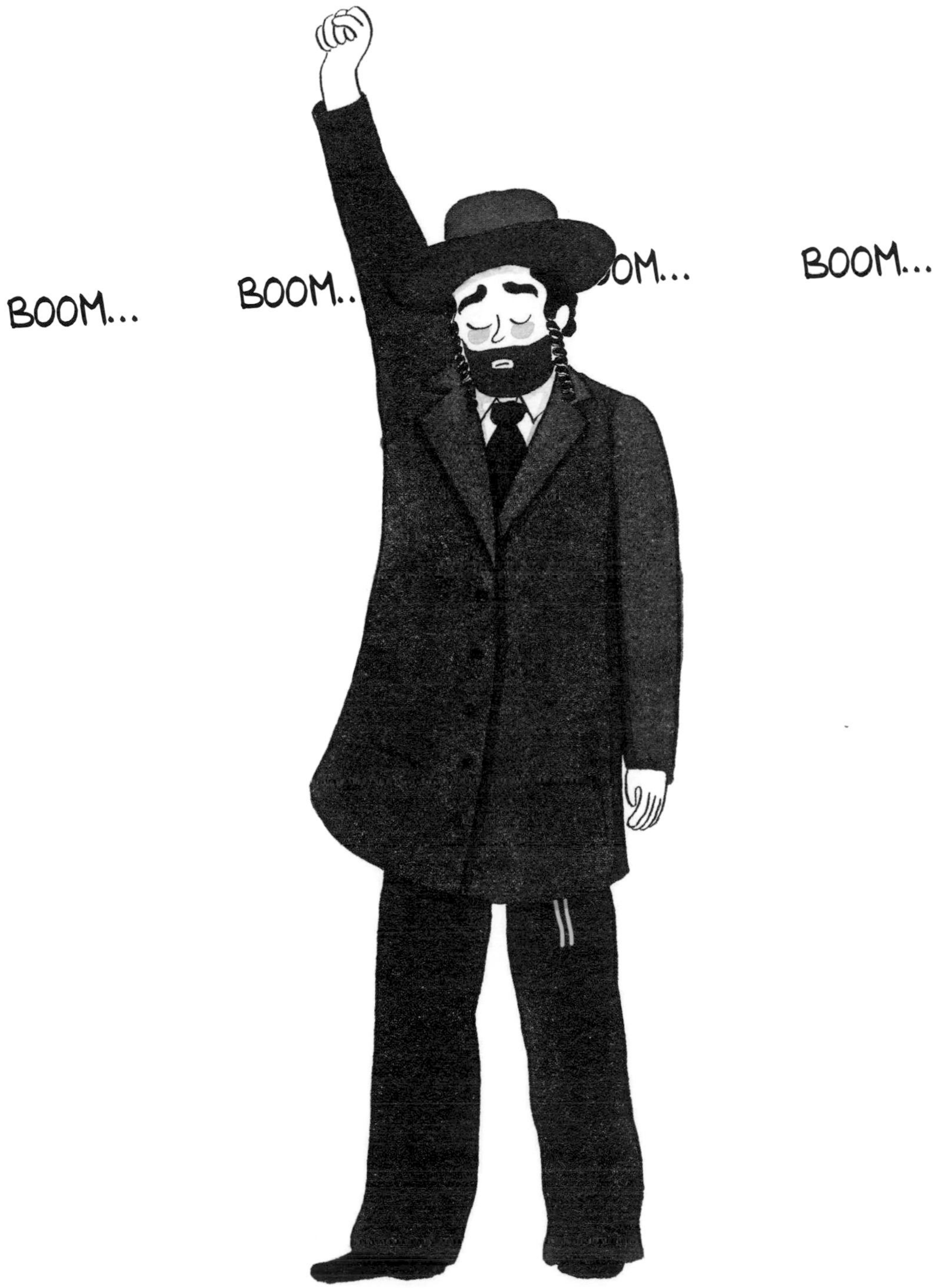
BOOM...
BOOM...
OM...
BOOM...

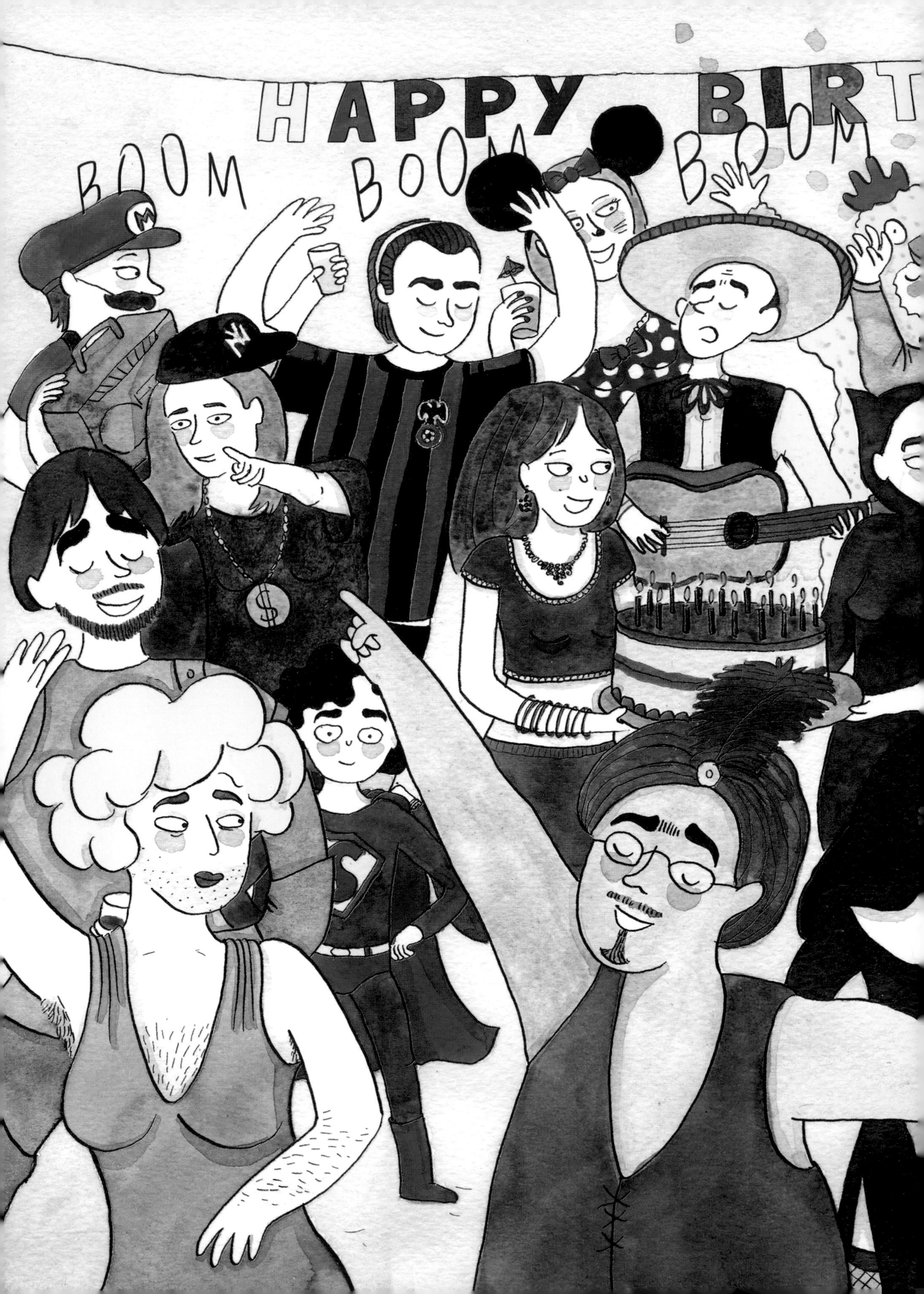
HAPPY BIRT
BOOM
BOOM
BOOM

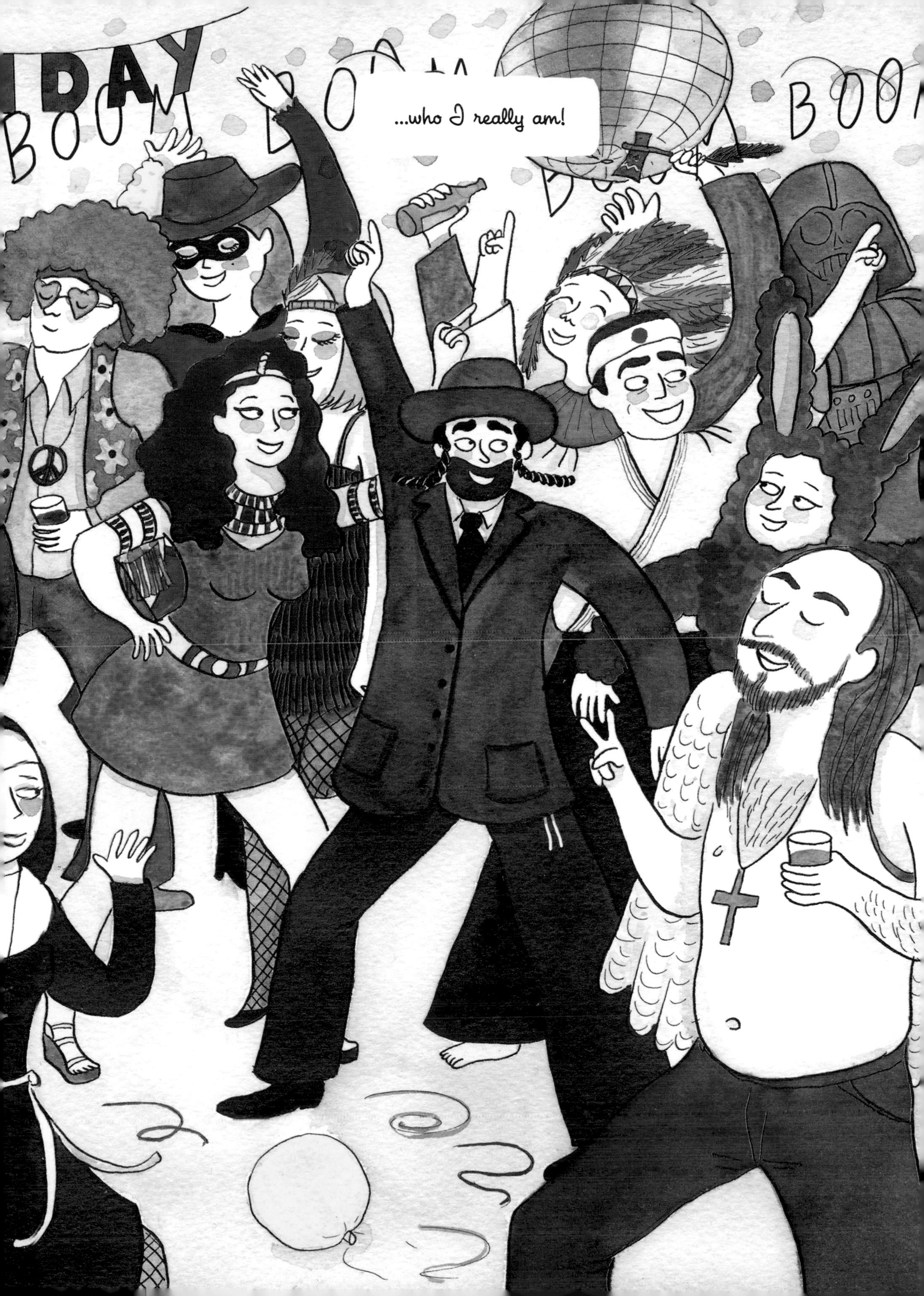
IDAY
BOOM
...who I really am!

Family Album

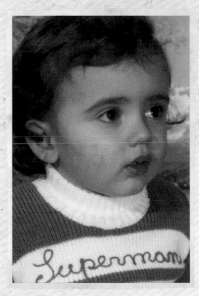

Thank you to my parents and friends, all of whom I used as inspiration
to create the characters in this graphic novel and who are infinitely
deeper, more beautiful, and more complex than their caricatures.

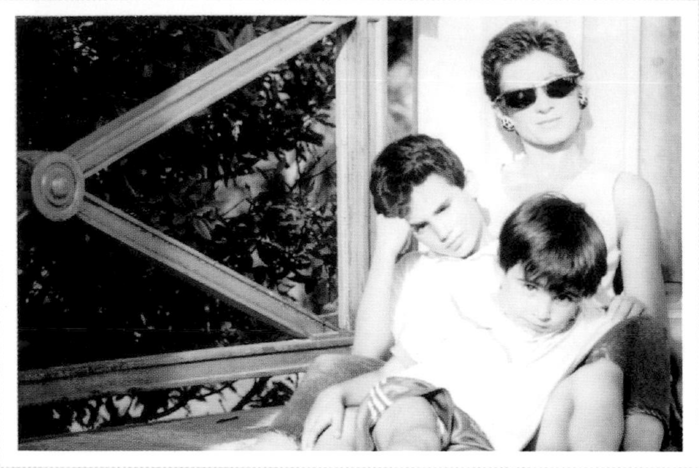

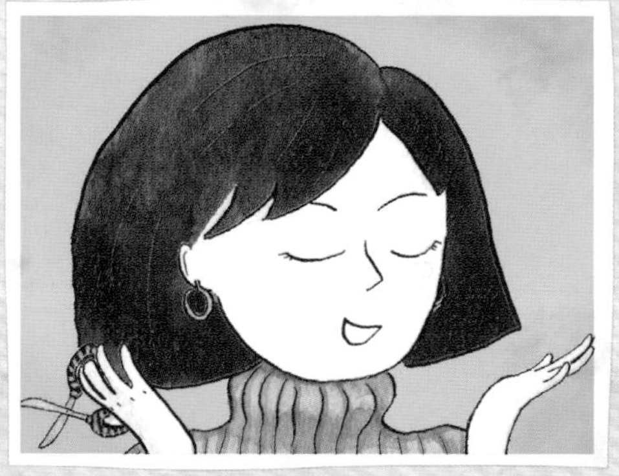

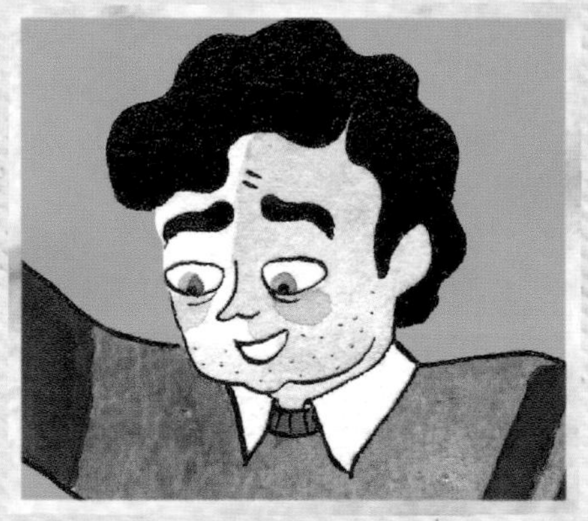

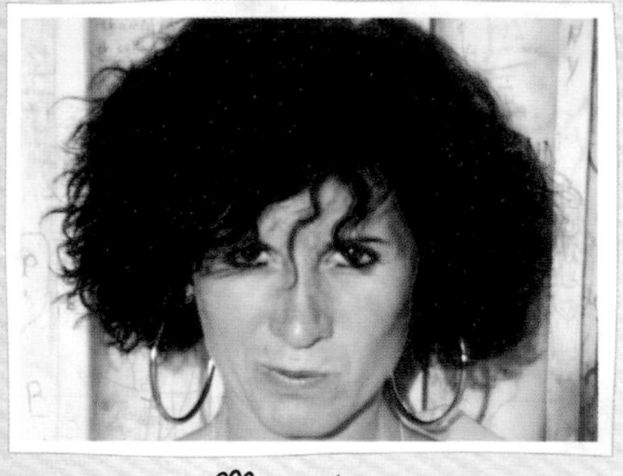

My mother

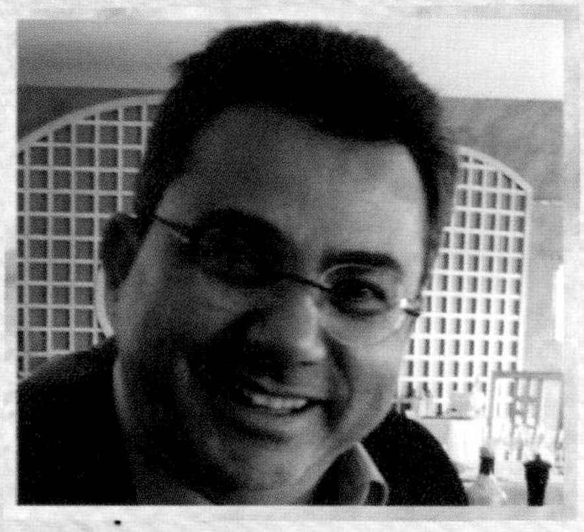

My father

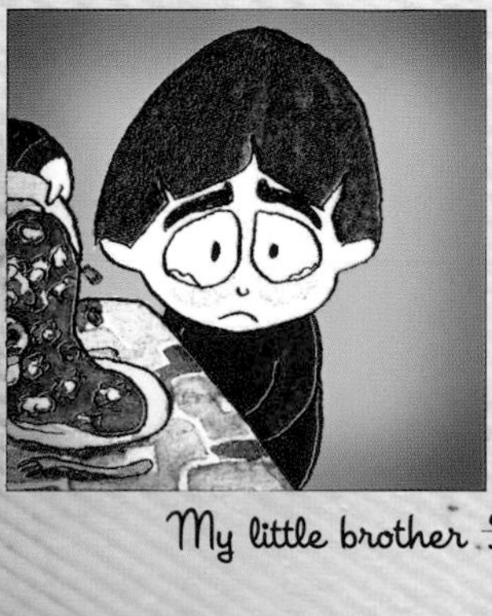

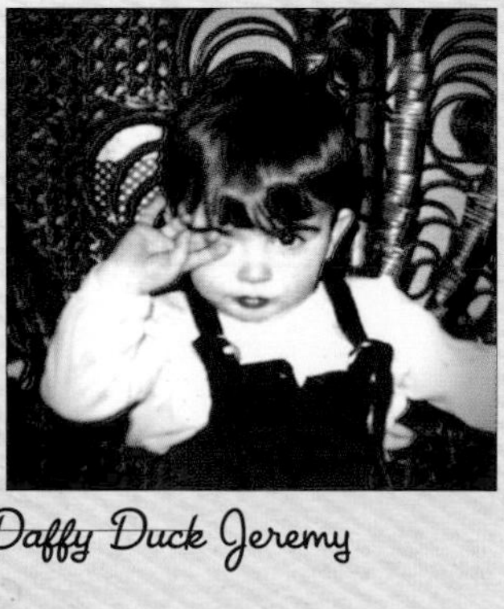

My little brother ~~Daffy Duck~~ Jeremy

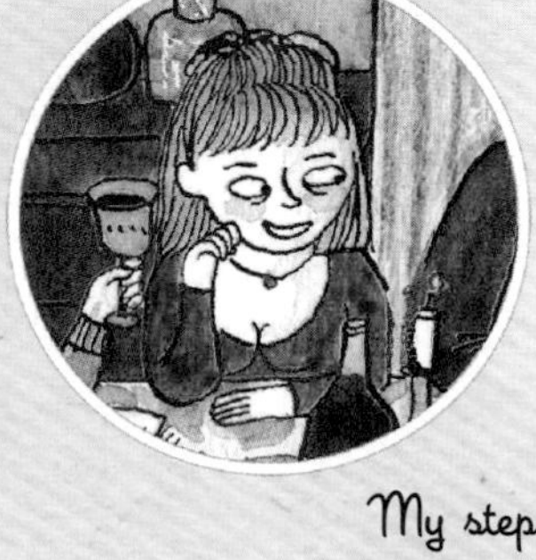

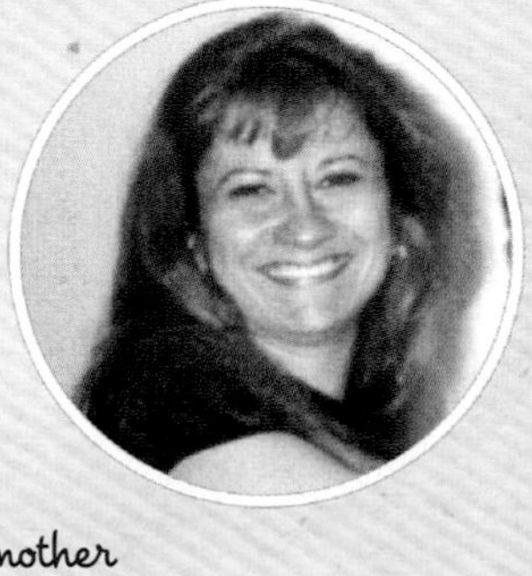

My stepmother

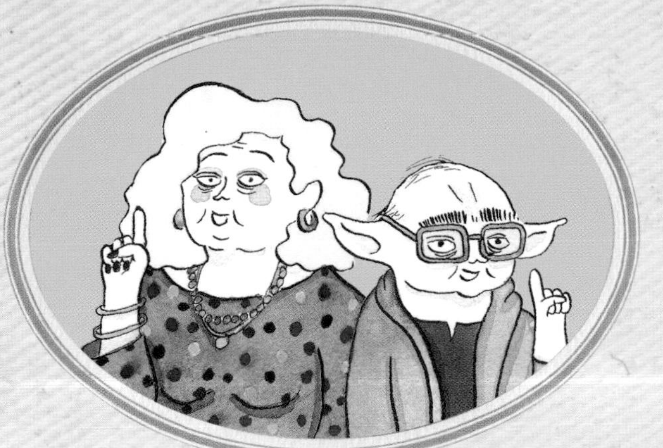

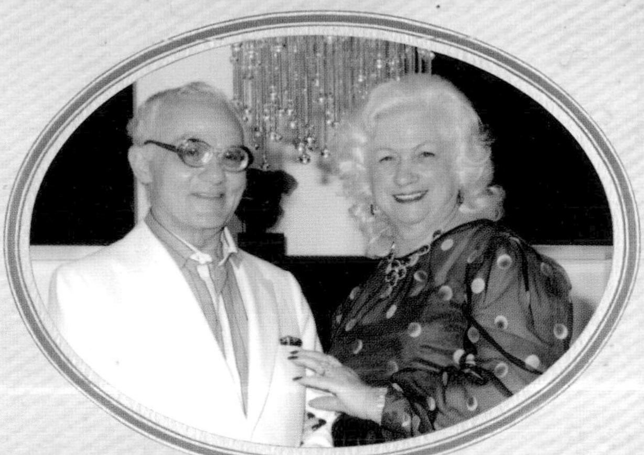

Grandmother Yvonne and Grampa Yoda Richard

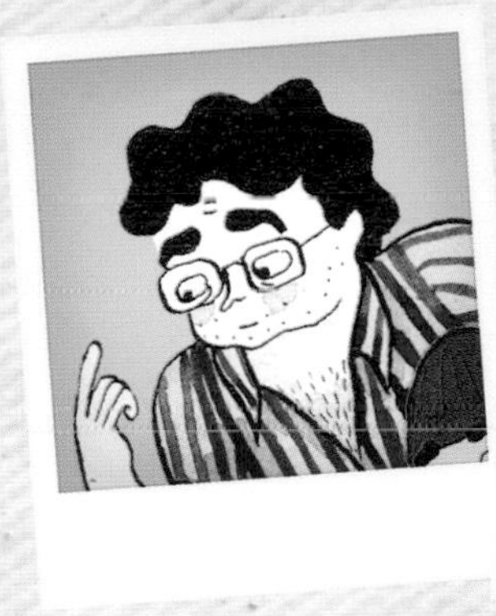

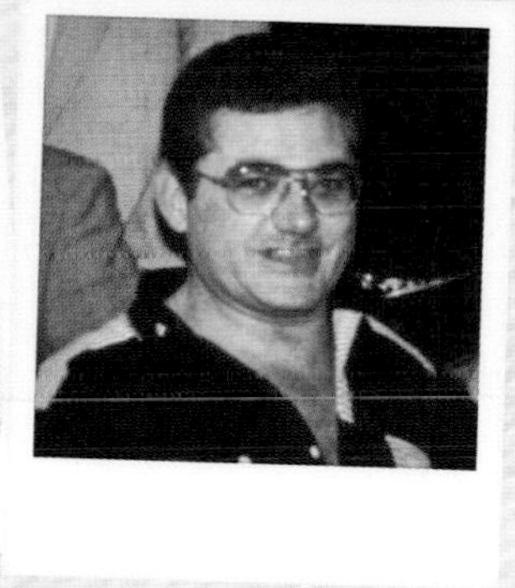

Uncle Yves

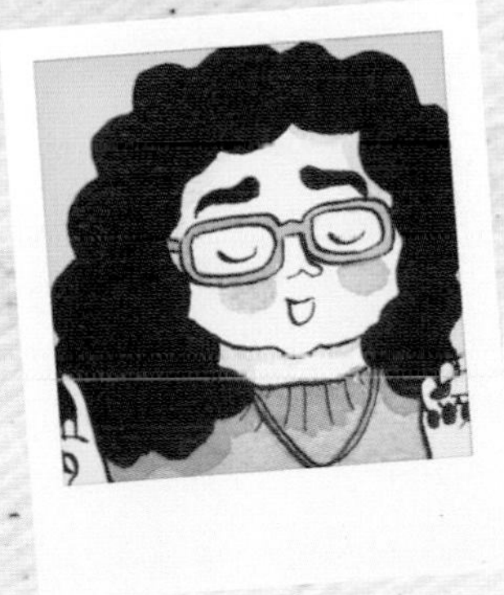

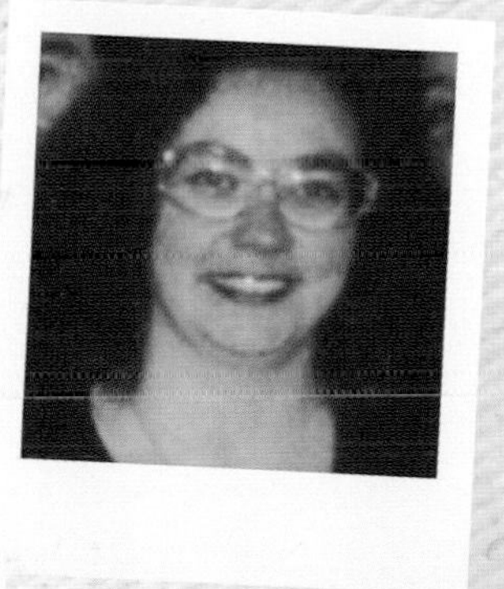

Aunt Genevieve

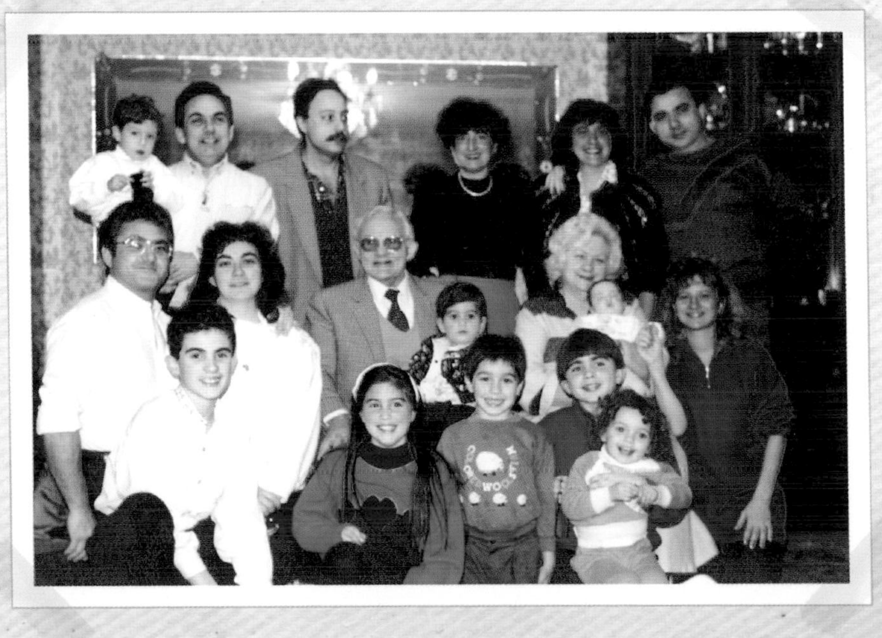

Recipe for Dafina

For Jews, Saturday is the day of rest, during which they are not allowed to work, cook, or use electricity or fire. Therefore, in order to be able to enjoy a delicious family dish on Saturday afternoons, Sephardic Jews (Jews from North Africa) invented...Dafina!

Every Friday before nightfall, Jewish grandmothers used to bring their cooking pot of Dafina to the baker, who put it in their bread oven and let it simmer on a low flame the whole night. The next day, each family would come to pick up its cooking pot so they could enjoy a delicious meat dish without having to cook on the day of Shabbat.
Caramelized and soft like jam, this ancestral dish is one of the most representative dishes of North African Jewish cuisine. Whether we call it Dafina, Dfna, Tafina, or Skhina, whether it includes beans, wheat, spinach, chickpeas or the famous small pieces of pasta, kawa, there are as many ways of cooking this dish as there are Jewish families in Algeria, Morocco, and Tunisia.
Everyone thinks the best Dafina is the one their grandmother makes, but the truth is that the very best Dafina in the world, THE one and only, is my grandmother's!

Here's her recipe, and it's a World Exclusive!

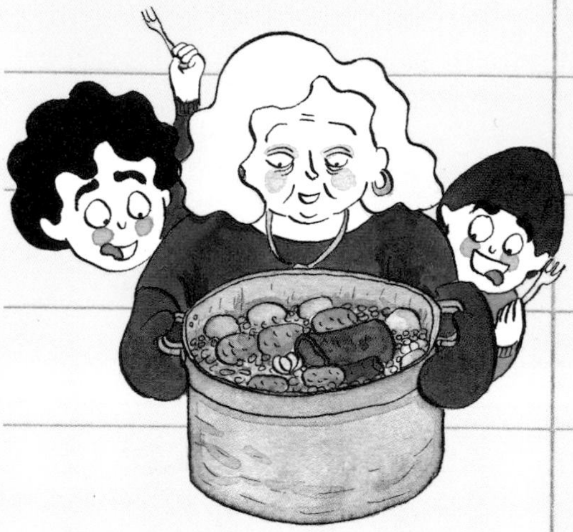

Ingredients

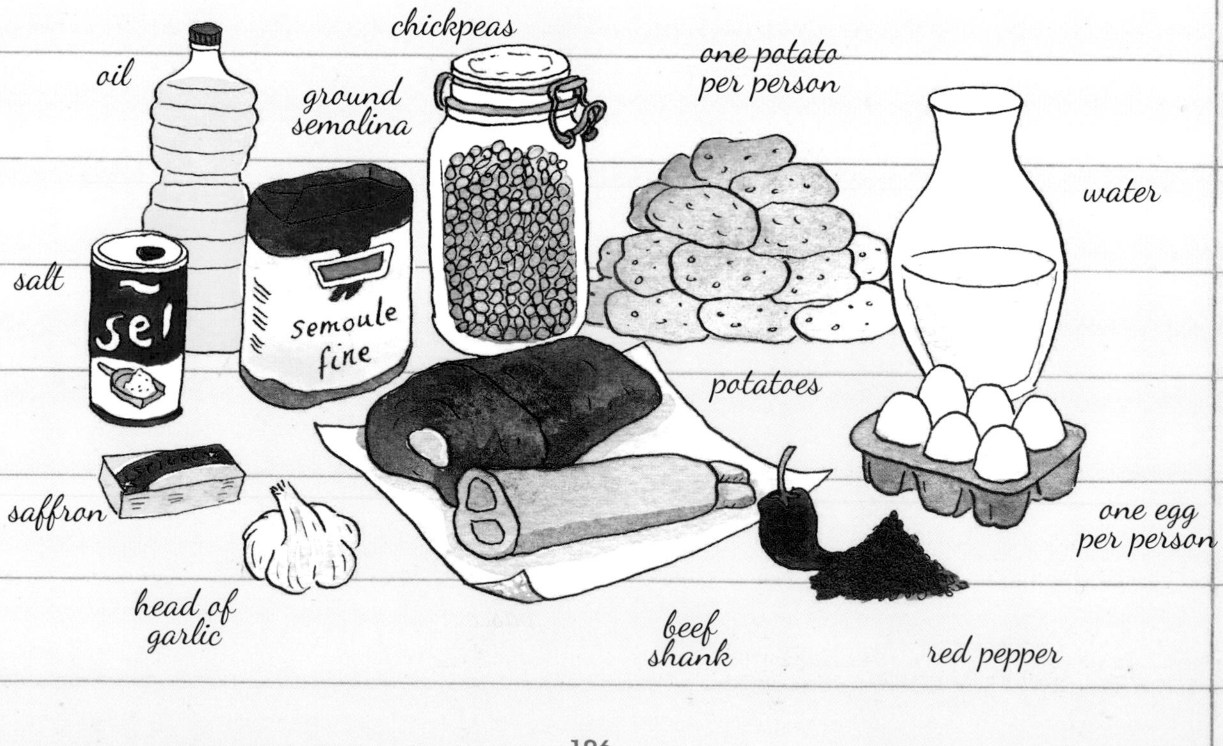
oil
chickpeas
ground semolina
one potato per person
water
salt
sel
semoule fine
potatoes
saffron
one egg per person
head of garlic
beef shank
red pepper

1 PREPARING THE "KAWA"* PASTA

*PRONOUNCED "KAWAY"

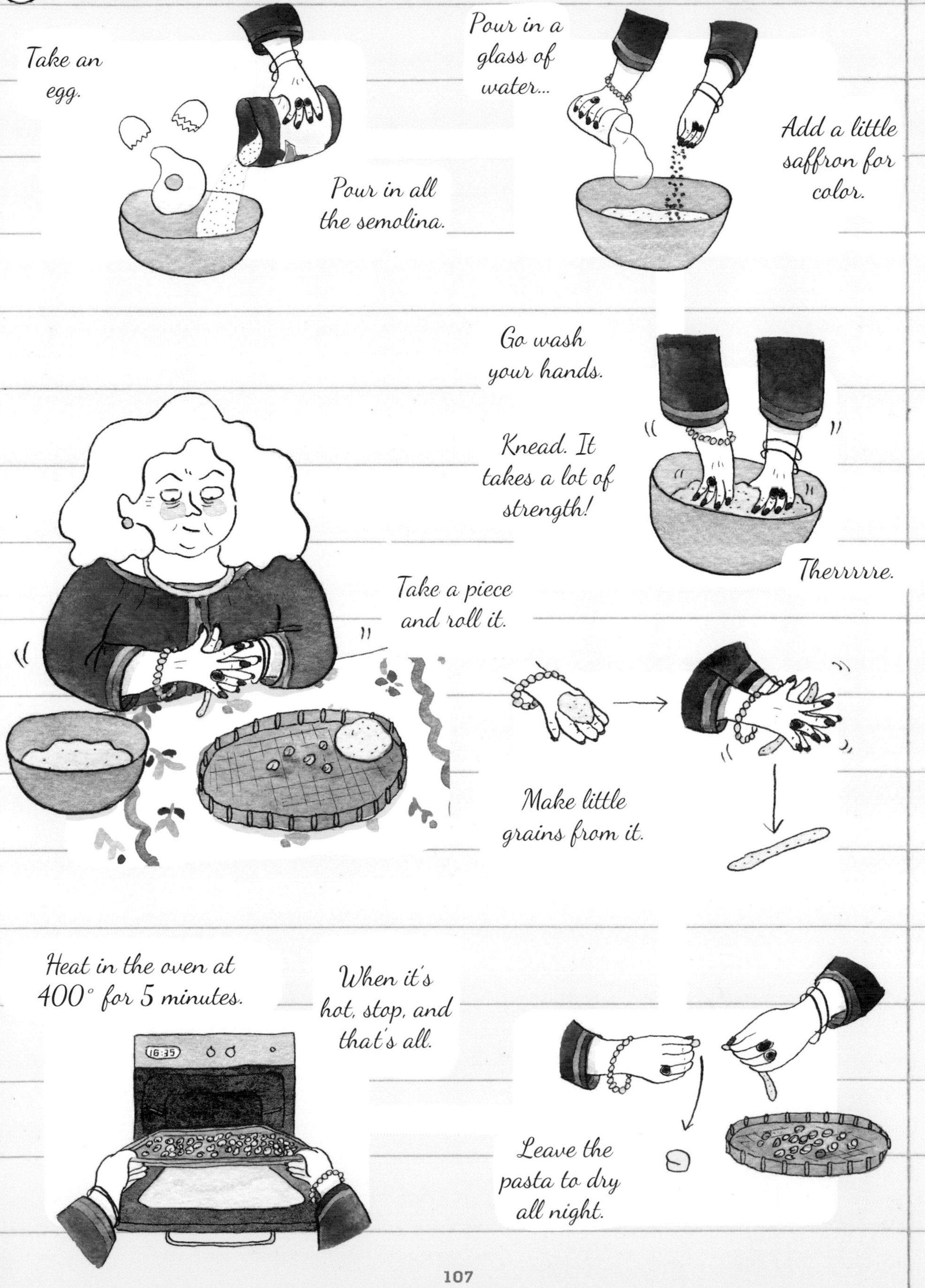

Take an egg.
Pour in all the semolina.
Pour in a glass of water...
Add a little saffron for color.
Go wash your hands.
Knead. It takes a lot of strength!
Therrrrre.
Take a piece and roll it.
Make little grains from it.
Heat in the oven at 400° for 5 minutes.
When it's hot, stop, and that's all.
Leave the pasta to dry all night.
16:35

2 Filling the cooking pot

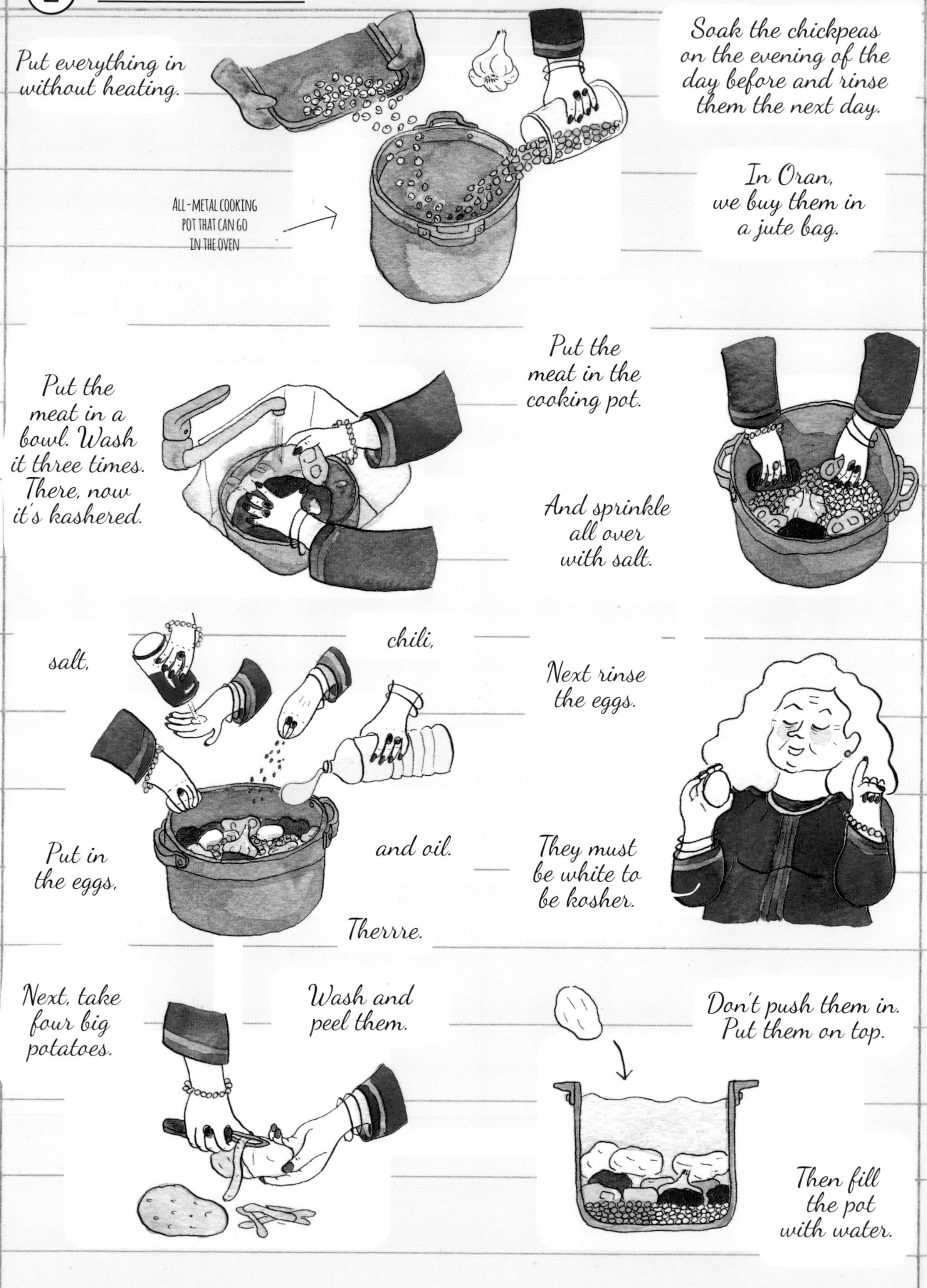

Put everything in without heating.
Soak the chickpeas on the evening of the day before and rinse them the next day.
ALL-METAL COOKING POT THAT CAN GO IN THE OVEN
In Oran, we buy them in a jute bag.
Put the meat in a bowl. Wash it three times. There, now it's kashered.
Put the meat in the cooking pot.
And sprinkle all over with salt.
salt,
chili,
Put in the eggs,
and oil.
Therrre.
Next rinse the eggs.
They must be white to be kosher.
Next, take four big potatoes.
Wash and peel them.
Don't push them in. Put them on top.
Then fill the pot with water.

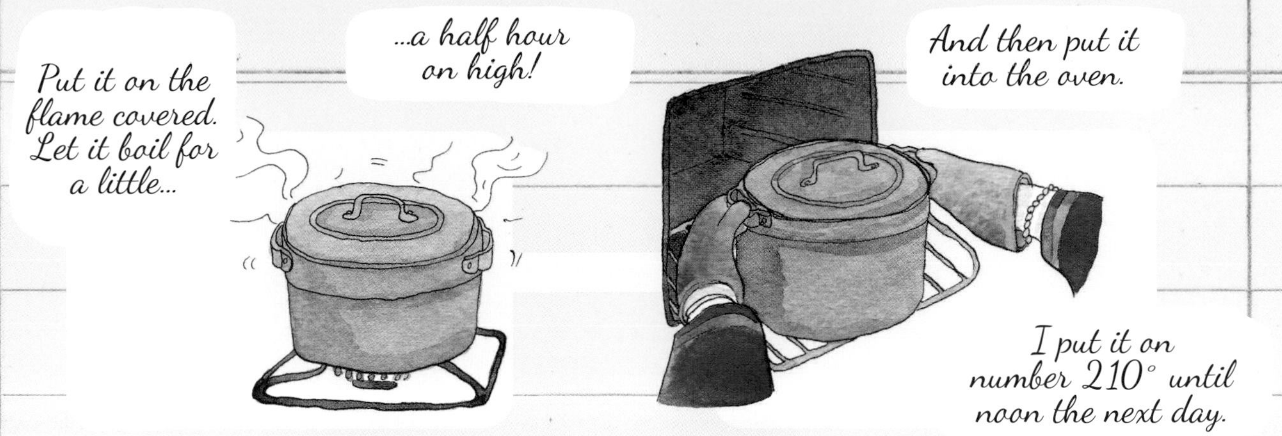
Put it on the flame covered. Let it boil for a little...
...a half hour on high!
And then put it into the oven.
I put it on number 210° until noon the next day.

③ Tasting

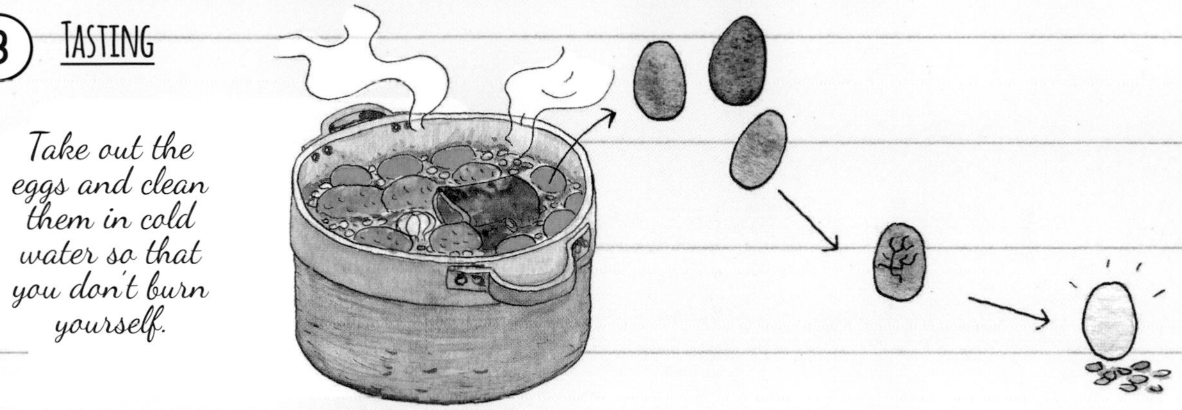
Take out the eggs and clean them in cold water so that you don't burn yourself.

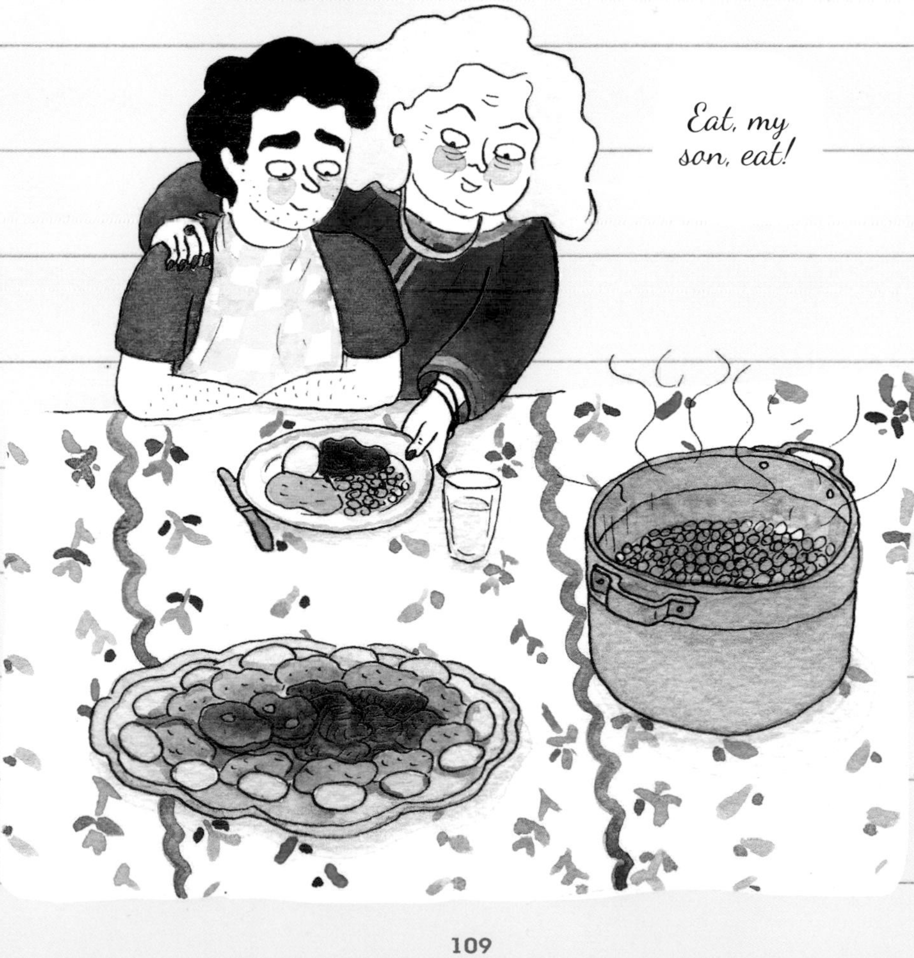
Eat, my son, eat!

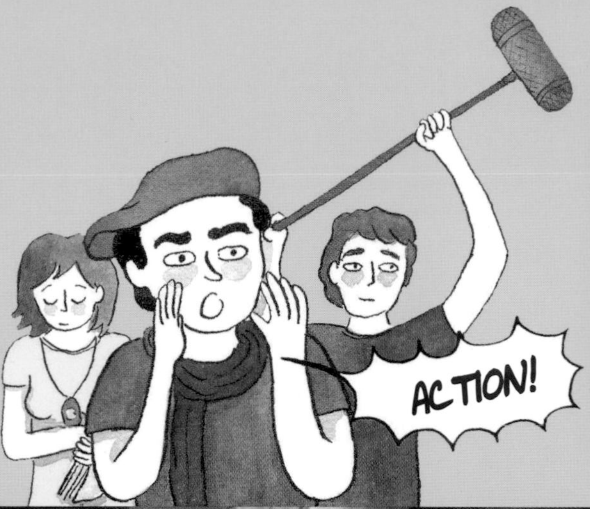
ACTION!
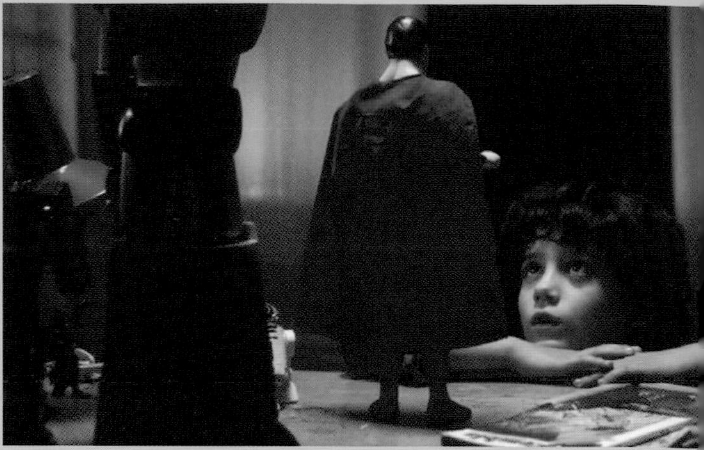
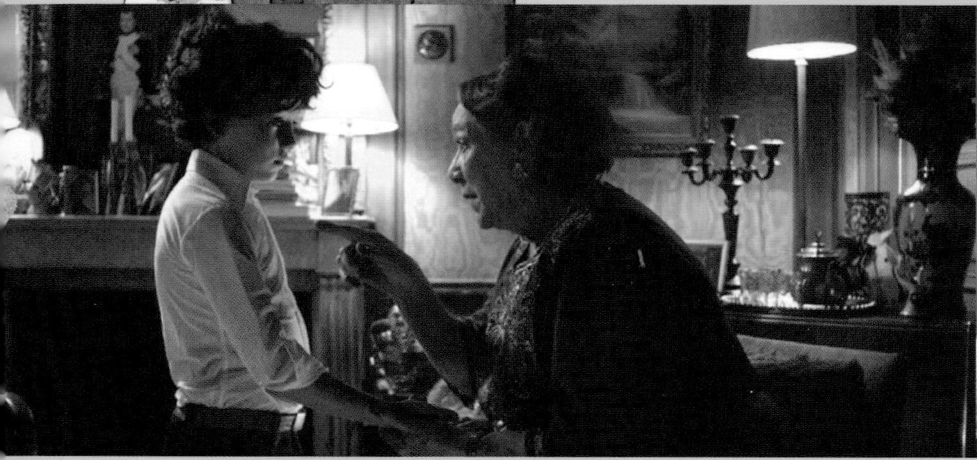
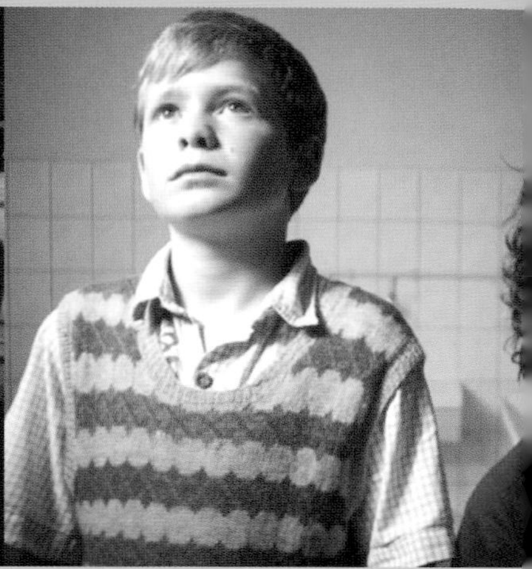
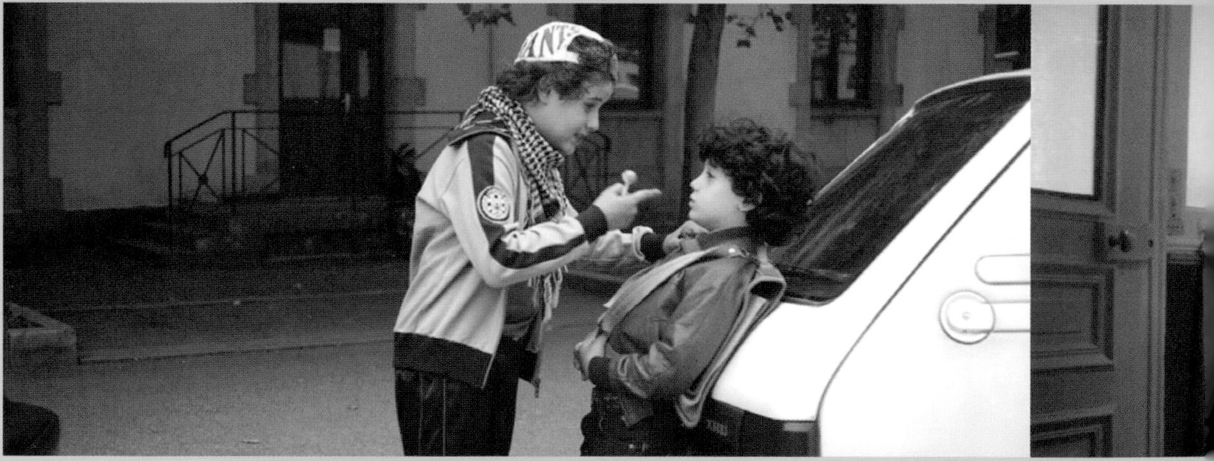
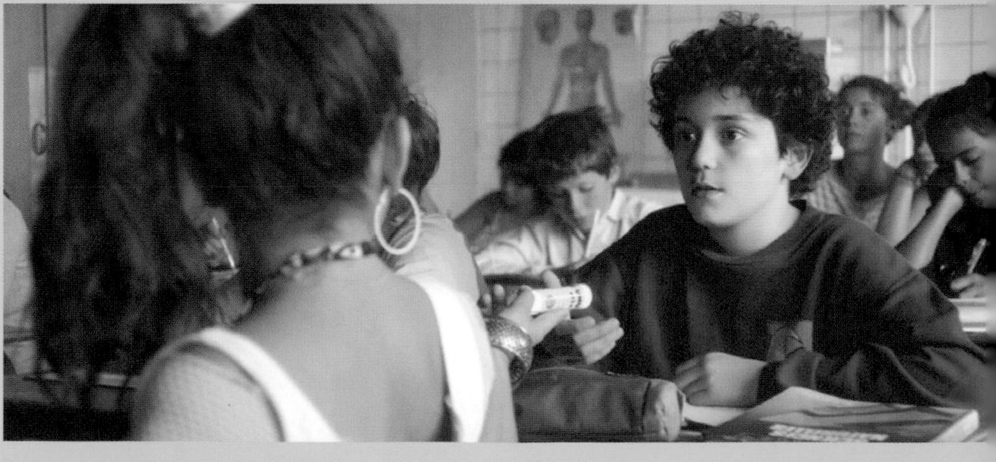

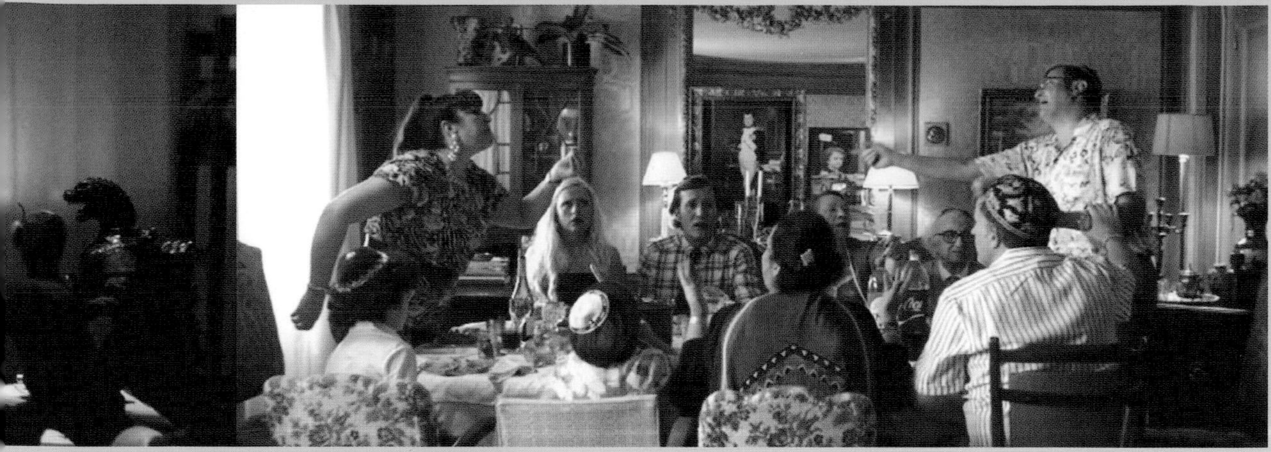

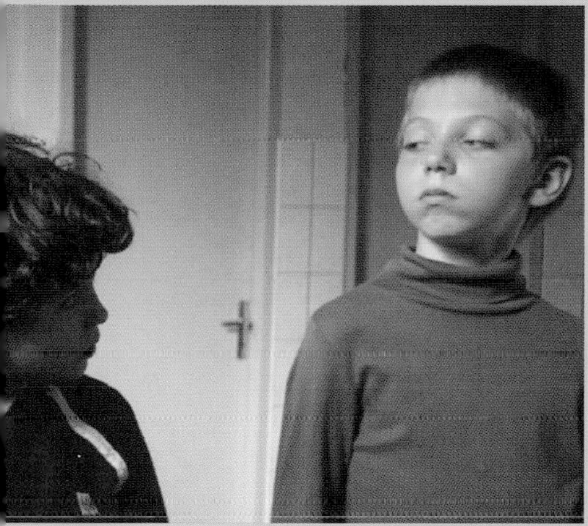

SUPERMAN ISN'T JEWISH
is also a 30-minute film written and directed by Jimmy Bemon and produced by Easy Tiger.

Watch the movie exclusively at:
www.humanoids.com/@sinjmovie
Password: Dafina1018

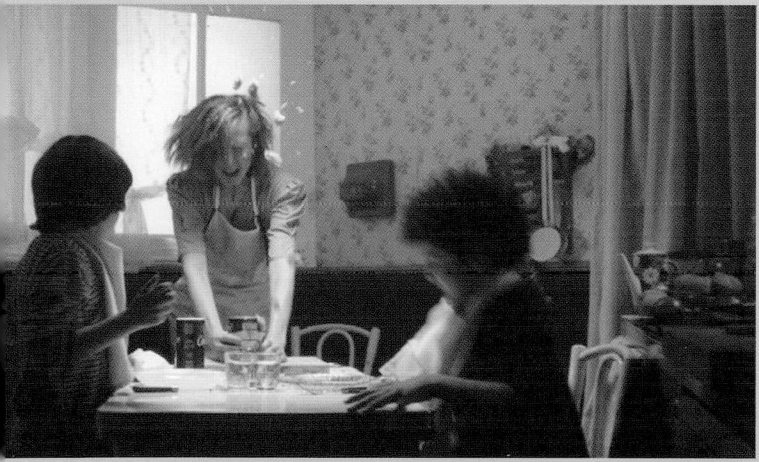

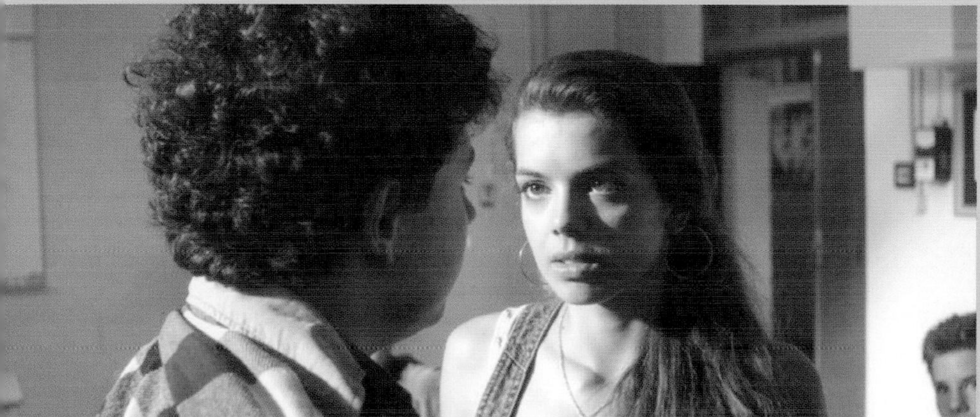

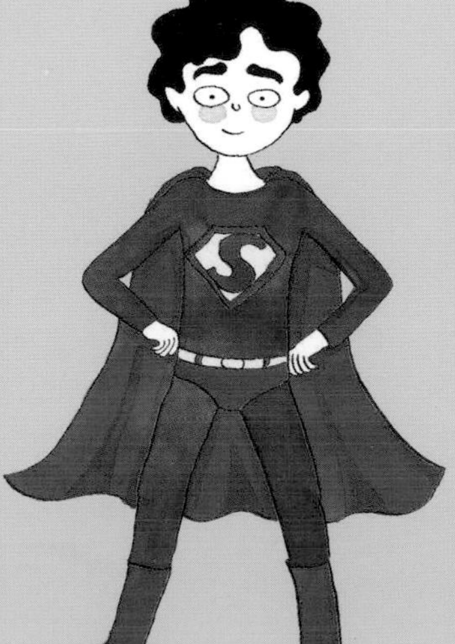

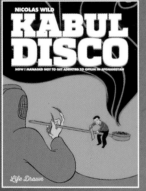

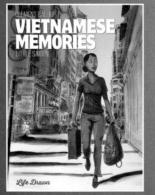